Caffeine

Smile of the Viper

Harry Dunn

13th. March 2018

For Katy,
With My Best Wishes,

Harry

Fiction aimed at the heart
and the head…

Published by Caffeine Nights Publishing 2012

Published in Great Britain by Caffeine Nights Publishing

www.caffeine-nights.com

British Library Cataloguing in Publication Data.

A CIP catalogue record for this book is available from the British Library

ISBN: 978-1-907565-24-3

Cover design by

Mark (Wills) Williams

Everything else by

Default, Luck and Accident

For Jen

Acknowledgements.

I wish to thank a number of people who read the early drafts and helped me improve the book. Nick and Kirsty Ede, Jeff and Barbara Brogden, Dorian and Sue Edwards and Lisa Lee. Their honesty and encouragement helped me to the finish.

For my dear wife Jen, daughter Rachel and son Andrew, who always believed in me and somehow knew I'd get there.

My never ending thanks go to my dear friend and author Judy Bryan. She not only proof read and edited the story, she taught me the craft of writing. She gave huge chunks of her precious time to transform the manuscript from its original state of chaos. I will be forever in her debt for her unswerving encouragement, patience and friendship. Without her, this book would not exist in its present form.

Finally, I would like to especially thank Darren Laws and the team at Caffeine Nights. Darren had faith in me and opened the door.

Smile of the Viper

Chapter 1

Approaching the perimeter, he switched off the lights, slowed to a halt, and reversed to within six feet of the weather-beaten brick wall. The only sounds were the ticking of his cooling engine and the distant hum of the night traffic from the M4.

He turned around in the cab of the 4 x 4 and retrieved a pair of overshoes and his industrial gloves. Pulling the low beam torch from the door pocket, he slid his feet into the rubber shoes before stepping out. He soft-clicked the door after him and moved to the rear of the vehicle. Raising the tailgate, he slid out two lightweight stepladders and placed one against the cemetery wall. He stood on the first rung and lifted the second ladder over the top, leaning it against the other side. Stepping off, he turned and reached inside the rear of the vehicle. He slid out the bagged body, grunting with the effort as he hoisted it on to his right shoulder. Within a minute he had clambered up and over the wall moving swiftly across the turf to the fresh grave, dumping the bag next to the raised mound of earth and its small temporary wooden cross.

He retraced his steps and returned in the same trotting motion with a long handled spade under his right arm and a tarpaulin under the other.

Spreading the sheet out on the left hand side of the grave, he removed three bouquets of flowers and the small cross and placed them carefully behind him. The sweat collected under his arms as he began rhythmically moving the topsoil onto the ground sheet. He worked quickly, removing three feet of loose earth. As if on cue he stopped digging, lay down the spade and using his feet, rolled the body bag into the shallow grave barely above the coffin which had been laid to rest only hours earlier. He quickly re-filled the hole and placed the flowers and cross exactly where they had been, standing back to catch his breath and examine the scene in the torchlight. Satisfied the earth mound looked exactly as it would have done to the cemetery's resident gravediggers when they left it twelve hours ago, he pulled the four corners of the tarpaulin together and dragged the surplus soil to the stepladder and over to his vehicle. Fit as he was, he stopped, bending forwards with his hands resting on his knees, breathing deeply to restore his oxygen levels.

He went back for the spade and made a last slow sweep with penetrating eyes to ensure he had left the grave as he found it. Satisfied, he moved swiftly and silently back to the wall and pulled the ladder up behind him. Climbing over the wall he placed his gear into the back of the vehicle next to the tarpaulin and removed his gloves and overshoes, stuffing them into a canvas holdall.

The Land Cruiser moved slowly away from the cemetery and rejoined the narrow lane which eventually fed into the motorway towards London.

The rhythms of the night had barely been disturbed in the 43 minutes the disposal had taken - his fastest time yet.

Chapter 2

Jack Barclay ran his hand through his grey-flecked black hair and looked out of the office window onto Kensington High Street.

It was going to be another hot day in the City. He wished he was anywhere but here where the phone remained silent with no one needing the services of a private investigator. He idly stretched his right arm to snag a cobweb caught in a shaft of morning sunlight and sighed as he turned away to pick up his personalised 'I'm all right Jack' coffee mug.

In the beginning, business had ticked over, maybe because of the goodwill of friends. He had been busy, often working long hours to complete projects quickly and surprising his clients. But he knew in this game, word of mouth could only keep you in work for so long. Few of his friends knew of others who needed the services of an enquiry agent. Maybe he shouldn't have picked his friends so carefully. Anyway he'd maxed out his MasterCard with a 6 x 6 Yellow Pages ad and it was just a matter of time. The phone rang, startling him from his thoughts.

'Mr Barclay?' said a woman's cultured voice.

'Yes, this is Jack Barclay speaking.'

'I need to see you.'

'Now?'

'Of course. When would suit you?' She spoke rapidly and there was nervousness in her voice. 'It's quite urgent.'

'How about one o'clock today?'

'That would be fine. My name is Jill Stanton and I know where your office is.'

'I look forward to meeting you.'

Jack sipped his coffee and thought about the call he had just taken. She was Jill and he was Jack. He hoped it wasn't someone's idea of a joke. The lady had given nothing away, but the urgency seemed real enough and he needed the work. He decided an early lunch would be a sensible move given his new appointment and tugging his keys from his jacket pocket, he moved towards the door. He closed it behind him and walked down the narrow, airless corridor noting the cracking blue paint and scuffed walls. He often wished his workplace was a little more imposing but hey, three months ago he was newly divorced and found out what it was like to be broke, so one thing at a time.

He walked out into the warmth of the Midsummer Day, his tall lean frame and rugged good looks turning the head of a young smartly dressed lady as he headed for Maggie's Deli.

Maggie was busy behind the counter filling a large ceramic bowl with her signature dish of prawns, pasta and flakes of pastrami. She would fill it three more times before the day was out. Her jet black hair, tied at the back, danced from side to side as she started to shake the bowl. She broke into a smile as Jack walked in.

'Hi, Maggie. What's new in the world of food?'

She laughed as she stretched across for the pasta bowl. 'Usual?'

'Well, you know me. A creature of habit.'

She filled his container, spooning in some extra prawns and clicked the top on. Jack paid for his takeaway and smiled.

'See you tomorrow, Jack?'

'Wouldn't miss it for anything.'

Back at the office there were no flashing lights on the phone. No urgent little bleeps. He settled into his chair and prised the top off the lunch box. Putting his feet up on the desk, he dug a fork into the mound of pasta and watched the old wall clock tick round to 12.30.

At one o'clock there was a soft knock on the door and almost immediately it opened. Well, there was no secretary on duty. He looked up to see a tall woman with ash blonde hair expensively cut. He'd been warned about moments like this. She looked to be late thirties, with a beige blouse above a light blue pencil skirt hanging just above the knee to show a pair of tanned legs. Tennis, he thought.

She gently closed the door, moved across to the front of the desk and stretched out her right hand as she said, 'Jill Stanton. We spoke earlier.'

'We did. Please have a seat.'

'You have been highly recommended Mr Barclay,' she said, placing an oversize tan handbag onto the floor and carefully crossing one leg over the other.

'Well that's always good to hear.' He leant back in his chair and looked her in the eye. 'How can I help you?'

'I need to find someone.'

Don't we all.

'From what I hear, you get results.'

'Well nothing is ever guaranteed but I'm persistent.'

'That's what I heard.'

She re-crossed her legs and looked down as she straightened her skirt. 'I'm a married woman Mr Barclay or at least I think I am. Seven days ago my husband Tom left on one of his regular business trips to Paris but never arrived. He didn't even get to Heathrow and was down as a no show with the airline. He should have phoned me on the first evening but I wasn't worried when he didn't call. He often entertains clients in the evening and I assumed he was busy and would get in touch in the morning. He didn't, so I called his mobile phone but it went into voicemail. I still wasn't worried.'

She paused and Jack leaned forward and asked, 'What does your husband do?'

'He's in finance. Investment and things. I never really take much interest.'

'Go on.'

'I rang his office first but they just assumed he was in Paris although they hadn't heard from him. I phoned around all our mutual friends and business colleagues, and no one knows anything.'

'The police?' interjected Jack.

'I phoned the local police station and reported him missing. They took details and have recorded him in the system.'

'Did you mention Paris?'

'Yes, and details will be circulated abroad too I'm told. They said they get missing person calls every day and invariably the person always turns up. Just gone off the radar for a while. He'll surface is what they said.'

Jack nodded as if in agreement.

'They asked me to keep in touch and if he doesn't turn up pretty soon, they will step up their enquiries. They didn't seem worried.'

'But you think he's in trouble, don't you?'

'Yes. He's a banker, a creature of habit. He doesn't go off the radar and he always keeps in touch when he's away. It's early days yet but I want to speed things up.'

Jack looked at her and said, 'Yes, I think maybe you should. I'll need an advance to get set up.'

'The money will not be a problem Mr Barclay. Just let me know how much you require to get started. Will a cheque do?'

'Of course.' He opened the drawer of his desk, pulled out an A4 pad and rummaged in the mug for a pen 'Do you have a recent photograph of your husband?'

She bent down and reached into her bag bringing out a red leather wallet and unzipped it. She passed him a photo. 'This was taken quite recently.'

'Description?'

'He's thirty-eight, six foot and about twelve stone. He has thick dark hair. Keeps it short. He has olive looking skin with brown eyes. He broke his nose playing rugby when he was at school so it's slightly crooked. Cute though.'

'Do you know if his passport is still at home?'

'I'll have to check.'

'You need to look out any recent credit card statements and I'll need details of his business partners.'

'God, you make him sound like a criminal.'

'I need information to make a start, that's all. I'm making no judgements.'

She nodded.

'Do you have children?'

'Yes, a girl and a boy. Sarah is fourteen and Oliver is twelve.'

'Have you been aware of any unusual phone calls to your home in the last few weeks?'

'Not that I know of. I'm not always there, but I always check the message service when I get in and I can't remember anything strange.'

'How long have you been married?'

'Fifteen years this August.'

'Happy ones?'

'Yes, on the whole, very happy. There were times at the beginning when he was spending what seemed like every hour of the day building the business and it caused friction but it soon passed.'

'Social life?'

'Mostly at our local tennis club.'

'Did you have a special group of girl friends there?'

'Yes, a few.'

'I'll need their contact details.'

'I can't see how they are connected to this.'

'We haven't even started looking for connections yet, Mrs. Stanton, but believe me, something will connect with something else at some time and it may surprise the hell out of both of us.'

Jack turned a page in his notebook and asked, 'Did Tom do business at the club?'

Jill Stanton held his gaze.

'Did he mix business and pleasure, you know, help club members with investments and things?'

'He didn't make a point of it. I mean, he was there to get away from all that type of stuff.'

'Did he ever discuss business with you?

'Never. He didn't speak about clients with me. It was our golden rule and in fact he made that plain to people he was dealing with, especially if they were friends of ours.'

'Do you think your husband was seeing anyone else?'

She shot a hard look at him but regained her composure. 'No, I don't.'

'Sure?'

'A woman knows, doesn't she?'

He moved on. 'Your husband's work. How much do you know about it?'

'As I said, we never spoke a lot about it and I really wasn't terribly interested. She smiled and said, 'I sometimes picked up the financial magazines he brought home. The headlines were usually enough to put me off.'

'Did he go out much socially? I mean without you?'

'He went out with his two partners, Charles and Bob for a drink every Friday after the business closed for the week.'

'Just the three of them?'

'I suppose they met other guys there. It was a bit of a meeting place for business types just slackening the ties and relaxing.'

Jill's mobile phone started ringing in her bag and Jack used the moment to make a couple of notes. When he looked up she was nodding into the phone and then said, 'No, nothing yet.' She placed the phone on the table in front of her and her face dropped. He wondered if she was hoping the call was from her husband.

'That was Bob asking for any news.'

He nodded and closed his note pad. 'Can you write down your contact numbers for me?'

Leaning across to the front of the table she began leafing through the pages of an address book, jotting down names and numbers. She added her own.

'There is one last thing I need you to do. It may sound a little unpleasant but it's important you do it. When you return home, would you go through your husband's suits and jackets?'

She looked directly at him. 'Do I have to?'

'I'm afraid so.'

'What am I supposed to be looking for?'

He shrugged and said, 'Receipts, pieces of paper with a name or a phone number, parking stubs, club memberships, address books or a diary. At the moment we know absolutely nothing.'

'I understand.' She stood up to run her right hand down her skirt to smooth any creases.

Jack stood up from behind the desk and stretched out his arm to shake her hand. 'I'll be in touch.'

'I'm pleased you are going to help, Mr Barclay. I really am.'

She turned round and made for the door and closed it softly behind her without looking back.

After she'd left Jack thought how much she reminded him of Kate. His thoughts went back to the pain of their broken marriage and the guilt he always felt at his part in the breakdown. He tried to push the thoughts from his mind.

Chapter 3

It was a balmy evening in Paris and the Saint-Germain area in the Old Quarter was crowded with tourists paying too much for everything. Lovers were strolling hand in hand, touching one another and laughing, oblivious to anything but themselves. Lamps had come on throwing long shadows over the medieval buildings. It was a good time to be alive, especially if you were intoxicated by this great city.

The Café Meurice in Rue St. Luis was doing its usual brisk evening trade. It was a destination for locals in the know and was rarely found by tourists. Tucked away in a narrow cobbled street, once you found this little gem you always returned. It had been serving beautiful food for over forty years and the taciturn waiters moving around in the dark wood panelled restaurant only served to improve the ambience.

The back room was in contrast to the part where patrons consumed their foie gras and petit cochon. The walls carried abstract prints and the lighting was modern but subdued. At the side was an oak bureau on which rested two computer screens and a cluster of mobile phones constantly on charge. In the centre of the room a round table had four high backed executive black leather chairs with a bottle of Perrier and a drinking glass in front of each. The two men sitting in the chairs were unsmiling. Both had seen the inside of Fleury-Merogis prison just outside Paris. One had been charged with the possession and distribution of 'les stupefiants' and the other with 'l'enlevement', although no ransom was ever asked for and no body ever found. Both wore dark two piece suits and white shirts opened at the neck but the likeness ended there.

Khalid had left Algeria as a young man and his enormous pock-marked face sat on a short bulging neck. His large lips and dark narrow eyes made him pig-like in appearance. Over the years his weight had ballooned to nearly 20 stone and the table creaked as he used his huge muscled forearms to move his weight in the large executive chair. Xavier next to him had been raised in the waterfront of Marseilles and in contrast to his partner seemed almost rat like in appearance. His face seemed too small for his aquiline nose and underneath it a thin moustache did little to detract from his cruel slit of a mouth. His black greasy hair hung long on his collar and the smell of stale tobacco smoke hung around him. Although, like Khalid, he had been in and out of prison all his life he had always managed to escape the long stretch. This was helped by a constant lack of witnesses to his crimes. His eyes darted around incessantly. He never felt comfortable in briefings.

When the mob needed some blood work doing or when slow payers ran out of time, you sent for Khalid and Xavier.

Masters of their art.

Sergei stared hard at them around the table but the respect he had earned was enough to get their attention. He was 35 years old and represented new school Russian criminality. His finely chiselled features with short cropped dark hair and slim build were due to his daily fitness regime at the gym. As was his custom, he wore a crisp white Ralph Lauren shirt, open at the neck to complement his immaculate black Armani suit. The Patek Philippe gold watch on his wrist left no one in doubt of the image he wished to create.

His quiet voice was enough to let his small audience know there was bad news coming.

'We have a problem. A large amount of money is missing and our financial man in London has disappeared. We're looking at £4m here and we need to move fast. You will travel separately and check into different hotels from the list. Collect your equipment including mobile phones from the safe house in Paddington. The usual lines of communication will be used.' He stopped talking as his mobile rang. He checked the caller ID and turned his back to take the call. When he disconnected he said, 'I have just heard that his wife has put a private investigator on the case. They've got a start on you so work quickly. I don't have to tell you what the stakes are.'

Sergei gave them names, locations and phone numbers. After ten minutes he leaned back in his chair and extracted a large Cuban cigar from the top pocket of his jacket and began the ritual of lighting it.

Speaking deliberately he said, 'Right. Do it. Any way you choose.'

The two men pushed back their chairs with a scraping sound on the grey flagstones, nodded at Sergei and retreated to a door at the back of the room partially hidden by a black curtain.

Sergei moved across and, using a key from his trouser pocket unlocked the door. He patted both men on the shoulder as they went out into the dimly-lit alley running along the back of the restaurant. They turned right towards Rue St Luis and melted into the evening crowds.

Sergei locked the door behind them and slumped back into his chair, drawing on his cigar. As he exhaled, he reflected on the situation facing him. He wasn't going to allow the money man in London to endanger his position. Some new boy who'd just joined the organization. He reflected on the years of hard work to get where he was now.

The memories of his rural upbringing on a smallholding twenty miles from St Petersburg always stayed with him. The eldest of eight, with a life of stress and constant hunger, he was forced to watch his father, fuelled by cheap vodka, abusing his mother every day without fail. Christmas day was not an exception.

He shifted uncomfortably on his chair as he recalled the shouted obscenities from his father and the screams of his once beautiful mother as the daily beating ritual began. He remembered the night he had seen and heard enough. The hatred for his father erupted as he watched his beloved mother lying on the stone floor trying to ward off the vicious blows. As his father lifted his arm to punch his mother again, Sergei felt an intense anger well up. He picked up the long poker from the hearth, crept up from behind and struck his father with all the force his fifteen-year-old body could muster. The blow to the back of the head felled him and his mother looked on in silence. Sergei dragged his father over the rough stone floor and outside as his brothers and sisters cowered in the bedroom doorway. What followed was a fog to Sergei. He dragged his father's unconscious body to the end of the yard, scrawny hens scattering in his path. He reached the disused well which was almost covered over with scrub and let his father's inert body fall to the ground. He lifted the rusting grate cover to one side and moved his father to the lip and heaved him in. Sergei's breathing was rapid and the anger was still coursing through him as he heard the thud of his father's body hitting the bottom eighty feet down. Without stopping, he walked to the outhouse and dragged two bags of cement to the well and placed them by the old round brick wellhead. He picked up old misshapen bricks six at a time from the nearby stack and piled them next to the bags of cement. After he'd dropped fifty down the well, he tipped in both bags of cement and went across to the hosepipe and cascaded water into the darkness for several minutes. The entombment was complete. His father had disappeared. His mother and siblings never asked what happened and Sergei just told them he'd gone.

He left a few days later and arrived in St Petersburg with nothing. The drug gang he joined saved him from starvation. He started as a foot soldier distributing in the most dangerous parts of the city but he was tough and it got noticed by the hierarchy.

He became the biggest earner and was given better pitches. One night he was asked to take out a rival dealer who had moved on to the gang's pitch. He knew it was a test. The dealer was never seen again. When it was known he could kill, he quickly rose to the top of the St. Petersburg distribution chain and it was only a matter of time before he was promoted to greater things.

In three years he was selected to command the Paris operation. He wrote to his mother every week, and without fail, a courier arrived at the farm once a month with an envelope containing 30,000 roubles. More than enough to feed the family and put some by for the future.

Chapter 4

Patrick Flynn was doing well. He was a big man and just the wrong side of thirty five but prided himself on staying fit enough to tackle anything which came his way. Plumbing was his line and he'd built his business from scratch. The work ethic was in his genes and he had certainly proved what could be achieved from sheer hard graft.

In the space of fifteen years he had a large house which was getting close to being paid off, a jet ski in the garage and money in the bank. He knew he was sound financially because he'd always followed the same mantra - spend a third, save a third and keep a third for the taxman.

Actually it had been his wife Lauren who had come up with that idea but he was happy to go along with it. The little he siphoned off on the quiet from cash jobs paid for poker every Friday night and nobody got hurt.

Patrick was a provider. He delivered everything a woman could need except maybe position in the local community. Her parents had high hopes for their only child and would have been happy to see her follow her father's footsteps and go into the insurance business, but after being blessed with two grandchildren whom they adored, any disappointment faded like snow off a spring flower.

Patrick met so many people in his line of work - pipes backed up on all sides of town - and he always got paid. It could take three hours to fix a blockage but five minutes to jam it up again if the customer suddenly found himself a little short. No one owed Patrick money. He vowed no one ever would. If things got a bit slack he'd just take himself off to Eden Lake for a spot of fishing. If his mobile rang he had his gear packed in minutes, got back on the road and put his foot down to the next pile of shit.

Three weeks earlier, when they were lying in bed one Sunday morning, Lauren mentioned her friend at the tennis club.

'You know Patrick we've got too much cash hanging about now which just isn't working hard for us. My friend Jill at the club is married to quite a financial wizard. Knows his stuff apparently and is helping a lot of the members to get the best returns for their savings. What do you think?

'Well my lovely, I make it, you take it.'

They'd both laughed. Patrick gave Lauren a quick peck on the cheek, threw back the duvet cover and launched his big frame out of the bed towards the wet room. He stretched out his hand and moved the shower control to full volume shouting through the half closed door, 'Fine by me, see what's going on.

A week later the Flynn's had met Tom at his office. They shook hands enthusiastically and were ushered across to the sofa at the side of the room. His PA, Cindy, quietly knocked on the door and came in with a large pot of tea, biscuits with china cups and saucers on a silver tray.

Patrick's sheer size took up most of the sofa. He was a giant of a man. If you didn't know, you would have guessed he was Irish. The large honest face and rust coloured hair with hands the size of hams. In them, his tea cup looked as if it had come out of a dolls house. Lauren, by his side, looked quite petite with piercing blue eyes in a cute pixie like face with long auburn hair. Opposites often attracted and they were the proof.

Patrick listened as Tom had begun with a rundown of SMG. 'The company had come from humble beginnings and were proud of their reputation. They found the best investment platforms and always put the clients' interests first.' The Flynn's had listened as Tom outlined a personalised investment strategy. 'You would be just as important to us as clients we have looked after since we started out. Your success is our success.'

They had been made to feel quite special and any concerns began to recede.

Patrick and Lauren became more relaxed as they realised the world of finance wasn't some murky business after all. It was actually very friendly and by all accounts they could easily begin to increase their savings quite substantially with little risk. Their investments would be spread over a wide range of well established products. The calm and authoritative manner of the presentation reminded them of a doctor dispensing wise counsel. They were hooked.

Even to Patrick, who'd had initial reservations, it seemed a 'no brainer.'

They all stood up after their two hour meeting. Patrick looked towards Lauren and nodded his approval. 'Let's do it honey.'

As Patrick moved his large frame from the sofa to the large oak desk, he pulled a wallet from his inside jacket pocket wrote a cheque for £97,000 and handed it to Tom. Everyone looked relieved and shook hands.

Patrick and Lauren were now serious investors, looking after their futures.

Chapter 5

Bob Goldman stared at his mobile phone after making his call to Jill. He ran his hand through his thick black hair as he tried to fathom out the possible reasons for Tom's disappearance. Where the hell was he? Why hadn't he got in touch? All sorts of scenarios had gone through his mind and self interest was the first one to rise to the surface.

He was in the office waiting for Charles who had cut short a client visit and was on his way from Fulham, delayed in heavy traffic. Bob went back into their computer system and punched in his password. For the third time in so many hours he trawled through pages of the company's financial data to check for anything which wasn't there two days ago. All their bank details seemed intact. No big or unusual withdrawals from the main account. Everything looked just fine. He came out of the finance pages and went to the week's diary. It was to be a fairly quiet week and only Tom was down to travel outside the UK. He was seeing an old friend and client, the finance director of Canard Bleu, a medium sized restaurant chain based in Paris. It was just a routine financial health check and there had been no reported difficulties or problems with the company or investments held by them. He picked up the phone and called a couple of their Friday night chums.

He knew it was a long shot as the Friday crowd hardly met outside the weekly meeting at The White Hart but it was somewhere to start. He decided to ask if they had seen Tom in the last couple of days and not mention his disappearance. No need to start speculation unnecessarily.

No one had seen him. Bob sat and nervously tugged at the lobe of his right ear. In the ten years the business had been going, this was the first time he had felt a pang of fear.

The company had grown quickly but no one ever questioned how success had been so rapid. There was no need. Their reputation was sound and their clients had stayed with them through the various ups and downs in the economy. Tom had played a big part in making them all successful and Bob knew that as the front man, he was probably irreplaceable. If Tom was the acceptable face of the company, Bob was the one who never shied away from the hard decisions. He was the dealmaker and his two associates just left him to it. He would do anything to grow the business and he had convinced himself he had always stayed within the rules. And anyway there was always risk attached to an investment, wasn't there?

As Charles came into the office he looked even more worried than usual. 'What the hell has happened?'   He almost shouted at Bob, 'Have you heard anything?'

Charles was a large ruddy- faced Scot, standing at six feet and with a waistline which had benefited from many a corporate lunch. His shirt was unfastened at the neck and his shock of sandy hair was looking tousled.

'Nothing yet', said Bob as Charles moved across the office and dropped his bulk into a large chair near the window.

'So what do we know?'

'Not very much except Tom was on his way to Paris for a regular meeting with Peter at Canard Bleu and never made it. As far as we know he never even got on the plane. He left the health club at around 8.00am for Heathrow and hasn't been seen since.'

'Someone must have seen something. Are the police involved?'

'Yes. Jill has reported him missing and they have circulated a description but as far as I know they are not treating this suspiciously yet. Too early I suppose.'

'Well it might be early to them but it isn't to Jill and the kids and to us. We need to start digging around a bit. The health club must have CCTV. There has got to be something which will throw some light on this.'   Charles began tapping the side of the chair in irritation.

Bob eased himself up from behind his desk and came to join him in the other easy chair by the round meeting table. 'Look Charles, I don't have any idea what has happened to Tom and we mustn't jump to conclusions, but yes I am worried and we need some answers fast. There's a hell of a lot at stake here, not least his family who must be worried sick.'

Charles closed his eyes in concentration and said, 'Disappearances are usually about sex or money but I can't see this applies to Tom. Got to be something else. Anyway we need to meet up with Jill and make sure she knows she has our support.'

'When did you last speak with her?'

'About an hour ago. She was with someone and didn't say much but I don't think there was much to say. There was no news, that's for sure.'

Charles rose and said, 'Give me a few minutes would you? I'm just going to ring round a few people. You never know.'

Alone in his office again Bob began to feel a knotting in his stomach. Charles was right about the sex and money bit. He hoped it was sex and nothing to do with Stanton, McIntosh and Goldman. Anything but that. He placed his elbows on the desk and held his head in his hands

Chapter 6

Jill Stanton went to the ladies washroom as soon as she left Jack's office and studied herself in the mirror. She had never felt so scared and her legs began to tremble. She closed her eyes, bowed her head and tried to shut out any negative thoughts.

I've got to pull myself together. She checked her image in the mirror and quickly walked down the corridor and out into the warm sunlight.

She hurried across to her black Audi convertible, climbed in and pulled her mobile out of her bag. She scrolled down to Tom's listing and with her hand shaking, pressed call and put the phone to her ear.

'Hi, you've reached Tom Stanton. Please leave a message and I'll get back to you as soon as I can.' She slumped down in the seat trying not to believe what was happening. She rang Bob and sensed before he spoke there was no news.

'Where are you Jill?' The concern in his voice was audible.

'I've just left a private investigator and he is going to help.'

'What about the police? Why not let them find Tom?'

'I don't care who finds him but I just know something awful has happened, Bob. I'm going to throw everything I can at it. I'm just going to ring the police now. If there is anything to tell you I'll call straight back.'

'Look Jill. Charles and I are here to help. Anything at all, day or night, just call.'

'Yes of course. I must go.' She phoned the police direct number she'd been given and identified herself before being put through to the duty sergeant.

'I'm sorry Mrs Stanton, we've circulated your husband's details but as yet we have had no reports of any sighting.'

'So what happens now?'

'We can assign an officer to the case and step up our enquiries but we need to see you and get as much detail as we can from you.'

'OK. Look, I'm on my way home now. You have my address and I expect to be there for the rest of today.'

There was a pause and some muffled conversation.

'Alright, we'll have someone with you at 3'oclock this afternoon.'

'Fine, will you call me if anything happens?'

'Of course. Good bye Mrs Stanton.'

She started the engine and glanced in the mirror before moving off. She realized how pale she looked and ran her hand through her hair. Driving through the traffic, she was aware her concentration was straying and she fought to stay focused on the road. What was it her English teacher, Miss Bellingham, had said to her all those years ago?

'You reap what you sow Jill, always remember that.'

'Dear God, please let her be wrong.' As she headed west out of London towards the motorway, a black Toyota Land Cruiser followed six vehicles back, the driver obscured by tinted windows.

Chapter 7

In London, one thing that has stayed constant over the years is the congestion which begins early in the morning and never lets up. Many of its streets were not designed to take today's traffic volumes and if you add in street closures from the crumbling 18th century water and sewage systems, which are in need of constant repair and renewal, then it is a perfect recipe for urban chaos.

Jack Barclay was negotiating heavier than normal early evening traffic in Kensington High Street as he headed towards Knightsbridge and a meeting with Mike Hayward, his contact for mobile phones. In all the years they had known each other, Mike never conducted business on the phone. Well if anyone should know about phone privacy, he should. Jack never asked how he got his information and Mike never raised his prices. An ideal arrangement.

Jack edged his ageing Saab 900 round yet another red bus and moved on thirty yards. These journeys did at least provide thinking time and he mulled over his meeting with Jill Stanton. He could almost guarantee she had been economical with the truth, especially about her own lifestyle. She was an extremely attractive woman with no shortage of money and time on her hands. There was bound to be a story somewhere and if her husband was not to resurface quickly, the pressures would mount and the skeletons would start tumbling out.

Jack knew a lot about skeletons and since his own divorce, and realised, as if he didn't already know, nothing is ever as it appears. Everyone thought he and Kate had the ideal marriage and so did he. Although he worked long and often unsociable hours, he had talked this through right at the beginning of their relationship and it was agreed they would build in and plan time together to ensure resentment didn't build up. However, visits to their boat moored on the south coast in the early days became fewer in number. Excuses were made and the months drifted on with work dominating both their waking hours.

The end was sudden and shocking for them both.

Jack had been in central London for a meeting with Mike Hayward and was headed for a small pub they often used just off Marylebone High Street. He had turned into Marylebone Lane and quite literally bumped into his wife. What were the odds of this happening in a city of eight million people? Trouble was that she was arm in arm with a man. An exceptionally good looking man and she was managing to walk and kiss him at the same time.

Jack had moved out of the marital home that night and they had done their best to make the end as civilised as possible.

The business had suffered as he tried to recover his equilibrium, but he knew he was drinking too much.

Without Kate he had too much thinking time and his re-acquaintance with whisky had sent him into spirals of retrospection. One morning he couldn't remember who he was. It became the turning point. It was the start of a return to sanity and the possibility of a future.

It took three months to rebuild his self respect and a little longer to kick start the business. But he was getting there and he hoped life would throw some kinder things at him if he stayed clean. Input equals output he remembered reading in one self help book and they are always right. Bastards.

Mike Hayward was at a table near the back with two glasses of Coke in front of him. Jack shook his outstretched hand as he sat down and just said, 'Traffic'.

He wasn't sure what Mike did for a living except that he was something in telecommunications.

It was always good to see him and they had become friends over the years if not exactly bosom buddies. There was a shared respect and not a little excitement what with the element of risk attached to Mike's services.

Jack passed over Tom's mobile phone number on a slip of paper and Mike looked at it as if he could tell something from it. It was another number which would no doubt yield some interesting data given the brief background he had just been given.

'I'll need three or four days. Maybe a bit longer given the workload on at the moment.'

'Fine Mike. Look for call repetition and any frequency overseas. All the usual stuff. The guy went missing at around 7.00am on Tuesday last week so any activity just before then could be helpful. His mobile is still charged as far as we know.'

They finished their drinks and stood up.

'Good to see you again Jack. I'll get back to you soon and we can meet up nearer your place. It's the usual arrangement unless there is something different. OK?'

'No problem Mike. Good to see you too.'

They made their way out and parted company on the pavement. The crowds had thinned now as Jack made his way back to the High Street and there was a pink glow in the sky as the shadows of the evening sun began to set over Bond Street.

Chapter 8

When Jill eventually reached her driveway she felt exhausted. The whole dreadful happenings were beginning to sink in and she just could not believe the reality of it all. 'Christ, Tom, where are you?'

She parked quickly and let herself in through the huge oak door which fronted the large mock Tudor property.

Inside it was airless and after opening one of the back windows she headed for the kitchen and went straight to the fridge. In the recessed door she knew there was an opened bottle of Pinot Grigio and stretching up into an overhead cupboard, she took down a large wine glass and filled it. She took a sip of the chilled white wine, then another.

She just wanted to delay what she knew she had to do and on refilling her glass, picked up her mobile and phoned Tom. It went straight into the message service.

She walked to a chair, sat down heavily and wept.

She had never known such desolation. Only the grandfather clock in the hallway pierced the silence and after a few minutes she gathered herself and headed for the bedroom.

All his clothes were in the walk in wardrobe and she gazed at them, almost afraid to start the task in hand. Tom's business suits were nearest the front and his casual clothes were towards the back. Taking three suits off the rack, she moved over to the king size bed and sat down. Almost without realising it she brought one of his jackets towards her face and inhaled his scent.

The first was charcoal grey from Saville Row and she started with the jacket. Most of the pockets were empty and all she found was a handkerchief and a pen. The second had some loose change and a London tube map. She put the map to one side. The third suit was dark blue and one of Jill's favourites as she thought it made him look even more debonair. The jacket pockets were empty but she felt a stabbing in her chest as she pulled out a scrap of paper from the trouser pocket. It looked as if it had been ripped from a small desk jotting pad and bore the words 'Eurostar? 7.15.Tuesday.'

As she searched the rest of his clothes she became increasingly uneasy. After a few minutes she had moved on to his trousers and casual shirts. Most pockets contained nothing at all but as she was about to give up on the exercise she felt something in the back pocket of a pair of beige chinos. It was a tiny packet and opening it she saw what looked to her like washing powder. She froze and instantly knew what she might be looking at.

'Oh my God! Not this.'

Chapter 9

Stanton, McIntosh and Goldman had not always been so successful and at the beginning, Tom and Charles had worked hard to build the client base. They had pulled in many of their friends and set them up with good solid investments, pensions and endowment mortgages. They had bought some existing investment business but eventually they knew new blood was needed to build turnover. Charles had known Bob Goldman for about six years and always rated him. He knew he was frustrated with his present company and his earnings were capped. Charles also knew he was very well connected in the City. Something he and Tom needed badly.

It had been two years since Charles had sounded Bob out over a long lunch at Smithfield Market.

'We are turning over £3m a year but we need help to move forward. We think you are our man and we would bring you in as a full partner from the start. We'd like you to give it some thought.'

Charles could see Bob was flattered.

He had joined SMG the following month and the Company quadrupled its profits in the following year. They were on their way to the big time.

***

Charles McIntosh drew a blank when phoning round his business associates. Most of them already knew about Tom and were as mystified as Charles as to what had happened. On the business front, this was bad. In the financial world it was all about confidence, confidence and more confidence. The slightest whiff of uncertainty spread quicker than a Greek wildfire and money quickly moved out to what was thought to be safer havens.

It was clear word had spread fast, very fast, thought Charles. He put the phone down and started to trawl through his e-mails. Nothing jumped out and there seemed little that was immediate. He picked up the phone, thought better of it and made his way down the corridor to Bob's office. He walked in without the usual tap on the door and Bob looked up from his phone conversation and nodded Charles to the chair by the side of his desk. He finished his call with a rather weary, 'OK, be in touch' and sat back staring into space for a second.

'This is going to sound uncaring and mercenary Bob, but we've got to limit damage to the company. The word is out about Tom.'

'So what do you suggest?'

'We just have to be careful not to make things worse by digging a bigger hole. I think we say nothing and wait for the next bit of drama in the City to knock this into the back pages as it were. The way the market's going, that could be today.' He shrugged. 'Let's carry on with our appointments and keep in touch with each other.'

Bob cleared his throat. 'I think we must meet with Jill too. How about early evening today if she is up to it? She can update us and who knows, there might be something positive by then. What do you think has happened?'

Charles laid his pen down carefully and said, 'I don't really know, but it is so out of character and I can only think the worst. I mean Tom has always been ultra cautious about image. He built the company on it. He always said trust was everything, that's why clients give us their money to invest.'

Bob grunted in agreement and asked, 'Have you gone through the accounts?'

'Yeah I had a look through them this morning and there's nothing jumping out at me. We've hit 60 per cent of target for the month at the half way point. Nothing spectacular but given the state of the market, we're doing fine.'

'Was Tom working on anything we didn't know about?'

'Not as far as I'm aware. His French trip was really routine, but he has been to Paris three times recently which is a lot for the size of the account.'

Bob frowned at him and said, 'Maybe it wasn't so routine.'

'Maybe not. Anyway, look Bob, I'm going to carry on with my meeting at the Marriott. I'll ring Jill and see if we can get together tonight and I'll phone you from the car.'

***

Charles took the call from the bank at 4 o'clock and excused himself from the small meeting room, walking out into the hotel corridor.

The manager at their branch was John Parsons and he was rather blunt. 'Is there something you should be telling me Charles?'

'What do you mean?'

'Your client business account has been cleaned out.'

Charles felt a chill spread over his gut. 'Jesus. By whom?'

'Well, I was hoping you would tell me that.'

'What are we talking about here John?'

'Nine hundred thousand withdrawn with all signatures. All above board but given the amount, I thought I'd better run it by you.'

'Christ. Where has it gone?'

'We can't tell. It was withdrawn as a bankers draft and is immediately cashable.'

Charles felt his heart beginning to race as he tried to grasp what he was hearing. Suddenly light headed, he sat down. 'You've got to cancel it John. Bob and I didn't sign anything.'

'Charles, the money's gone. The account is showing a nil balance.'

He could feel the sweat trickle down his back and the hair at the back of his head was soaking. 'Give me a few minutes and I'll be right back to you.'

He flipped his phone shut and began pacing up and down the corridor. For the first time in his memory he didn't know what to do. His hands began to shake. He suddenly knew everything he had striven for was about to explode in his face. 'We're fucked,' he said out loud.

He opened his mobile and punched the office number.

'Bob, I've just had a call from John at the bank. Our client account has been cleared out. No explanation.'

There was a pause at the other end then, 'Holy Jesus.'

Chapter 10

Jack woke early and went to the kitchen to percolate the coffee.

He drank half a mug but breakfast would have to wait. He knew he had lost a lot of time on Tom Stanton and he had pushed Mike Hayward for some mobile phone information.

Time to meet up with him. It was only 7.30am but Park Lane was already at a crawl and Jack eventually made it to the underground car park near Marble Arch. He emerged and made his way to The Rendezvous in Curzon Street and ordered a bacon sandwich and a filter coffee.

Mike arrived as Jack's breakfast was delivered to the small table on the pavement and he stood up to welcome him. 'Breakfast?'

'No thanks, coffee will be fine. Cappuccino please – large. 'Mike sat down and exhaled loudly. 'Sorry I'm late. Traffic was shit, but then I'm sure you know that.'

He took out a wad of folded A4 sheets from his inside pocket and passed them over. 'I haven't had a chance to analyse them, but there is considerable foreign traffic. France mainly. A lot of repetition on specific numbers and a lot of calls each way to Paris.'

Jack took the papers and quickly looked through them. Dates, times and numbers. Everything but the conversations.

Mike's coffee arrived and they changed the subject to London and how you had to move around before sunrise to get anywhere on time nowadays.

Jack called for the bill and passed an envelope to Mike as the waiter disappeared inside. 'There's a bit extra there. I appreciate you turning this one around on the hurry up.'

'No problem Jack, but I can't promise this so quickly again.'

Jack nodded and gave a note to the waiter on his return.

After Mike had gone Jack called the waiter back and ordered another coffee. He might as well start looking at Mike's lists now rather than go back underground to his car. His eye was moving down the first page when his phone rang.

'Jack, it's Jill Stanton. Can you speak?'

'Yes I'm OK.'

'I did as you asked and I think I found something.' Her voice quivered as she spoke and Jack knew she was struggling to sound calm. 'I went through Tom's pockets and really only came up with one thing which I thought you should know about. I found a day return Eurostar ticket to Paris in his pockets. It was for the morning he left.'

'We thought he was flying.'

'Yes, that's what everyone thought.'

'Well, thanks for that. There may be a simple explanation but no doubt we'll find out. Was there anything else of interest?'

Jack sensed her hesitation. 'Nothing as far as I could see. Just normal stuff.'

'OK, Jill. Is it alright to call you Jill?'

'Of course.'

Jack sat back on his chair as the office workers walked quickly by him, clutching their takeaway coffees. He knew Jill was scared and he knew she was covering something up. He sipped his second coffee and studied the lists he'd been given from Mike. The calls went back almost two months and he pulled a highlighter from his inside pocket and started marking in orange. He went through the first few pages and realised there were three numbers continually showing up and all were in Paris. The durations of two of them were relatively short and during the day, indicating business. Calls to the third one were made in the evening. Tom Stanton had frequent contact with Paris and he had at least somewhere to start.

Chapter 11

The costs of buying a house anywhere in or near London had always been high and as families grew, many owners opted to extend what they had rather than try to move to a larger house.

With Windsor Castle rearing up majestically in the background, Datchet was one of the most desirable of neighbourhoods on the River Thames west of London and at times it seemed every home had scaffolding and blue tarpaulins around it.

It was at such a home the skip lorry had come to collect the full container of rubble from the small unmade road running along the back of the property.

The BMW was parked so tightly its front bumper was almost under the edge of the battered yellow skip. The lorry driver checked for an occupant but found no one inside the vehicle and went round to the front of the house to check with the building workers. No one knew anything about the car except it had been there for a couple of days. He phoned in to the office and his supervisor asked him for the registration number and said he'd get back to him. His supervisor phoned his mate at the police station. When the skip driver answered his mobile fifteen minutes later he was told to stay where he was.

The police arrived soon after and two uniformed officers looked around the car without touching it.

It was registered to a Tom Stanton and after it had lain collecting builders' dust, it was about to get a lot of attention.

***

Jill was at the door of the lounge as her children watched The Simpsons on TV. She knew they were bound to see speculative reports about their father appearing on the television and the newspapers. The abuse would follow from children at school and they would begin to suffer. She had to be completely honest with them and the time to speak was now. She saw Sarah sitting on the sofa, her intelligent green eyes focused on the screen and her right hand playing with a strand of her long fair hair. Jill suspected she already knew something had happened. Her daughter was usually one step ahead on most things but she had not asked too many questions. Mature beyond her years.

Jill's thoughts drifted as she saw Oliver flop deeper into the sofa opposite his sister, one leg dangling with his foot resting on the floor. The spitting image of his father, he was waiting for his next rugby lesson from his Dad, a player who had made county level. A sports mad father whom he worshipped. She knew he was confused and blotting out the telephone conversations he must have heard over the past few days.

The programme ended and Jill walked in. 'Hi kids, we need to have a little chat about dad.' Sarah snapped the TV off with the remote and Oliver glanced up with a startled look. 'What's up Mum?'

Jill sat down next to Oliver and with her hand, beckoned Sarah over to sit next to her. 'Something's happened.' She felt Oliver's hand twitch on her arm. 'We don't know anything yet, but your dad seems to have gone missing. He's on business and hasn't turned up where we thought he would. It's probably all a mistake but you know, we have to stick together on this.'

'What do you mean, stick together. Where is he?' Oliver sat up, glaring at his mother.

'We just don't know where he is at the moment Olly. It's probably nothing to worry about at all.'

'But where could he be?'

'We don't know.'

Sarah turned to Jill. 'Do the police know?'

'They are looking for him but they aren't worried.'

'Are you Mum?'

Jill leant back on the couch, exhaled and steeled herself. 'No. There will be a simple explanation to this and we'll know something very soon, I'm sure.'

'If you two aren't that bothered, then I am.' Oliver got up from the couch and stumbled from the room. Sarah turned to her mum and hugged her and they both began to sob quietly. 'Oh God, Mum.'

Chapter 12

Jack Barclay tried to make some sense of what he had just been told. Tom Stanton was nowhere to be seen. He had an air ticket to fly to Paris but never got on the plane and he was in possession of a Eurostar ticket for the same day. If he was trying to confuse things, he had done pretty well.

Jack pulled Mike's printouts from his inside pocket and began studying the detail. He knew there was more to Paris than looking after the financial investments of a restaurant. As he mused over his notes his phone rang and checking the ID, saw it was Jill Stanton.

'Jack this is not about the bank cards. They've found Tom's car.' She sounded panicky and her voice cracked as she told him it had been found empty three miles from his health club in a back lane of Eton.

'Do you know if there was anything on show inside the car?'

'Not as far as I'm aware. The police have taken it away for forensic examination and closed the area off.'

'What about the boot?'

'Oh God, Jack. I'm told they would have known if it had...you know, had anything in it.' Her voice trailed off.

'Yes, they would have known, believe me. Look Jill, try and stay calm. It could have been worse news and at least there is some physical evidence for us to go with.'

'I'll get back to you later Jack. Sarah has a field trip today and we need to look out some extra stuff. I've told them about their dad but they don't know about the car yet.'

'OK, we'll speak later.'

He called the waitress, paid his bill and headed for the door.

Making his way north he walked to Oxford Street and moved across into a side street. He found the unobtrusive entrance and pushed open the door. Climbing some worn stairs he entered a small cluttered electronics shop. The strip neon light picked out a small balding man in a brown lab coat who appeared to be in his seventies. He looked up and smiled as he saw Jack.

'Well it's been a couple of months at least. How's things?'

'OK, Pop. How about you?'

'Fine, back still playing me up but who's interested? You after the usual?'

'Yeah, sure am but could you make it two? I'm in for some heavy use this time. They need to work from anywhere.'

'Sure, no problem.' He turned and went behind a crumpled grey curtain, re entering the shop after a minute with two small boxes. 'Same price as usual to you.' Jack paid cash and always put a generous tip on top. He took four fifties from his pocket and passed them over. 'Thanks, I appreciate it.'

'No problem son, look after yourself out there.'

'Sure will, see you again.'

Jack knew the two prepaid mobile phones he had just bought were completely untraceable..

Chapter 13

As Jill Stanton turned left to make her way up towards the school, the coach arrived for the field trip. Tempers frayed at the congestion and she pulled in to the side of the road well short of the school. It had been a sombre journey with Oliver asking lots of questions before he was dropped off at his school and Jill unable to answer any of them.

Sarah was subdued as they had travelled on to her school. It should have been a light hearted journey with a field trip really meaning a bit of fun with her mates and a day away from the classroom.

As she moved across the rear seat to get out she put her arm through the gap in the front seats and hugged her mum. 'Will you be OK?'

'Sure honey. Stay cool. I'm sure Dad is fine. Try not to worry and I'll pick you up at 4.30.'

Sarah wiped a tear from her eye as she opened the rear door and stepped out onto the pavement. She had to keep hold of the extra rucksack packed with her walking boots and spare clothes in one hand and picnic lunch in the other. She turned and closed the door with her hip and started walking towards the school. Jill saw her look back and try to wave. She waved back and pulled away from the kerb, narrowly missing the Land Cruiser parked in front of her. The driver of the 4X4 watched it all in his rear view mirror.

It was after midday by the time Jack parked in his allocated space at his Maida Vale apartment. He put the key into the lock and heard the hissing sound of mail being pushed along the floor as he opened the door. Bending down he picked up the pile of what looked like a mixture of real correspondence and junk. He flicked through the envelopes and seeing nothing of great importance, dumped them on the coffee table. He hadn't eaten properly all day and moved through to the kitchen, throwing his keys on the sideboard as he went. He boiled some water and poured it into a saucepan with some dried pasta. He added a tin of chopped tomatoes and turned the gas ring on. He placed a pack of fresh basil next to the stove so he wouldn't forget to add it. After waiting till the pan boiled, he turned the gas to low and went through to the lounge and sat down on the small sofa.

He had tossed a lot of thoughts around on the drive back from central London and kept coming back to the Paris connection. The call frequency was high for the apparent low importance of the client. He knew there had to be more to Le Canard Bleu. He looked into his briefcase for the mobile phones, pulled one out and decided to call one of the Paris numbers.

'Bonjour, Restaurant Meurice.'

'Hello, I am bringing some friends along next week and wondered if I could have some directions to your restaurant. I hear you are very good.'

'Of course. We are in St Germain, off the Rue St Luis.'

'Thank you so much. I will call with reservations nearer the time.'

'OK. Au revoir.'

'Au revoir.'

Jack clicked the close button and sat back. Another restaurant to add to Canard Bleu. Tom must like his food!

'Food!' He leapt up and went through to the kitchen. He checked the pasta and saw it was cooked. He remembered to add the basil before pouring his Italian masterpiece into a white bowl. After grinding some black pepper over it, he picked up a spoon and went back through to his chair. As he ate he reflected again on what he knew. He felt sure he had some inside track on Tom Stanton but was it legitimate SMG business or something else?

***

Jill Stanton drove away from the school with her mind racing. Where the hell was Tom? Why was he doing this? Her right leg started to shake as she depressed the accelerator. She was going to go straight home in the hope her husband would be there but as she approached the tennis club, she slowed. Her group would be there for coffee this morning and almost without thinking made a late left turn into the club. Throwing her mobile into her bag she climbed out and made her way to the clubhouse.

As she entered she knew from the stares that word had got out.

Everyone looked up and Jill felt like a rabbit caught in the headlights but Lauren immediately stood up and came over to her.

'Jill, we've heard about Tom. It's so awful but I'm sure you'll hear from him soon.'

'Thanks Lauren. I don't really know why I'm here but I couldn't face going back to the house.'

'Come on over and have a coffee.' Everyone moved up and made space for Jill on the sofa and as she sat down Lauren came back from the bar with coffee.

Suddenly, Jill wished she hadn't come to the club at all. She didn't know everyone round the table and the women she knew were unsure how to handle this new situation. Everyone seemed to be thinking before they said anything.

She was saved by her mobile ringing in her tote bag and excused herself, and moving away to the window overlooking the court used for competitions. She saw Mark, the club coach, giving a lesson and a wave of guilt washed over her. She had found him a great antidote to Tom's perpetual absences on business but suddenly she felt alone and ashamed. She felt a flush burn her face. She quickly turned away and answered the phone.

'Hi, it's Jack. Is there any news?'

Jill walked towards the exit and out into the sunlit car park. 'No, nothing. I was hoping you might have heard something.'

Jack paused. 'How often did Tom go to Paris?'

Jill walked towards her car. 'It was quite a lot, sometimes four or five times a month. He said he had a big new corporate client there and they needed some high maintenance, especially in the early days. Something in engineering but he never went into much detail about them.'

Jack knew Canard Bleu had about as much in common with engineering as a duck had with dry land but followed up with another question. 'Where did he normally stay when he was in Paris?'

'He mentioned a small hotel he used on the Left Bank. I think it was called Le Petit Maison. He liked the feel of the place and said it was friendly and near the Metro.'

'OK, Jill. I'm looking at a few things but we need to meet up so as I can get the background stuff from you. Could I come and see you early evening?'

'Sure. Give me a ring before you set off.'

Jill leant against the side of the car as she finished the call and opened the driver's door to seek refuge inside the vehicle. She had to compose herself before going back into the clubhouse.

Chapter 14

Charles McIntosh arranged another meeting with Bob at the office at 6.30 that evening. The feeling of apprehension gripped him as he tried to change lanes to hasten his journey through the rush hour traffic. Why had he not spotted anything? Why had Bob not spotted anything?

Tom was the company. He was Stanton, McIntosh and Goldman.

If anyone should take credit for the success of SMG it was Tom. By sheer drive, energy and charisma, he had been the lynch pin in building up the business. Many of their clients were high achievers and used to success. Just as many were personal friends of all three partners and had placed absolute trust in them to look after their portfolios. Even when times were not so good, they kept faith with them and rode out the market lows.

By the time Charles reached the office he could feel the wet in his armpits. He swung his car into his space at the front of the building. He swiped his security card on the panel at the side of front door and made his way to the first floor. Bob was on the phone and finished the call as Charles came in. Bob Goldman was chalk white and his hands shook as he nodded at Charles. Without sitting down, he said, 'Anything new?'

'I'm not long back myself but as far as I can make out, the general client account money is definitely gone. £900k. Around 20 new clients involved. I don't know about Tom's personal client portfolio. I can't access his system but we can only hope everything is in place.' Charles fell into the easy chair next to the desk and looked up saying, 'I don't believe this. What the hell do we do?'

Bob Goldman threw his pen onto the desk and slumped in his chair looking suddenly like a small boy lost in a forest. 'I think we've been had. He's has taken off and we're in it up to our necks whatever happens but don't ask me what we do. Finding Tom would help.'

Charles sat staring into space wordlessly and unbelieving. In his own thoughts he was trying to predict how this would play out. How it would affect him and his family? His friends who were already affected. Jesus, even his own house on vast mortgage could be in danger. His car. His whole lifestyle. The thoughts tumbled into the forefront of his mind as he realised the nightmare was just beginning.

***

Jill had sent the children to the family room to watch television and poured herself a chardonnay. The phone had rung constantly and she could tell the callers nothing. No, she hadn't heard anything about Tom and yes she would get back to them as soon as she knew anything. She felt as if she was dealing with a family bereavement and it was something she was not used to. She picked up her mobile and scrolled to Tom's number, her finger trembling so much she almost hit the next name on the memory. Straight to voice mail again. Jill shouted out in frustration. Oh God Tom, please ring me. Please. Please. She jumped when the phone rang.

'It's Jack. You sound upset.'

'No, I'm alright. I just thought it could be Tom. Come round when you can. Have you eaten?'

'Not really since lunchtime but I'm not particularly hungry.

Jill took a sip from her glass and said, 'Nor me.'

'We have a lot to talk about Jack'

'I know, but I have more questions than answers for you.'

Chapter 15

Jack pulled into Jill's driveway just after 7.30 that evening as an orange glow was beginning to appear in the sky to the west. He saw two cars parked in front of the house. He thought it could be Tom's partners and if they had arrived unannounced it would present him with an opportunity to do some digging. He slid his Saab behind the two cars making sure they could manoeuvre and leave before him.

He rang the doorbell and Jill came to the door. Considering what she was going through she looked even prettier now than when he first met her.

Her white blouse was buttoned up just enough and her tight jeans showed off her toned figure. Jack had never seen her like this. So casually dressed but aware of the possible effect.

'Charles and Bob are here. I hope that's OK.'

'Of course.'

She led him through to the back of the house into a large softly lit conservatory. The space was broken up with two chocolate coloured leather sofas and an armchair with an antique coffee table in the middle.

Three floor standing lamps, one at each side, threw a warm glow over the room. Bob Goldman sat in one of the sofas and Charles McIntosh was in the armchair. Both looked as if they had just been told they had a terminal illness.

They glanced up and stood as Jack preceded Jill into the room.

Before Jill could say anything Bob Goldman introduced himself and stretched out his hand. Jack took it and returned the introduction. Charles did the same.

'Drink, Jack?'

'Tap water would be fine thanks.'

She left the room and went to the kitchen. Jack sat down on the armchair looking at both men in turn.

'How is Mrs. Stanton?' he asked.

'Holding up pretty well on the outside I'd say.' Bob had beaten Charles to the reply and carried on. 'This has come as a huge shock to us all Mr. Barclay. It's just so out of character and frankly we are utterly mystified as to Tom's disappearance.' He paused and said, 'You'll find out very soon anyway but we have just discovered there is money missing from the company as well.'

Jack tensed and asked, 'How much?

'We found out today from our bank. £900k is missing from our new client account and it looks as if it must be connected to Tom's disappearance. It has been removed in a cashable cheque and carried all our signatures but we, that's Charles and I, haven't signed anything. Jill knows and the police have been informed. They need statements from us but it looks as if signatures have been forged.'

'Would that be two signatures or three?' asked Jack.

'That we don't know till the cheque goes through the system and is returned.'

'I would like to think three were forged but if not, Tom must have had a gun at his head before doing that to the company.'

Bob stopped talking as Jill came back and handed Jack his water with some ice cubes tinkling in the glass. She collected her own drink from the coffee table and sat next to Bob. Jack looked across the room and said to no one in particular, 'There could be a logical explanation but some people are going to think the worst.'

Charles cleared his throat. 'Mr Barclay, our company has been successfully built up with absolute integrity. You have to understand, there must be some logical explanation for all this. We aren't some boiler room, fly by night operation.'

Jack put his drink down at the table next to him and addressed Bob directly. 'I'm sorry to have to be so blunt, especially with Mrs Stanton here, but you must know that everything points to Tom being involved in a large scale fraud. He may have been coerced into this and is in danger. You may as well start thinking along those lines.'

Bob and Charles looked startled at his directness.

'I need your complete co-operation. No holding back. Is there anything you know about Tom which could give us something to go on? I'm sorry, but we may as well face reality here.'

Jill's head dropped and she let out a pained moan.

'I know, I know' she said, lifting her wine glass to her mouth and taking a gulp.

Charles crossed his legs and stared hard at Jack. 'Are you saying Tom is a crook?'

'I'm afraid that's one of the possible options.'

'That's ridiculous. Tom was, is, one of the straightest guys in the business.'

Jack glanced at Jill who was now ashen faced. He decided to go ahead anyway as he had created an atmosphere which could lead to an opinion or fact which had hitherto been off limits.

'Charles, when you are dealing with a new client who is still perhaps a little wary of committing, how do you help him or her to make choices?'

'How do you mean?'

'Well it's a big decision to hand over your well earned money to someone whom you may have never met before. Put yourself in their shoes.'

'You have to weigh up how much risk you think the client wishes to live with and there is a recognised method of gauging this. You then give the client as many choices as you can within the parameter set. It is a position of trust you are in and confidence plays a very big part.'

'So, you are offering choices to help gain trust?'

'Yes, that's one of the reasons.'

'Well for choices just say options and that is what we need to examine very carefully. You may not like it, but it is possible Tom has absconded with a great deal of money. But there are other possibilities. He may have been kidnapped and forced to pay the money. He may have been blackmailed. If you have any other theories, let's hear them.'

Charles rose and began pacing the room.

'You need to think of anything you have heard or witnessed about Tom which could steer us in the right direction.' There was an uncomfortable silence and Jack pressed on. 'How much did you all know about each other's investment portfolios?'

Bob spoke for the first time. 'We had formal weekly meetings but we are a small firm and we all knew what each was doing most of the time.'

Jack interjected 'Most of the time?'

'Well you know what I mean. There were no business secrets between us.'

Jack picked his moment. 'What did you know of Tom's business in Paris?'

Bob looked a little quizzically at him. 'Paris was pretty small beer to us but had potential if new restaurants were opened'.

Jill's head snapped up. 'What about the engineering company he had brought as a client? It was called FRM or something.'

Charles turned and looked at Bob for assurance.

She carried on. 'He said it was his baby and it could get big for SMG.'

Bob looked at Jack and held up his hands. 'Look, we never took much notice of the Paris portfolio and it didn't feature much in our regular update meetings. In fact Tom's expenses for the trips often didn't cover the commissions we were getting from the investments but we let it go.'

'We just assumed Tom was building a larger investment from Canard Bleu. Its owner, Peter, came over once or twice to London and we took him out to dinner. Nothing too glitzy but he did live in Paris and he was in the restaurant business so we pushed the boat out a bit. Usually around Notting Hill, which he liked.'

Charles sat down again and ran his hand through his hair. 'This FRM thing needs to be looked at. We'll have to get back to you on that.'

Jack glanced at Jill and saw confusion on her face. He turned to Charles. 'How did Tom usually travel to Paris?'

'Flew usually. Liked to keep his Air Miles up.'

'Never on Eurostar?'

'Nope, he had a thing about tunnels.'

Jill managed to nod.

'OK', said Jack, 'here's where we are now. Tom hasn't used his mobile since he went missing. We have still to check with the bank as to any use of his credit cards but I suspect they won't have been used.'

Looking across at Jill he carried on, 'He hasn't been in touch with Jill or either of you since he disappeared and now there's the money missing from your company. The police will have a lot of questions for you now there is a potentially large fraud involved. Until yesterday it was a missing persons investigation and frankly they don't get too worked up immediately an adult goes missing. Hundreds do every day and most turn up. Be as honest as you possibly can with them because a lot of time has elapsed. If you don't have any objections, I would like a few minutes with Mrs Stanton.'

Bob and Charles looked at each other, shrugged and made to get up. As they moved towards Jill to say good bye, Jack pulled some business cards from his pocket. Both men pecked Jill on the cheek. 'Call us at any time if we can be of help.' As they turned round, Jack stood up and handed them his card.

'Ring me if you hear anything, however small. And thanks.'

Jill rose wearily and showed them to the door, her eyes beginning to look puffy. On her return she sat down heavily on the sofa next to Jack and stared into space.

Jack noticed the black circles below her eyes and felt immense pity. It was all beginning to get to her. 'Why don't you get someone over to stay for a couple of days? Your mum, a girlfriend, just someone to share the pain a bit.'

'My mum and dad are abroad but they'll be back in the morning. I've phoned them and they know Tom is missing.'

He brought out his pocket notebook and said, 'Jill, I know this is not the best time but I need Tom's credit card details and any other contact numbers which may have been in his wallet. I also need to speak to his health club and the airline. Could you also ask your bank for a statement on your current accounts? Everything up to the time he went missing.'

Tears welled up in her eyes and almost without thinking, Jack put his arm around her shoulder. 'I'm sorry Jill, I really am.'

She sagged and as she put her head next to Jack's he could feel the wetness of her tears against his face as she began sobbing quietly. He held her for several minutes and as he began to feel a calmness come over her she pulled her face away and said, 'Will we find him?'

'Yes, we will, but it may not be soon. Tom has vanished into thin air and it will take time to find out why. You're going to have to be very brave for the kids and it's going to be tough.'

Jill tried to smile. 'Thank you.'

He slowly raised his hand and gently wiped the tear tracks from the sides of her face. 'You must trust me and tell me anything you know which may help. And I mean anything. Tonight might not be the best time but just be straight with me'.

She nodded, 'Let me check on the kids, would you? I'll be straight back.' She got up and tugged her blouse down at the waist and ran her hand through her hair pushing it back from her forehead before going through to what Jack took to be a television room just off the hall.

She was away for about five minutes and when she came back, she picked up her wine glass and sat at the end of the sofa.

'How are they?'

'Fine. Better than their mum.'

Jill had clearly composed herself for the kids and he knew he had to ask the difficult questions.

'Is there anything you know about Tom or anything in your lives which would have some bearing on what's happened?'

She was startled by his directness but quickly gathered herself. 'Not really. We were just motoring through life in a pretty normal way. Nothing I can think of.'

'When you went through Tom's pockets, did you find anything which surprised you? Anything which puzzled you?'

Jill hesitated and he knew.

'What did you find?'

She stared down at her feet, her knees clamped together, lifted her head and said, 'I found some drugs, I think.'

Jack's expression didn't change. 'How did you know they were drugs?'

'Well, I can't be absolutely sure but we all watch television. It was a small packet with white powder inside. It was in a pocket of his chinos.'

'Assuming you are right, did you have any idea he was into that sort of thing?'

'No. If he was, it was never obvious and you know, it's as upsetting as him not being here.'

Jack exhaled and said, 'It may not be what you think. Was there anything else?'

'Nothing as far as I could tell. It was just all the usual stuff.'

'Could I see what you found and the card details too?'

'Yes, of course.'

Jill rose and went through to the hall and climbed the stairs to the master bedroom.

As he waited for her to come back he knew this changed everything. The big new dimension. The secret he kept from his family and probably everyone around him. So he was capable of deception, but what else lay hidden?

Jill returned a couple of minutes later and handed Tom's wallet to Jack. 'Take it. Give it back to me when you've gone through it. The packet is in there, too.'

'Sure. I'll ring you first thing in the morning to make sure you're OK. See if you can get some sleep.'

'I'll try.' She followed him as he made his way out of the conservatory and headed towards the front door. As she opened it, he turned and squeezed her arm gently. He looked into her eyes and said, 'We'll find him Jill.'

He felt her eyes on him as he crunched down the driveway and climbed into his car. He started the engine and turned towards the road.

Casting a glance left and right across the darkened hedgerows on each side, she closed the door and switched off the porch light.

Chapter 16

Khalid and Xavier always used Eurostar. Slacker security compared to CDG and LHR or at least it seemed that way. As Khalid went through the carriage at Gare du Nord to find his seat, people stared at him. It was a miracle children didn't scream. He knew why and he was quite used to it. After all, he had to look in the mirror every morning. Knocking against passengers as they sat reading their morning papers, he pushed his bulk through the central aisle to carriage six. He knew he was in seat twenty five on the left because he had sat in it often enough. Superstition was his only weakness. The well dressed young business man sitting with his laptop on his knees didn't look up as Khalid towered over him. As if it mattered, Khalid noted his reservation tag on the chair back.

He effortlessly hooked his hand over the carry on bag sitting in the overhead rack and dropped it on to the floor. The man was startled and his jaw dropped as he looked up and saw Khalid jerk his thumb in a gesture to vacate the seat. Wordlessly he got up, snapped his laptop shut and stumbled away dragging his case behind him. Passengers around him pretended not to notice as Khalid placed his case in the rack and sat down heavily. He closed his eyes, thought of nothing and waited for his arrival at London St. Pancras.

Later that morning Xavier made the same journey with a little less drama. In fact no one noticed him at all. Just as he liked it. His only thoughts were whether the pistols at the safe house would need cleaning.

Their new temporary home in Paddington was one of the few neighbourhoods which had yet to be gentrified. Too close to Central London to get property on the cheap and a history of all-night street activity around the cheap hotels and kebab joints. Perfect for anonymity. Perfect for Khalid and Xavier.

***

News of Tom Stanton's disappearance spread quicker than flu in January.

Everyone knew just as soon as people could be contacted by phone and lurid detail given. Not that anyone actually knew anything. They just made up what they didn't. And then added more to it. By the fourth day of his disappearance, Tom was variously in Bolivia or maybe Venezuela or sailing the South China Sea. With a woman.

The phones at Stanton, Goldman and McIntosh had started ringing at 7 o'clock in the morning on Wednesday and the car park began to get busy by 7.30am. Charles had realised the news was spreading and arrived at the office at 6 o'clock. Suddenly he wished he was somewhere else. The staff didn't normally get in til just before the nine o'clock official start and he couldn't handle all the calls. Bob arrived before 8.00am and said he couldn't get into the car park outside.

Huddled inside Charles's office on the first floor they realised the situation could get out of hand. Fear was the factor and some reassurance was needed.

The outside doorbell started ringing and knocks were heard at the door.

Bob clutched a black coffee and said, 'We've got to scotch the rumours. That's all it is. Rumour. They don't know about the money. All they maybe know is Tom is missing. We've got to calm things down and appeal for some logic.'

Charles looked out of the window as a car horn sounded. 'OK, he said. 'You go out and tell them that because I'm not.'

'We need some help here, Charles. The press will be onto this soon and people will expect answers. Trouble is, we haven't got any. We're going to have to stall things. We need some time to find out what's happened. Where the money is. Let's draft a statement and release it in an hour. Get the heat off.'

Bob was increasingly nervous. 'The staff need to be filled in on this too, you know, and they'll be here in half an hour. 'Let's get it drafted.'

Patrick Flynn had an early start for the new extension at the Carter's house.

Some extension. It was about as big as the house itself and involved amongst other things, a recreation room, an extra bedroom and a wet room. Cash as they went. A third to start, a third in the middle and a third on satisfactory completion. Everyone happy, everyone thinking they'd had a good deal. Life was just a bowl of cherries.

He and Lauren had been in Cornwall for three days with the kids and he wanted to make sure this job was going right. He eased his way through the early morning commuter traffic in Pimlico and signalled right to pull into the Carter's 'U' shaped driveway as his mobile phone rang. He parked his van behind a plumber merchant's lorry and answered his phone.

'Pat, it's me,' said Lauren.

'What's wrong honey?'

'Tom Stanton's gone missing.'

Patrick felt a quick tightening in his gut and stayed in the cab.

He knew. He just knew his world was about to crash. The bastard had taken them. Lauren was sobbing uncontrollably on the phone. He said, 'I'll be home in an hour.' And hung up.

***

It was an everyday traffic offence on the Marylebone Road. Its many junctions had cameras ready to film any vehicle that drove a red light. What a revenue earner. Vehicle registration details were recorded and an automatic fine would be posted to the registered owner. The camera flash was just another split second in the busy life of this affluent capital city.

Shame on the driver of the black Land Cruiser who transgressed the law.

He'd seen the flash high above in his rear mirror as he drove west across the Baker Street intersection. 'Fuck 'em.' He drove on and headed down through Shepherds Bush to the Chiswick Flyover towards the M4. The traffic was as heavy as ever and he constantly changed lanes as if it would help him reduce his journey time. He was agitated and the camera incident had annoyed him.

The light was draining from the sky and a bright orange glare had begun to hit drivers full in the face as they made their long way home to the more affordable towns far from the capital. The never ending daily grind.

When it happened, it happened without warning.

A large dark 4X4 vehicle thought to be of Japanese make had become involved with another vehicle as they exited at junction 5 on the M4 for Windsor.

The vehicles came into contact with each other and both stopped on the slip road exit. The driver of the Ford Focus, a young man in his twenties, got out and moved forward to speak with the driver who had got out of his vehicle. As the young man approached him, the driver of the lead vehicle raised what was thought to be a sawn off shotgun and shot the other driver in the chest at close range. The victim had raised his hands perhaps in surrender, perhaps in a vain attempt to ward off what was about to happen. His body lifted off the ground and he was thrown backwards landing on the grass verge at the side of the slip road.

The attacker walked calmly back to his vehicle and drove off. As other motorists stopped to help they found the young man sprawled on his back, already dead in a widening pool of blood. His unseeing eyes were wide open and there was a look of terror on his face.

The M4 was closed following the attack and caused gridlock back to Central London.

Police said they were looking for witnesses and would also like to interview the driver of a dark Toyota Land Cruiser with tinted windows. The driver of this vehicle is described as around forty years old, about 6 feet tall, white, muscular build and with light brown hair. He was wearing black trousers and a grey top with dark trainers.

No name of the victim had been released as it was thought his family were out of the country on holiday and had yet to be informed.

Other drivers told of their shock when they saw what was happening.

'It was so quick and almost unbelievable. The guy with the gun, he was just so cool and calculating. Terrible, just terrible. That poor lad.'

***

After leaving Jill's place, Jack Barclay headed for home but pulled in to his favourite take away as he neared his flat. Shankar had opened the Kohinoor twenty years ago and was always busy in the evenings. He waved to Jack as he saw him enter and immediately walked over to look after his regular customer and friend. They shook hands as they always did and Jack ordered his usual chicken Madras with plain rice and one naan. No popadums. A little too fattening he thought. He sat down in the small waiting area as Shankar went into the kitchen to prepare his food. The TV high on the wall was showing breaking news and the message running along the bottom was reporting a serious incident on the M4 near Windsor. The motorway was now closed westbound and diversions were in place. Jack had wondered why his journey against the evening rush hour seemed busier and now he knew why. Must be something big to close the motorway at this time of night.

Shankar came back with his meal neatly packed into a greaseproof brown take-away bag and went round to the till to get the change from Jack's ten pound note.

Jack looked up at the screen to see the message had changed to a shooting incident on the motorway and he shook his head slightly as Shankar came back. 'See you soon my friend' he called out as Jack opened the door and made his way back to his car.

He drove back to his flat and parked in his usual place. Pushing open the door he was surprised at the lack of mail. Not even junk variety.

He walked through the darkened hall and placed his takeaway on the kitchen table before turning left into his small living room. The walls were painted with a mustard colour theme and a beige carpet was set off by a dark brown leather sofa with two matching easy chairs. The wooden fireplace surrounded a very real looking gas fire and his flat screen Samsung was big enough without dominating the room. On the other side of the fireplace was his Bang and Olufsen music system. His pride and joy. He switched on two side lamps which gave a friendly glow and used the remote to hear some instant jazz on the radio. Home sweet home.

He walked through to the kitchen, took a plate from the cupboard, emptied his rice and curry on to it and placed the naan on a side plate. He selected a Peroni from the fridge and some cutlery from the rack. Turning round he picked up a tray which sat next to the cooker and put everything on it before going through to the living room and sitting down on his favourite seat.

He ate slowly as he listened to Thelonius Monk playing 'Round Midnight' and began going over what he knew. And what he didn't.

The drugs changed everything. Everyone had a secret but this was a serious secret. Any investor with SMG would take their money and run if they knew. If their money was still there that is. He had no doubt SMG would take a huge financial hit and complete oblivion for the company was a real possibility. He had to get to Paris and delve around.

Tom's frequent trips to the restaurant or elsewhere in Paris were key to his disappearance but he had to find who else Tom had contact with. He was feeding the habit and he was almost certainly taking all the risks an addict takes. Assuming he was addicted.

If Tom was leading a double life, he had fooled everyone including those closest to him. Those who loved him dearly.

He finished most of his meal and placed the tray at the side of his chair.

He pulled his notebook from his inside pocket, swigged his beer from the bottle and started to read his notes.

He'd scribbled 'check the long calls to Paris' at the side of page two and he looked again at the number and made a note to check in which arrondissement Tom had been placing the evening calls to.

He suddenly thought of Jill. She must be going through it tonight. Picking up his mobile he rang her.

She answered almost immediately. 'Jack?'

'Yeah, it's me. How are you doing?'

'Not so good. I've drunk a bit too much wine and I'm sitting here in the dark. Kids are in bed but Sarah's upset. So is Oliver but he's trying not to show it. 'The phones have calmed down but it's good to hear from you.'

'I just wanted to know you were OK, that's all.'

'I appreciate that. Will I see you tomorrow?'

'Probably not. I'm just about to book a flight to Paris. I think the first one goes about six but I'll probably go on the next one if I can get a seat. I just need to check a few things out. I'll be back on the evening flight tomorrow. I'll give you a call when I get in if it's not too late. Will you ring me if you hear anything?'

'Of course I will. Take care of yourself.'

'Always do.'

He hit the end button and eased himself up from his chair and brought out his laptop from its case. He logged on and searched for a flight next morning.

Chapter 17

The safe house in Paddington was just behind Sussex Gardens.

When Xavier arrived, Khalid was already in the kitchen, eating a Big Mac. It was the biggest burger Xavier had ever seen and as he looked away in disgust. As if it was the worst thing he'd ever seen.

Xavier wanted this job done quickly so he could go home to his little place by the Vieux Port in the heart of old Marseilles. He dreamt of his favourite table at Chez Fonfon with the best bouillabaisse in the world. The killing and inflicting of pain he found enjoyable. It was having to share his time with Khalid and his disgusting habits that he objected to.

They had separate bedrooms and Xavier put his bag in the back one away from the traffic. That fat bastard can sleep in the front. He won't hear a thing anyway.

The apartment was basic and had three bedrooms, but the third 'guest' room was much smaller than the other two. Access to it was by a small door at the end of the corridor. Khalid probably wouldn't get his gut through it. As Xavier made himself a black coffee he checked the notes he'd made the previous night in Paris.

A private investigator was on the case and that was trouble. Not big trouble but it had to be dealt with. The address of the missing man was known and he had a wife and family. That was always helpful.

As Xavier looked at his notes he recognised all the things he had seen before in his profession. The names were different, the location was different but the solution would be the same. He'd be out of here and home in 72 hours.

After his gourmet meal, Khalid had fallen asleep in a chair. Xavier left him and went to bed.

Next day the sky over London was clear blue, broken only by the high vapour trails of the jets as they criss-crossed Europe. At 6 am the City was coming to life and the prospect of a warm day seemed to make everyone more cheerful.

Jack Barclay headed west to Heathrow and parked in the long term car park for Terminal 5. After its disastrous opening problems, it was indeed a showpiece building to match the best the world's airports had to offer.

He had printed off his boarding card when he booked online last night and with no luggage he went straight through security and past the myriad of upscale shops in departures to tempt the traveller with time to spare.

He headed for one of the coffee shops and ordered. He resisted the calorie laden muffin and sat down with The Times.

Apart from the world being in its usual mess, the front page carried the account of a brutal murder on the M4 yesterday. Shocked witnesses told of the horrific shooting of the defenceless young man and the callous indifference of the murderer as he walked away. The photograph taken at a distance clearly showed the dead man's feet protruding from a grey blanket which had been placed over him. Given the trauma that Jack had experienced over the years and the gruesome scenes he'd witnessed, he read the report with growing unease. This was an unusual level of violence given the seemingly innocuous circumstances leading up to these two men meeting each other. It seems they were complete strangers. A gratuitous slaying of an innocent young man in broad daylight with witnesses all around. The perpetrator had shown no mercy as he carried out the execution.

Jack realised he had not even started his coffee as he absorbed the hideous detail of yesterday's events not five miles from where he was sitting.

He skimmed through the paper not taking in too much. He couldn't get the slaying out of his mind. He checked the screens every fifteen minutes and his gate opened at 7.10am. He joined a quiet group of business people and waited for the flight to be called.

After they were airborne he accepted a cup of coffee from the stewardess and simply looked out of the window as they climbed to cruising height over the English Channel and eventual descent to Charles De Gaulle.

It was just another routine flight mainly with business people and passengers who were processed quickly through immigration and into the sunshine of an early summer's morning in Northern France.

***

His day was going to be busy and he took a taxi into central Paris asking the driver to take him to Hotel Le Petit Maison. He wasn't sure of the exact address but the driver knew it and set off through the heavy morning commuter traffic.

The driver didn't speak much English which suited Jack. He was in contemplative mood and was happy to sit back and enjoy the scenery such as it was. Suburban landscapes giving way to urban areas as they neared the City. As they began crawling through the streets of Paris stopping and starting in dense traffic, he began to wish he had used the fast train instead but at least he would be taken directly to his destination. He got out 15 minutes later and paid off the taxi.

Le Petit Maison was a small three storey hotel with a modest double glass door entrance set into a traditional stone frontage. It looked to be a turn of the century building, warm and beckoning to the weary traveller. Although it was now light, two coaching lamps either side of the doors were still illuminated. Jack stood in a doorway on the opposite side of the street just watching. Habits die hard. As he watched, a smartly dressed middle aged lady in a pale blue coat came out of the hotel carrying a small dog. She looked both ways but set off up to the left stopping after a few yards to set the tiny animal down and attach a lead. It made an immediate escape as far as the nearest tree and peed against it. All normal Parisian life really. Jack waited another ten minutes when nothing much happened, looked both ways then moved off and ambled across the street.

The hotel reception was small and by the looks of it, most guests had already checked out. An old lady with a yellow and green flowery apron was slowly vacuuming the carpet next to a blue sofa and low coffee table near the window as Jack went up to reception. He picked up a tariff brochure from a small display card and was just about to glance at the details when an attractive young looking woman with auburn hair appeared from a curtained off area behind the desk.

'Bonjour monsieur'.

'Bonjour mademoiselle.'

'Vous desirez?'

Running out of French fast, Jack said, 'Do you speak English?'

'Of course', she replied.

'I wonder if you could help me? A few days ago a good friend of mine stayed here and left a leather jacket in the hotel. Maybe in the breakfast room. As I was in Paris today he asked if I would call and see if it had been found. '

'Ah. OK just a minute. Do you know when he was here?'

'It would have been about ten days ago.'

'And his name please?'

'Tom Stanton, from London.'

'I will just check with the restaurant.'

She came out from behind the desk and went through a small corridor to the left of the reception area. Knowing there was possibly a covert camera trained on reception, he waited without looking at the visitors book.

The woman was back in a couple of minutes shaking her head as she went round the back of the desk again. 'No monsieur, nothing has been found here.'

'Could we just check the book as I'm not sure when he was here exactly.'

'Of course. Let's see.'

She turned the register round and leafed back a page. 'You say it was a Tuesday?'

'Yes, I'm sure he said that.'

'Well there's no sign of him staying here then, sir.'

Jack gave her his friendliest smile and said, 'I wonder if it was maybe earlier in the month. He travels a lot and sometimes gets confused, you know.'

She smiled and started to slowly leaf back through the book and stopped after turning over another three pages.

'Here we are. Mr. and Mrs. Stanton stayed with us two weeks ago. They had the quiet room at the back of the hotel.'

Jack showed no reaction and said, 'Oh they must have left the jacket somewhere else in the City I think. I'll tell him when I see him tomorrow. Thank you so much for all your help mademoiselle.'

'My pleasure Sir.' She returned his smile.

Jack dodged round the lady with the vacuum and left turning right down the tree lined pavement. He walked up to a small café about 100yards from Le Petit Maison and sat outside. He ordered a café au lait and wondered if Tom had ever sat here either on his own or with 'Mrs. Stanton'.

A small piece of the jigsaw had just fallen into place although it would not be that small a deal to Jill struggling to come to terms with the situation back home. Best she didn't find out till he knew more. Jack now knew Tom Stanton had a secret life going on here. As his coffee arrived he chewed over some possibilities. Now he knew of Tom's mistress, he was inclined to think he may have disappeared with a view to starting something new but it was an extreme move. Not many people manage to disappear without trace. A mistake is usually made be it a minor traffic offence, the use of a bank card or even a sighting. That would be assuming he had not changed his identity or physical appearance. The removal of £900k from the company account would fund a lot of false documents and some facial surgery and plenty besides, but some very high level connections are needed to pull it off.

As big as finding about Tom's mistress, was Jill's discovery of the wrap of white powder in his suit pocket. Taken together, the web of deceit had deepened considerably. Both those hobbies are expensive. In Britain they can be socially unacceptable but in the business Tom was in, probably terminal in terms of integrity. If found out it would be the end for Tom Stanton's standing in the local community. And the end of his part in SMG.

It was only 11am and Jack ordered another coffee. As he did so he took one of his new phones from his inside pocket and rang London. 'Mike, it's Jack. Can you speak?'

'Yeah, it's OK.

'What can I do for you?'

'You know the two main Paris numbers being called regularly?'

'Yeah, I remember.'

'Would you be able to find the areas in Paris being called from the phone codes?'

'That's easy. I can do that now for you. Hold on.'

Jack held his phone to his right ear with his left hand and took a sip of his new coffee with his right. Not easy.

'OK. One is Madeleine and the other St Germain. The longer calls are to and from St Germain and are often made in the evening.'

'Thanks Mike. I owe you. Again.'

'No problem. See you soon. Bye now.'

Tom had used the office phone to call Canard Bleu and Le Petit Maison so they didn't feature much on his mobile account. He probably deduced no one was counting his office calls to anywhere in Paris. It was legitimate business. Jack checked his watch and decided to have lunch at the Meurice. He paid his bill, left and found a taxi.

Chapter 18

Jill rose early next morning after sleeping fitfully. If it hadn't been for the wine, she wouldn't have had any sleep at all. As she padded downstairs to the kitchen, she stopped and glanced into the hallway mirror. She saw the dark lines under her eyes and knew the physical and mental strains were beginning to show. She would give the kids a cup of tea in bed before jumping into the shower.

They both grunted as she brought them their drinks and Sarah turned over. Jill retreated to her en suite and luxuriated under the hot water for almost ten minutes before getting out and towelling herself down. It was going to be a difficult day and she wanted to be ready. As she was preparing breakfast, the phone rang and she picked up the kitchen extension and almost shouted, 'Hello.' It was her mother.

'Any news dear?'

'No, nothing Mum. We're still waiting to hear.'

'Oh Jill, we're so worried for you. We've just got in but we slept a bit on the flight. Would you like us to come over?

'No, Mum. Thank you but I've got so much to do today and I have to meet with the police and all sorts of things. I'll keep in touch and ring you tonight.'

'All right dear but just let us know if we can do anything. How are Sarah and Oliver?'

'They're holding up pretty well but they're frightened.'

'Give them our love won't you?'

'Of course I will, thank you Mum. I'll call you later today. Bye.'

'Bye dear.'

After breakfast, Jill loaded the dishwasher and herded Sarah and Oliver into the car for the school run. It was a subdued journey through heavy traffic and the children knew it was probably going to be another day with no news. Word had got out and the comments had started at school. Jill was determined to stay as calm as possible and tried to reassure them they were bound to hear something today. 'Dad will get in touch. It'll be all over soon.'

***

Xavier got up at 7.30am and Khalid tumbled out of bed at 7.45. They said little and went round to a café along the street for an English breakfast. Xavier thought it was awful and Khalid went back for more sausages. They got back to the safe house just after nine o'clock and Xavier spread out the maps. They knew approximately where their target lived but no precise address had been given to them. What they did know was where his offices were and Xavier said that would be a good place to start. Khalid just grunted and went to the toilet.

By 10.00am they were ready to go. Xavier felt better having shouldered his gun and Khalid had a spare little .22 tucked in his inside pocket just in case.

They left the house just after 10am and walked for fifteen minutes before Khalid complained and they flagged down a black cab. They argued on the journey. Khalid peered out of the window, 'What's London got that Paris hasn't?'

Xavier said, 'You.' Khalid didn't get it and said, 'God, I hate this place. They can't make coffee and the food's shit.'

'You could have fooled me.'

Khalid sulked for the rest of the journey and thought about lunch.

Xavier thought about what he was going to say when he got there. If they got this right, it was a big payday. Enough to get him a new boat. In his best English Xavier asked the driver to stop near the offices of SMG.

'No problem guv'nor.'

The taxi pulled in to the kerb four hundred yards from where Xavier thought the target's office would be and they both got out. Khalid paid him off with a tip but not one to remember. As if the cabbie would forget Khalid. They stood in a doorway and looked up the street. It was busy and there were plenty of people moving around. A traffic warden was walking slowly up the other side of the street checking meters and tax discs. No other uniforms were around. Xavier nudged Khalid and they stepped out of the doorway and turned left towards the offices of Stanton, McIntosh and Goldman. Both instinctively patted their clothes to check their weapons.

***

Inside SMG everyone was in a strange mood. Some clients had taken the trouble to make the journey to SMG in person and the atmosphere was tense. Some of the senior PAs were manning the phones to help placate anxious clients and the telephone lines at SMG were on overload.

Xavier and Khalid entered the building at 10.55am. Bob Goldman saw them first and stared at Khalid unbelievingly. He could not take his eyes off this ugly mountain in front of him. Khalid just smiled.

'Can I speak with Mr Stanton?' said Khalid in very broken English.

Bob said, 'He isn't here today.'

'Well that's too bad because we have travelled a long way to see him. Where is his office?'

Xavier and Khalid pushed past him and started to walk down the heavily carpeted corridor towards the back offices.

Bob ran after them, 'Hey, you can't do that. Who are you?'

'We're asking the questions,' Khalid followed up with a shout. 'So who are you then?'

'I'm Bob Goldman, Mr Stanton's partner.' Khalid just looked straight at him and shouted. 'So where the fuck is Stanton?'

'I told you he's not here.' Bob pushed past and spread his arms as if to shield the offices but Xavier looked past him and saw 'Tom Stanton' on the name plate. He pushed past and tried the door but it was locked. He stepped aside as Khalid launched his shoulder against it and with a splintering of wood the door flew open. They both crashed in and quickly surveyed the plush interior. An imposing desk was near the large window and two upholstered easy chairs were in front of it. The carpet was a thick wool in burgundy. They moved to the desk which had a laptop sitting in the middle, next to a large blue phone. As Khalid went round the desk he found all the drawers unlocked. He started with the bottom one and worked up. He didn't know what he was looking for but he found a black notebook and stuffed it in his pocket. Everything else seemed to be financial stuff. Xavier leaned on to the desk and took hold of the laptop and wrenched it away from its connection.

As Bob Goldman ran in behind them shouting for them to get out, Khalid turned round and slammed his right fist into his face smashing his nose into a kind of red mess.

As Bob fell to one knee, Khalid lashed out with his foot and caught him in the ribs sending him crashing against the side of the heavy desk and onto the already blood spattered carpet. Before all Khalid's instincts kicked in, Xavier took hold of his arm and said, 'Let's get out of here.' Xavier tucked the laptop under his arm and pulled Khalid towards the door. They walked out and up towards the office with girls cowering behind the reception desk and people shouting. They left by the front door and out to the street. They took their customary ten minute walk after making a 'visit' and hailed a taxi. Xavier was due to call in to Sergei. At least he could tell him they had something.

Chapter 19

The taxi pulled up outside the Meurice. Jack climbed out and moved across to the other side of the street to an ATM to get a better look at the building. It was a quaint ivy- clad restaurant with a few tables running along the pavement and two globe shaped bay trees in large terracotta pots on each side of the door. The only giveaway to the name was a small highly polished brass plaque on the right hand side of the door with Restaurant Meurice in three inch high letters.

He moved along to the cash machine and entered his card. The ATM was out of money and his card was returned. Checking his wallet, he thought he would have enough to cover the restaurant bill. Cash sale, no trail was one of his mottos. He looked at his watch as he saw a party of four business men approach and enter the restaurant. It was now 12.30pm. Giving them a couple of minutes to get settled at their table, Jack looked up and down the street and walked across and entered the Meurice.

The maitre d' came over and welcomed him enquiring as to the numbers.

'Just one.' He was ushered to a small table by the side wall, and he sat with a view of the interior and the front door. A young waiter dressed in a starched white shirt and black bow tie with a long black apron arrived and offered Jack a lunch menu. The interior was dark, with wood panelling set off by two small chandeliers casting a pale light which struggled to fill the room. As Jack studied the menu, the maitre d' glided up with some freshly cut bread in a small wicker basket. He set it on the table and Jack asked, 'Has my friend Tom Stanton been in lately?'

Surprise crossed his florid face and he accidentally tipped one of the pieces of bread onto the tablecloth.

'I don't know him,' he said as he picked up the fallen bread with a white gloved hand and placed the bread back in the basket. 'Are you ready to order, Sir?'

'Yes I am.'

The Maitre d' turned and made a small signal to the waiter and then moved away from the table.

Jack enjoyed a lunch of rabbit slow cooked in a red wine and onion sauce with fresh vegetables. Because he was in Paris he had ordered a half bottle of Cote du Rhone to go with it and finished off with homemade crème brulee and coffee. As he sank his spoon into his dessert he saw the maitre d' from the corner of his eye. He had moved behind a curtain next to a bookcase set into the wood panelled wall and hadn't re-appeared. Had to be a door. Jack watched and waited as he finished his wine and sipped his coffee.

The maitre d' emerged a few minutes later and resumed his rounds of the tables in the crowded room, stopping and talking with regulars. He was giving Jack a wide berth and when the young waiter brought the bill, Jack realised he didn't have enough cash to cover it. He had underestimated the amount by around 10 Euros and he knew he was going to have to use a card. He added 10% and the transaction was processed at the table. He rose and left thanking the young waiter as he moved towards the door. The maitre d' was nowhere to be seen as Jack walked out of the restaurant, cursing. He was annoyed with himself for having to use the credit card. They now had his name and if it was any consolation, they might think he had done it intentionally but it was a stretch. He turned right past a couple eating outside and walked along till he got to a narrow alleyway. He wanted to have a look behind the restaurant and found a service road running along the back of the terraced buildings. The area was lined with commercial rubbish bins and strewn with pieces of paper and empty plastic bags. A rat scurried behind one of the bins where rotting food lay. It would have appalled customers who used the restaurant. He sauntered down the alley hugging the buildings as he moved. He came to the rear of the Meurice and saw two doors. One looked scuffed and marked as if it had constant contact with deliveries. There was a wedge of cardboard at the bottom keeping it ajar. The other was about three meters further along and was, to all intents and purposes, like a normal front door on a suburban house. It had two substantial locks on it and was firmly closed. Jack moved on without breaking his step but unknown to him, had already been captured on a covert camera fixed discreetly high up on the wall on the other side of the alley. He noticed a rusting wrought iron gate leading to a small park area and walked in looking for a bench. He needed to sit and think. Most of the seats were already taken by down and outs some holding beer cans and others wine bottles and as they looked up in anticipation, he made his way back to the gate. He felt bad seeing them but couldn't give the time. The soiled, wine sodden men sitting around had been down a much longer and lonelier road than him.

He exited the park and started looking for a taxi to get him back to the airport and the 7 pm flight to London. He suddenly felt the need to get home.

***

Sergei took a call from Xavier as they were in the taxi leaving the SMG offices. 'What have you got?' Xavier leaned forward and asked the driver to shut the glass dividing panel. 'We've been to Stanton's office but he wasn't there. Nobody knows where he is. We got his laptop and a notebook.'

'Nothing else?'

'There wasn't time. Too many people around all screaming and shouting. We had to get out.'

'OK, I'll need to see what's on his computer but it's probably been looked at already. Check out the private investigator next. I've got his office address now and we think he's in Paris so you should have enough time. Get over there now.'

Sergei gave Xavier the address in Kensington. 'Where are you anyway?'

'In a taxi in London somewhere. What will I do with the laptop? I can't just carry it around.'

'Buy a fucking bag or something.' Xavier wished he hadn't asked. 'Get back to me as soon as you can. And don't forget to look in the bathroom.

Xavier knocked on the window and the driver slid it open.

'Can you take us to Kensington High Street?'

'Sure, where about?'

'Just by the tube station will be fine.'

'OK.' An oncoming truck driver slowed and allowed him to make a U turn. Only in London.

Khalid said he was hungry when they got to Kensington but Xavier rounded on him. 'Shut up. Let's get in and do it.'

They found the office just off the High Street and looked up and down before pushing open the communal door. The first office they passed had a sign on the door saying 'Hammer & Hammer Solicitors.' Xavier smiled. Even Khalid found that one amusing. Both paused and put on cotton gloves. They moved along the narrow corridor with its well-worn brown carpet and although it was only 4 in the afternoon, it seemed as if it was dusk. They walked up a short flight of stairs to the second floor and saw an office up on the right. The sign said 'Jack Barclay, Private Enquiry Agent'. Xavier reached it first and could see it was a standard lock. He searched in his jacket pocket and found his pick. It took him 2 minutes before he heard the familiar click. They were in.

The room was fairly well lit and they noticed how modest an office it was compared with the one they had just left at SMG. Xavier went straight to the desk and started with the drawers. There was nothing of any interest on the left hand side and on the right even less with stationery taking up three of the five drawers.

Khalid was looking through the unlocked filing cabinet but what little there was related to different times, different people, different problems.

Xavier looked round and a leather briefcase tucked under the desk caught his attention. In it he found mail which Jack Barclay must have taken from his home. They were all addressed to Mr. Jack Barclay in Maida Vale, London. He wrote down the address, left all the mail intact, closed the briefcase and put it back where he found it.

Meanwhile, Khalid checked the small fridge and took out some pastrami and started eating it. He was going to get to 300 pounds if it killed him.

Xavier looked round to see if there were any adjoining rooms but there were none. No bathroom. No cistern to search. They knew Sergei would be still be pissed off they were no nearer finding Stanton, so they pulled out every drawer from the desk and the filing cabinet and tipped everything on the floor. Then they left. Xavier called Paris again when they were back outside. Sergei still sounded gruff but his mood changed a bit when he learned they had found Jack's home address.

'Get over there now and wait for him. Call me back when you get a result. It doesn't matter when, just call me.'

Chapter 20

Patrick Flynn was knee deep in someone else's shit. He was in a shopping centre in Slough and there had been a blocked waste pipe from level one.

He had called out for some help from his part timers but the job was going to be bigger than he thought and it was getting dark. He could not remember ever feeling this way. Even at the darkest times of building the business when he thought he had visited hell, he had never felt like this. It had taken years of purgatory to save the money. Years of fifteen hour days and coming home smelling like a sewer. His anger was boiling over and he knew he had to be alone. He stumbled out of the complex and went out to the darkened car park. He walked blindly on and on reaching his vehicle, climbed in and just sat still. He rang Lauren. 'Heard anything?'

'No.'

'Patrick honey, where are you?'

'At work.'

'I've cooked some dinner. Why don't you come home?'

'I'll be late. This one's a bitch. I'll call you later'.

He sat back and lit a cigarette, still shaking with anger and unable to move till it subsided. After ten minutes he climbed out and went back to his gang trying to fix the leaking waste pipe.

'All right boss?'

'Yeah, fine. Let's get this thing sorted. I've got some stuff to do tonight.'

It was 8pm by the time Patrick climbed back into his vehicle and his mood was worse after an argument with the night security manager of the shopping centre.

'Why has it taken you guys six hours to fix a leak?'

Patrick just managed to stop ripping his head off as he explained they had to use a mini cam to find where the break was.

'Yeah, sure,' he said smiling and showing rotten teeth. 'Like you need sat nav to find your dick?'

Patrick felt the shakes coming on again. 'Fuck you pal.' He managed to walk away. He drove out of the precinct and headed west.

Lauren had spoken of where the Stanton's lived and it was an area he knew. He was used to finding people's addresses but this one was special.

As he approached, he recognized the house from Lauren's description. He noted the imposing drive but kept driving past it. He parked 100 yards beyond, tucking his van onto the grass verge. Walking back and finding no gate, he sauntered up the driveway and rang the bell.

***

Jill Stanton knew she was descending into a kind of new hell. She had no idea how to cope with what was happening to her. To her children. To her life.

Panic had led to a feeling of grief then puzzlement and now, fury.

She had no doubt her life was about to disintegrate. She was pouring her third glass of white wine when the doorbell rang. She looked at the clock on the kitchen wall and saw it was 10pm. 'Oh my God.'

She put the bottle down and almost ran to the door. The man at the door meant nothing to her except he smelled of drains.

'I'm Lauren's husband,' he shouted at her.

Jill stepped back and was about to slam the door shut when he lunged towards her. She fell backwards and as she recovered her balance, her arms went up defensively to cover her face. She stared at the wide eyed man and screamed out in panic.

'I need to see you about my money. Now.'

'I don't know what you mean.' Turning to face him she gasped, 'What do you want?'

'I want my money back.'

The stink from his work clothes was overpowering and she moved back from him. He stood aggressively in the large hall next to an ornate mahogany antique table, with his arms by his sides, hands clenched.

She looked straight at him. 'Look, Lauren had a conversation with me a few weeks ago and said she wanted to speak to Tom about investing some money. I gave her his office number and that is all I did. I don't even know if she called him.'

Patrick started jabbing his finger at her. 'We met with your husband at his office and I gave him 100 grand. I know he's gone and I want my money back. All of it.'

He had a wild look in his eyes and she wondered if he was on drugs. He moved further towards her and she shrank back till she was close to the phone on the small table by the sitting room door. She felt the panic rising in her belly.

'I told you, I don't know anything about his business life. I can't help you.'

The noise had been overheard by Sarah and Oliver and out of the corner of her eye she saw them standing motionless at the top of the stairs. As Patrick began moving towards her she became aware of his huge build and the coarseness of his hands. He had raised his right arm as if to strike her but looking round she realized she couldn't retreat further and knocked the phone off its holder onto the floor.

Sarah called out in warning as she peered down from the landing and Jill screamed 'Get back.' She turned to Patrick shouting, 'I'll pay you. I'll pay you the money. If you've lost anything I will give it back to you.'

Patrick stopped advancing and lowered his arm. 'I want a cheque.'

'All right I'll do that for you', was all she could say, her voice shrill. 'Will you leave us if I do this?'

'Yes, if the cheque is good.'

'Stay here and I'll write you one now.'

She turned and went into the kitchen rummaging in her handbag. Two cheques left. She picked up a ballpoint from the kitchen top and ran back to the hall. Oliver was sitting on a high step with Sarah still peeking round above him.

'What do you want me to write?'

'Make it out to P Flynn for £97,000 and phone your bank and tell them to express it.'

She wasn't sure what that meant but said she would.

'If it bounces, I'll be back. Next time it will be different. Speak to your bank first thing in the morning and make sure the funds are there. Borrow it if you have to. I don't give a shit.'

She almost laughed at that. Maybe it was the relief that the danger was over.

Patrick turned round and without a further word left by the front door. The children came running down the stairs and they all stood in the hall hugging each other. Sarah looked at her mum and said, 'I'm scared.'

It was after midnight by the time she had settled the children and bathed. She went back downstairs and rang Jack's mobile. He answered the phone with a tired voice and she asked if he was OK to speak.

'Sure. I've just arrived at Heathrow. Something happened?'

She blurted out the story of Patrick Flynn's visit and Jack said nothing as he listened.

'Phone the police.'

'He didn't actually do anything except frighten us. He was drunk.'

'Up to you, but I'd let the police know about it. Tell them he said he would be back if the cheque bounced.'

'I'll do that because the cheque won't clear.' Jill looked around for her unfinished wine and said that to some extent she could understand his anger. 'I mean it's a hell of a lot of money Jack.'

'Maybe so but he can't go around people's houses behaving like that.'

She sat down on the couch. 'What sort of day have you had? Any news?'

'I found out a few things but there's no sign of him. I need to make one or two more enquiries and then we could meet for a catch up.'

'OK.'

'How was Paris?'

'Hasn't changed much. I was pretty busy and didn't see too much of it apart from a bit of the Left Bank and the scruffy parts from the Airport.'

Jill unfolded her legs and pushed herself up from the couch. She walked towards the window and pulled back the curtain an inch and looked out.

'Are you still there?'

'Just a bit jumpy tonight that's all. Will I see you in the morning?'

'Yes, I'll call you. Lock up tight tonight.'

'I will. Goodnight Jack.'

***

By the time he pulled into his parking bay in Maida Vale it was just before 1.00am. Jack felt physically and mentally exhausted and realised he'd been going for almost 20 hours. All work and no play…

He climbed the stairs to his apartment and pushed the door against some mail. He turned to close it, bending down to pick up the envelopes as Khalid ran down the short corridor hitting him with his full force, crashing him against the wall. Jack's right shoulder took most of the impact and he felt the wind knocked out of his body as he tried to regain his balance. Khalid immediately followed up with a crushing right handed punch to the side of his face and his gold ring caught Jack near his left eye.

Jack knew he had to get away from the door before he took another hit and he gathered all the strength and dived towards Khalid using a foot against the door for leverage. He brought his foot from the door and bent his leg using the momentum to bring his knee forward and into Khalid's groin. Khalid let out a scream as the pain shot through him and began doubling up. Knowing he had him off balance, Jack reared up and caught him full on the chin with his clenched fist. Khalid screamed again as his teeth went through his tongue and he fell against the wall as Jack finished with a full kick into his kidneys. As he slid down the wall Jack rose up and desperately tried to heave air back into his lungs. He winced as he tried to move his arm and wondered if his shoulder had been dislocated. He felt wetness on his face and touching it with the fingers of his good arm found blood. He could still see but he knew his cheek had been gashed.

'Not bad Mr Barclay. It takes a lot to put my partner down.'

Jack turned and looked into the muzzle of Xavier's Sig-Sauer. He stood far enough away from him to get a shot in if Jack tried anything.

'Just move slowly forward and go into the living room. I'm very happy to use this if I have to.'

Jack had little difficulty in understanding his broken English and as he was still trying to get enough oxygen to live, he walked into his living room. Xavier switched on the hall light as he followed behind him. Jack couldn't believe what he saw as he entered. The place had been completely trashed and there was hardly room to put one foot in front of the other. His CDs and DVDs were scattered over the floor and the stuffing had been ripped from his chairs. Ornaments had been smashed open and the carpet had been pulled up around the edges. Every drawer was empty and on the floor along with their contents.

'How did you find my place?'

'Not difficult. Your office has had similar treatment. You are not as clever as you need to be in this game.'

After all he had just been through; criticism was the last thing he needed.

Jack heard a noise behind him and half turned to see Khalid standing groggily behind him, his face twisted in pain. Xavier waved his gun indicating Jack should sit on the ripped sofa.

'Now. Where is Tom Stanton?'

Jack looked at the scene of devastation around him and said, 'Fuck you.'

Xavier moved so quickly he didn't have time to protect himself. He smashed the pistol into Jack's face and a searing pain shot straight to his brain. He fell back but managed to stay upright. He wished he hadn't as Xavier pistol whipped him again. Jack fell sideways onto the couch and Xavier moved forward and pulled him back up by the front of his blood stained shirt.

'One more time. Where is he?'

'I haven't a clue. No one has. He's gone and you know it.'

'Why did you go to Paris today?'

'To look for him. Why do you think?'

'I'm asking the questions Mr. Private Detective. Why go to the Meurice?'

'I liked the look of the menu.'

Xavier nodded to Khalid and Jack braced himself for another blow.

Then they all stopped as they heard a police siren in the distance. Xavier looked quickly at Khalid.

'I've got good neighbours. They've heard the commotion. As Khalid tried to take a last swipe at Jack, Xavier moved between them and pushed Khalid away. 'Go,' he said and they both moved towards the door with Xavier half turning to keep the gun on Jack. They shut the door and were gone as the sirens got closer. Jack felt his face again and wondered if his cheek bones were broken. He made his way through to the bathroom and switched on the mirror light. His face was covered in blood and it had dripped onto his shirt and trousers. He ran cold water over the hand towel and began cleaning his face to staunch the blood flow. Then he heard loud knocking at the door and his name being called. He opened it and saw a policeman and a policewoman. They took one look at him and reached for their truncheons.

'No need. They're gone.'

The constables looked over Jack's shoulder into the hallway as if to make sure and the PC asked, 'Mr Barclay?'

'Yes, I'm Jack Barclay. Did a neighbour call you?'

'Yes, Sir. He heard a great deal of noise and thought you were out. So he called us.'

The WPC couldn't take her eyes off Jack's bloodied and swollen face. 'Do you need an ambulance Sir?'

'No really, I'll be OK.'

As distant sirens could be heard, the constables both nodded towards Jack as if to get him to move aside. 'Come on in if you can. It looks like a hotel room after a rock band has stayed the night.' The two officers stepped around the debris and stared at the chaos. A soft knock at the open door heralded two more police constables and they too looked inside and grimaced.

'We'll need some details from you Sir', said the first officer to arrive. 'Do you have any idea who did this to you?'

'I'm a private investigator and I work on more than one case at a time. Just like you, no doubt. I don't know to which case it relates but as you can see, I got a visit tonight. There were two men here and they broke in and ransacked my apartment. They waited till I got back then attacked me in the hallway. They heard you in the distance and made a hasty retreat.'

'Do you know what they may have been looking for?'

'Well as I said, I work on more than one case at a time so I'm not sure who sent them.'

The officer gave a knowing look and said, 'We'll need some descriptions from you.'

'Of course.'

By the time all the details had been exchanged it was after 3am.

'You need some rest.' Everyone helped him tidy up some of the mess. Two of them put his bed back together and another made a pot of tea. It had turned into a family affair.

Jack thanked them all for all their help and as he shut the door he almost staggered as he made his way to the bedroom. He lay down on the bed and eventually fell into a deep sleep.

Chapter 21

Jill woke at 7 am and felt the effects of last night's wine.

She lay mulling over what had happened the previous evening before swinging her legs out of bed at 7.15am. She put on her favourite white silk gown and went down to the kitchen, made a pot of tea and put some toast on before bringing out the cereals. The children were subdued after the trauma of the previous evening. They were being collected by a neighbour today for the school run and Jill was pleased. She had so much to do and she suddenly remembered about the bank.

As she pottered about tidying up after the kids she felt miserable. Her whole life had been turned upside down and she didn't have a single clue as to her husband's whereabouts. Had their marriage been a sham? Did she really know her husband at all?

She finished her third cup of tea and went back upstairs to get dressed.

She didn't spend too much time on it and picked a pale green blouse and a pair of black Whistles trousers and black shoes with a little heel. She'd hardly bothered but she would still turn heads in the High Street. It was after 9 o'clock when she went downstairs to call Jack.

At first she thought she had missed him and waited for the message service to kick in. Then he answered in a voice which could have been from the bottom of a swimming pool.

'Hello.'

'Jack, is that you?'

His voice was hoarse as he said, 'Yeah, it's me.'

'What's the matter?'

'I got in late from Paris and then got beaten up by two gorillas.'

Jill waited a second to see if he would say anything else. 'Was that because of me?'

'No. I made a mistake in a Paris restaurant and paid for it. I'll explain later. I need to see you today but I have to get myself cleaned up a bit.'

'Jack, I'm coming over. What's your address?'

Jack gave her directions to his apartment in Maida Vale and she said she would be over as soon as she could.

'I'm sorry,' she said almost whispering.

'Don't be. It's all in the line of business.'

'Is there anything I can bring?'

'A first aid kit would be handy.'

She flinched but said, 'I have one in the car. I'll bring it in.'

'Good, see you soon then.'

'I'll be as quick as I can. Have some more rest.'

She locked the back doors and windows before collecting the car keys from their hook in the kitchen. She double checked that the front door was properly locked and climbed into her Audi and belted up. Her hands free phone rang after five minutes.

'Jill, it's Charles. Any news?'

'No, nothing I'm afraid. How about you?'

'We had trouble at the office yesterday afternoon.'

'What do you mean?'

'Two guys arrived and barged in looking for Tom. Bob challenged them after they made for Tom's office and got beaten up pretty badly.'

'Oh my God. Is he all right?'

'Yes, he'll be OK but he took quite a beating. We haven't a clue who these guys were. Where are you now?'

'I'm on my way to meet with Jack Barclay. He got beaten up last night by two guys. Too much of a coincidence Charles. This is turning into a nightmare.'

'Would you give me a call later today?'

'Yes Jill, I will.'

Remembering the visit from Patrick Flynn, she said, 'I need to have a chat with you anyway. I had a visit from one of Tom's clients and he threatened me. I'll give you a call later today. Would you tell Bob and Cath I will phone them later and that I am so sorry this has happened.'

'Will do. Speak with you later.'

'Bye.'

She made slow progress into Chiswick and she still had to turn north towards Maida Vale. Her mind was racing. Now Bob had been hurt too. Everything was spiraling out of control.

Jill parked in a street lined with horse chestnut trees and checked her makeup and hair in the interior mirror before getting out to feed the meter. She paid for two hours, picked up the first aid kit, locked her car and started walking back in the warm afternoon sun. Jack's apartment was in a stucco fronted period building just off Elgin Avenue. She found his name on the entry panel and rang his bell. His voice sounded croaky when he answered after a few seconds.

'It's me.'

'Come on up. Door on the right, first floor.'

Jill heard the click and pushed the front door open then closed it before walking along the darkened corridor leading to the stairs. Lights came on automatically as she climbed the stairs to the door and pressed the bell.

When the door opened she saw a beaten up face for the very first time. She must have looked shocked as Jack stood back and waved her inside. His left eye was completely closed up and badly swollen and his bruised face was matted with dried blood. She could see the gash on his cheek and it was still oozing blood at the bottom of the wound.

'Oh my God, Jack.' She stretched out her arm and touched him on the good side of his damaged face. 'How are you feeling?'

'Pretty lousy, but thanks for asking.'

He closed the door and Jill walked through to the living room which still bore the marks of the trashing it had suffered the previous night. DVDs and CDs were stacked in a haphazard way against the wall and broken ornaments were in a corner by the damaged B&O system which had been ripped from its wall fixing.

'Can I make you a cup of tea or coffee?'

'Coffee would be nice. Maybe through a straw.' He managed a small smile on his undamaged lips.

She took the coffees through and found him on his knees trying to sort out his CD collection. As she placed his coffee on the low table she put her hands on his shoulder and half whispered, 'I'm sorry Jack. I caused all this by coming to see you in the first place. This is all my fault.'

'Don't say that. It's the business I'm in. It's my choice.'

He got up painfully and sat across from her on the sofa, cupping his coffee in both hands. 'We need to put all our cards on the table. Tom has got himself involved with some very dangerous people and they'll be back. The only reason I'm still here is because a neighbour below heard all the noise and phoned for the police.'

She was beginning to realise the full extent of the danger they were all in.

'I couldn't tell them where to find Tom and I think they knew that. They will get more desperate as the hours go by. You must realise you and the children could be a target. You have to take precautions.'

Jill felt a knot forming in her stomach as the implications sunk in.

'I am going to give you the name of a home security expert to call. When you get back you must contact him. I will have already spoken to him and he will advise you what to do. It will involve infra red cameras outside your home - back, front and sides and a sophisticated alarm system. You'll need a gate on your driveway. It won't be cheap but you must do it. You need to protect yourself and the kids.'

'Yes, I know, I'll do that as soon as I get back but other things have happened too.'

She stretched down and picked up her coffee mug. 'Yesterday afternoon two men forced their way into SMG and demanded to know where Tom was. They attacked Bob and beat him up. He's going to be alright but he's badly bruised and shocked.'

Jack's head jerked up. 'It'll be the same two goons. Talking of violence, have you spoken to the police about your visit from Patrick Flynn?'

'No, I thought it would be too embarrassing at the club. I mean look how much damage has been done now. Tom invested money for others there and most don't know about his disappearance yet.'

'Look, you must let Charles and Bob know about what happened and ask their advice. That cheque is going to go through quickly. Are there funds in the account to cover it?'

'No, there won't be enough.'

'With the threats he made, you must involve the police otherwise he is going to come back at you. Share the problem.'

'You're right. I hadn't really thought it through properly. I'll call Charles and the police. Why is there so much violence Jack? Is there more to this than the cash missing from SMG.

'Your husband had another life. I don't know what it is but if he was involved with drugs, the level of violence is going to escalate. It looks to me as if he has seriously upset someone.'

He waited for a reaction before going on.

Jill shook her head. 'I can't believe he has put us in so much danger. I miss him terribly but I can only think he is out of his depth and had to escape to save himself. I used to wonder what he did on his business trips? I suppose it's never all business.

Jack let it go for now. He felt the wetness on his cheek and realised the talking had opened his wound. Jill saw it too and got up from her chair.

From the box by his side she pulled a couple of tissues out and gently wiped the blood from his cheek. 'You might need a stitch in this you know. It's quite deep.'

'I've got a good nurse here'. He put his hand on her shoulder. 'I'm worried about you. I think you should send the children away for a few days. We should be able to track these two thugs sent from Paris and they won't stay in England for ever but you are going to have to think of your own safety too. Is there anyone you could stay with for a few days until the security system is in?'

'I can't believe all this is happening.' She moved closer to him as he put his arm round her and pulled her in close.

They held each other for several minutes, both thinking their own thoughts.

When she finally lifted her head, she managed a weak smile.

'Thank you Jack. I might look OK but I'm scared to death for myself and the kids. I'll call Charles and get some advice on the cheque I made out for Patrick Flynn. Then tell the police about last night.'

'Would you like some more coffee?'

Jack dabbed his cheek and nodded.

She rose and walked through to the kitchen.

Coming back with the mugs on a tray, she asked. ' I'll call Charles now?'

'You should. The sooner the better really.'

She picked up her mobile from the table and scrolled down to SMG. A female answered and Jill asked for Charles.

'Who's calling please?'

'It's Jill Stanton.'

'Of course. I'll put you straight through.'

'Charles, it's Jill. Something happened last night which was extremely disturbing and I need your advice. Patrick Flynn, a husband of one of my girl friends at the tennis club, handed over what I believe is pretty much their life savings to Tom for investment and he came by my house late last night. He wants his money back and was threatening to harm us. To get rid of him I wrote him a personal cheque.'

'How much for?'

'£97,000.'

'Jesus!'

'The kids were terrified. I had to do something.'

'He asked me to express it and said he would be back if it bounced.'

'Have you the money in the account to cover it?'

'Probably not in our current account. I haven't actually checked on our savings accounts.'

Charles didn't hesitate when he answered. 'You mustn't do this Jill. We don't know the precise situation yet and anyway this should be a police matter. You should stop the cheque now and call the police. I would imagine they would want to interview Mr. Flynn in light of his behaviour last night.' Jill winced at the recollection.

'If you did this it could also affect the outcome for others who may have lost money. We can't have precedents. Could you call your bank now and then the police?'

'I will. I'm sorry.'

'Don't be. You just did what was right at the time.'

'I'll make the calls and speak with you later.'

She put the phone on the table and Jack nodded to say he'd understood the content of the conversation.

Checking her address book, she picked up the phone and spoke to her bank and told them to stop the cheque.

When she phoned the police station she was put through to the sergeant who took down details of last night's visit to her home. She told him she was in London but would try to visit them in the morning. Her main worry was what Patrick Flynn would do when the cheque was returned.

'We'll be visiting Mr. Flynn this morning to interview him. Don't answer the door to anyone tonight Mrs. Stanton, and make sure your home is securely locked up.'

'I will and thank you for your help.'

Jack had lain out on the sofa as she was on the phone and she suddenly realised how tired he looked.

She could hardly believe so much could happen in such a short space of time. That her life would change so dramatically and bring such violence to people around her.

Chapter 22

At SMG the situation was deteriorating by the hour and the staff were becoming fearful. Clients were arriving regularly throughout the day and any normal routines such as lunch breaks had become impossible. News was getting around fast and investors were becoming frustrated at the lack of information. Bob stayed in his office to avoid anyone seeing his injuries but Charles was out front trying to placate increasingly angry clients. People who until very recently had been the model of English reserve were now becoming shrill and accusative. Voices were raised and legal action was being threatened.

Some perspective was restored when at 3.00pm a young girl recently recruited to the company fainted and fell heavily against the edge of a desk gashing her forehead. Little did she know that by doing so, peace was suddenly achieved in what had become a form of bedlam.

Clients and staff rushed over to her and she was helped to a couch where she came round but was bleeding profusely from her wound.

Someone called an ambulance and a sense of guilt seemed to take the place of self interest as customers fell back silently to let the girl have first aid and a little privacy.

Charles took advantage of the situation to make an impromptu speech. 'There is no one sorrier than the staff of SMG that we have found ourselves in this situation. We are doing everything in our power to find out the exact position and as soon as we do, we will contact all our clients personally. I don't think we can achieve anything more this afternoon and I would respectfully ask you to let us resume our work here. Please leave your contact details with our receptionists and we will contact you within seventy two hours. Thank you all for your understanding.'

A siren was heard close by and as customers began leaving their names and contact numbers, two paramedics came through the front door. Charles heaved a sigh of relief and went over to the injured member of staff.

By 3.15pm the paramedics had decided to transport the young girl in an ambulance to hospital for a check on her head injury. She was wheeled out on a medical chair accompanied by one of the senior female receptionists and Charles closed the office to the public for the day.

Chapter 23

The midday temperature in Ciudad Del Carmen on the Gulf of Mexico was nudging 95F with a gentle breeze rustling the palm fronds by the promenade.

The couple enjoying a pre lunch drink on Playa Norte beach lay beneath a large yellow umbrella on matching upholstered sun beds which had been pulled closely together. They had been here for almost two weeks and were being feted by the staff at their five star hotel fronting the beach. It was assumed they were on their honeymoon and the husband was generous with his tipping. Although he was older than his young wife, their good looks drew sidelong glances wherever they went. He looked to be in his late thirties, tall dark and lean and his ready smile more than made up for a nose which looked as if it had been broken at some time. His French wife was thought by the staff to be the most beautiful guest amongst the beautiful people staying at the hotel. At five foot five inches she was very tall by Mexican standards but it was the long jet black hair and olive skinned figure which captured the imagination of the men in the hotel complex. Although she looked to be in her early twenties, she had the bearing of someone who had already experienced a great deal in her young life.

They were obviously very much in love and always displayed affection as they laughed and exchanged kisses. They were respectful towards other guests but never mixed and always had a table for two at dinner. They never seemed to be dressed in anything but designer clothes and their entrance each evening to the a la carte restaurant was an occasion. The passports lodged with the hotel on arrival showed they were Mr. and Mrs. Vanner from England and they had booked a suite overlooking the Gulf. He had made a point of asking if the room had its own internet connection.

'But of course, Sir.'

At the end of their second week a mildly agitated John Vanner walked up to reception. 'We will be checking out tomorrow. We've really enjoyed our stay but we're moving on now'

It had been during dinner the previous evening when Danielle announced, 'I want to move on.' Tom had smiled and seized his chance to talk about the Mayan ruins in the city of Chichen Itza.

'Sounds like a disease.'

Tom groaned. 'Look, Danni, it's been great here but we can't lie around a pool forever. We're in Mexico. Let's explore some of the history.'

She played with her food and said, 'How about Cancun then?'

'What's in Cancun of any interest?'

'Shops. Lots of them. I want to have some fun Tom. I want to go shopping.

Tom didn't want a scene in the dining room. 'Can't we do both?'

'Cancun first.'

'OK, but just for a couple of days, then we take off and do what I want to do.'

'Sure, Tom, whatever you say.'

That night in bed, Danielle couldn't stop thinking of the designer stores in Cancun. Jack was beginning to reflect on his situation. He was thinking of Jill and the children and how much he missed them. He would find a way to redeem himself. The air conditioning had chilled him and he rose from the bed and went over to the control on the far wall and switched it off. As the room began to heat up, he fell into a fitful sleep.

They checked out next morning and the bell hops managed to get all three cases into the Mustang before they set off towards the 180 and Cancun. The only trace of their visit was the passport details they presented on arrival and images from the discreet CCTV around the hotel.

As they drove towards Cancun, she detected a change in his mood.

'What's the matter? We're on holiday. Why so miserable?'

'You wouldn't understand.'

Danielle sulked and slouched in her seat. 'Can we stop soon? I'd like a cigarette.'

'We've hardly started. Wait till we get there.'

Danielle muttered something and Tom ignored her.

Chapter 24

Tom knew it had been the frequent trips to Paris which had changed everything in his life. The evenings spent alone after the day's work had ended, and the time sitting in small bars mixing with the young students from the Sorbonne in the St Germain area of the City. How he loved the company of young, intelligent and good looking female students talking about books, cinema and art. And how they warmed towards this good looking and entertaining businessman with impeccable manners who dressed so elegantly and casually. Without realising it, he had started buying friends. He was generous and would often buy a meal for everyone at the table and finish up back at one of the student apartments for late drinks. Soon they all knew him well enough to let him know they enjoyed something stronger and so he began to try out cocaine. Just a little to keep up with the youngsters. Nothing to worry about. Just being sociable. He began looking forward to his Paris trips and knew he would need to find more than the modest account with Canard Bleu to justify the frequency of his journeys. And so was born 'FRM', his imaginary new engineering account which would grow into a 'major client'. Using his own money he began building up the importance of his Paris portfolio. Bob and Charles never once thought to check it out but why should they. It was another piece of lucrative new business brought to the company by Tom.

His cover was complete and he was having so much fun with his new young friends on the Left Bank. No one was getting hurt. It was all part of the business.

Too many days in Paris. Too much cash going out to keep the charade going and too many new expenses at home. Worst of all, his habit was beginning to cost him.

***

It was at one of the many late night parties in an apartment on the Left Bank when Tom found himself standing next to Danielle. 'Can I get you a drink?' She was the most beautiful girl he'd ever set eyes on and there were plenty of stunning girls in Paris. Two nights later they made love at her apartment. After their first frantic lovemaking, she turned and reached out for her cigarettes on the bedside table. It was then he noticed the exquisite small tattoo on her right shoulder. The image was that of a viper and he smiled. This girl really did have it all.

As Tom took a taxi back to his hotel that night he was almost delirious with pleasure but he knew he had crossed the big line. He tried to put any negative thoughts at the back of his mind. It had been sheer ecstasy. He could handle it. It would be compartmentalized in his head. Shunted off somewhere. It wouldn't matter and life would go on just as before. No one had been hurt. A month later Danielle skipped classes and met Tom for coffee. It was the day that would change everything.

***

'I need your help with some money transactions.'

He looked up quickly, 'What do you mean?'

'You know how we use a little blow to liven things up back at the apartment. Well, I have a friend who distributes to London and he has asked for my help.'

Tom knew what was coming and felt uneasy.

'It's pretty simple really. There are lots of students from the university going to London all the time. They've got boyfriends and girlfriends over there and they're all short of money. They take the stuff over and nobody gets to know. They're students and never get any attention from customs.'

'So why do you need me?'

'We need to filter the proceeds back to Paris. We are looking for someone to manage the flow of cash to go offshore from the UK and back to the organisation in Europe. Might as well keep it in the family. I said you had the financial knowledge to set it all up. Your call really.'

Tom winced when she said 'family' and was taken aback by the sudden knowledge that she must be pretty high up in the organisation. 'What's the set up?'

Danielle sipped her coffee and placed her hand on his. 'I don't understand the money side. I just manage the couriers. The students travel by ferry and Eurostar. During the summer, the drugs are hidden in the soles of their built up flip flops. Each pair has a number written inside which identifies the wearer. In the winter months we change to them wearing shoes. It's foolproof. Weatherproof actually.' She laughed at her own joke.

Tom ran his hand through his hair. He was seen as a pillar of the local community and his integrity was essential in his business life. Clients entrusted large amounts of money to him and he had to be cleaner than clean. The squeakiest.

'We don't want the students to know the intricate parts of the operation and we need a little co-ordination at the London end. They get paid when we know the drugs have arrived.'

'How do you know that?'

'The students travel in groups of twenty. They are seen as just another chattering and excited bunch of kids going to London. When they get there, they go to the cafeteria at Victoria Coach Station. Andrei manages our London distribution and will be sitting at a table reading a copy of Top Gear magazine. The kids wander out to the toilets and change their flip flops for others they have in their rucksacks. There's so much going on in the toilets, no one notices anything. The kids just leave their old flip flops under Andrei's table. It's a busy place and easy to do.

'That's it?'

'That's it. Keep it simple.'

'So what happens next?'

'Andrei leaves and goes to check the consignment. Specifically the number of shoes and the contents. When he is satisfied everything is intact, he makes a call and each student gets an envelope on their return to Paris.

Danni touched his hand again. 'There's another service which you could help us with. The Paris hub needs working capital on a regular basis and I have been asked to arrange around £10k to come separately each month.' Tom knew that was the exact limit per journey from the UK.

'You're here twice a month so I suggested you might bring it with you and give it to me. You would get your cut. This is on top of your commission from the offshore laundering.' Tom sat staring at Danielle as his stomach started churning.

'Don't look so worried darling. Remember you have no connection with the packages. You will only be transferring money as a businessman who is a frequent flyer. Who's going to be looking at you?'

Tom's own financial crisis was crowding his mind. He needed to find money quickly. Maybe this was the answer. I'll just carry the cash in my luggage. Spread it around in my pockets of my clothes. It's my money. Nobody's business really. Who's to know where it's been or where it's going.

The waiter arrived and she ordered two more coffees. Tom asked for a cognac to go with it.

'I'm going to have to give this a little thought Danni.'

'That's OK, let me know when you can. The next group of students is going in three days and there is cash waiting to come back from London. It could be your first payday.'

As Tom flew back to London that evening he was surrounded by business people still tapping away on their laptops. God, if only they knew they had a trainee money launderer in their midst.

A young fair haired man in an expensive dark grey suit sat across the aisle. Half way through the flight he glanced at Tom as if searching for inspiration as he wrote up his day in Paris. Tom looked away quickly as if he had already been found out. 'Christ, do I look like a crook. Is it that obvious?'

He quickly buried his head in his newspaper and realised he was becoming paranoid before he had even started stuffing his pockets with dirty £50 notes.

As he landed at Heathrow and began walking towards 'Nothing to Declare' he felt his palms beginning to sweat and his stomach began to tighten. He had walked this path hundreds of times and had always found it a bit farcical.

There was never anyone in the customs hall. Just another load of 'suits' on the way back from Paris. But he always knew there were eyes behind the mirrors. Bound to be and tonight he hoped they weren't watching Tom Stanton.

He was convinced they would spot the difference in him as he tried to look straight ahead and give off the nonchalant look of a tired businessman. He quickly made for the long term car park and headed for his car. As he drove he began to calm down and called home on his hands free. Jill answered and asked where he was.

'Just got in honey. I'll be about half an hour.'

'How was the trip?'

'All the usual. Did some good business though. Tell you later.'

As he ended the call, he realised that soon some more lies were going to be heaped on those already told. He switched on the radio and searched for some classical music. Anything to avoid thinking.

It was good to get home. He always enjoyed getting back from his Paris trips but that was probably linked to the guilt he felt each time. Jill greeted him as he walked into the large kitchen and planted a kiss full on his lips. Tom put his arms round her and returned her kiss. She slowly broke away and went to the door leading to the hall. 'Oliver, Sarah, dinner's ready. Dad's home.'

He blanked out the past three days as the children came in to the kitchen. 'Hi Dad. How was the "Moulin Rouge?' If only they knew.

He moved across to the Aga and lifted the top off a huge casserole dish and the aroma almost filled the kitchen. 'You've cooked my favourite.' They sat down to Moroccan lamb casserole and Tom moved seamlessly into his domestic role.

***

He knew he needed the danger, the excitement that his secret life in Paris gave him. In boring financial meetings his mind wandered to Danielle and he would get aroused just anticipating his next trip to see her.

As the weeks had gone by he began to exaggerate the importance of his new Paris client to his business partners and to Jill. Bob and Charles were happy SMG had established a business link in Paris but were aware of the increasing costs both in travel and hotels, not to mention Tom's time. Charles had jokingly highlighted the increasing 'entertainment' costs at one of their regular meetings.

'Don't worry, you haven't seen anything yet. The returns are going to be big and it won't be long now.'

Bob and Charles smiled, took him at his word and moved on to the next item on the agenda.

His concentration on Danielle and his secret life in Paris had led to an abdication of responsibility and unbeknown to his partners, his portfolio was becoming toxic. He had begun skimming from existing and longstanding clients to fund his fictitious business portfolio in Paris. As far as his partners knew, he was on track to make quarterly target.

Chapter 25

That evening, Jack had two shots of 12 year old Balvenie and went for a third before going to bed and sleep. He winced as he turned over. The pain in his ribs had been dulled with the whisky but he felt it nonetheless. He contemplated having another drink but decided the effort would be too much and eventually fell into a fitful sleep.

He woke as dawn crept through his curtained window and as he moved to read the time on his bedside clock, his ribs sent a message that reminded him why he was hungover. He remembered yesterday's bedlam and lay back on the pillow. Eventually he eased himself out of bed and moved gingerly towards the shower. He stood under the hot jet for almost ten minutes and although his face stung, the heat started to ease some of the tension in his muscles. He wondered if he was getting a little old for this game as he stepped out and started to towel himself down. He padded back to his bedroom and wrapped himself in his dressing gown and walked through to the kitchen. He made a cafetiere of coffee and put two slices of bread in the toaster. Just the basics this morning. He ate his toast and sipped his coffee at the kitchen bar before retreating to the bedroom to get dressed. He took off his dressing gown and examined himself. The bruising was heavy around his rib cage and the tops of his thighs were a vivid blue. As he felt around he decided no other damage had been done in that area. Looking into the mirror he turned around and saw more bruising in his lower back. They hadn't missed much. He dressed and had a last check on his face in the bathroom mirror. The cuts were still looking raw and he missed out on the wet shave. It would be the stubbled look for a few days. In the living room he set down his coffee mug and checked his phone for messages. Unusually there were none. Jack felt the pain in his shoulder as he put the phone back on the table. It was 10 o'clock and Jill should have returned from the school run. He called her.

'How are you?'

'I was about to ring you and ask that.'

As he eased back on the sofa, he grunted as the pain gripped him'.

'Jack, are you alright?'

'I'll be fine but I've got bruises just about everywhere. Any word from Tom?'

'Nothing. Nothing at all.'

'I've got a few things to do but I've spoken to Alex Mason the home security guy and he could make it over around one o'clock to do a survey for cameras and stuff.'

'I can be in then.'

'He could be there some time. He's very thorough. I'll give you a call later today.'

As she hung the phone back on its wall cradle, it immediately rang. She jumped and quickly picked the phone up again.

'Mrs Stanton?'

Jill stiffened.

'Yes.'

'It's Alex Mason here. Jack Barclay asked me to give you a call about security at your home. I said I could do lunchtime today if that's ok with you.'

'That's fine. I've just spoken with him and agreed 1 o'clock.'

'Great, see you then.'

***

As Jill put the phone down she almost expected it to ring again but it didn't. She sat on the bar stool and thought of everything that had happened. She was angry and scared. Angry that Tom had brought all this violence into their lives and scared at what Patrick Flynn might do when the cheque bounced. God, Tom you bastard, please call. Please end this.

She collected herself, turned round and picked up the phone again and called her mother.

'Mum, it's me.'

'Oh darling, how are you? I was just about to call you. Is there any news of Tom?'

'Nothing since they found his car but something happened last night.'

'Are you alright Jill?'

'Yes, I'm fine but I was wondering if you and Dad could come over later.'

'Of course we can. What happened last night?'

'Oh Mum, I'll tell you when you get here. I've got someone here at lunchtime to look at alarms for the house but maybe you could get here later in the day. Would you like to stay for a couple of nights?'

'Of course. We'd love to.'

'Give me a call when you get near and I'll have the kettle on.'

Chapter 26

Before his disappearance, Tom's performance at SMG's weekly partners meeting had been worthy of an Oscar. He was the only one with a real chance of meeting target for the quarter and Charles and Bob felt a little envious at the new business he was writing. He had brought in almost £100k from a new client connected to the tennis club and the new income stream from FRM in Paris was shaping up very well. The blue eyed boy could do no wrong.

They rattled through agendas without any dissent and Tom had casually mentioned that he may have to spend a little more time in Paris in order to progress things there. His two partners just nodded as if it was to be expected. Meetings finished early and they often enjoyed an 'executive lunch' sent in by the local deli. Tom used to excuse himself as soon as he had finished to 'catch up on correspondence'. The last thing he wanted was to be drawn into a jokey discussion about current nightlife in Paris.

After meetings he would close his office door and go to the computer on his desk. He would open his clients' folder and scroll to his 'old clients' file. Many of them never got in touch and probably didn't even remember how much money was under management at SMG never mind where it was invested. He often wondered if some of them were still alive. He would select six clients who had not responded to any recent correspondence from SMG and siphon off money from each. He never touched the capital amount, just removed some of the interest accrued over the years from a wide range of investments. This helped cover his phantom 'income' from FRM in Paris. But he knew this scam in itself was not going to generate enough capital to cover his secret life in Paris. That was the moment he made the call to Danielle.

'Bonjour ma cherie, ca va?'

Danielle had sighed and said, 'I miss you. Have you thought about what we talked about?'

'Yeah, and I think I should be involved.'

'So, I'll set it all up?'

'I think so, yes.'

'Mon cherie, it will be good for us both.'

'I love you Danielle.'

'I love you too.'

***

She disconnected the call and smiled at Sergei as he rested after their afternoon lovemaking. She reached over for her cigarettes. She lit two at once and passed one to him. Exhaling through her nose and mouth before kissing him on the cheek, she said, 'You can stop worrying about the money side. Tom will set up the offshore banks and bring the cash across from London every two weeks. I can guarantee it.'

Danielle watched him inhale deeply, lift his head and exhale smoke at the ceiling. He was smiling. 'That's good. I like it.' He half turned and picked the cigarette from Danielle's fingers, stubbing both out in the ashtray. He pulled her towards him and said, 'Let's celebrate.'

'I thought we just had.'

Sergei just smiled. 'That was the hors d'oeuvre, now for the entrée.'

Chapter 27

Joan Kennedy visited her husband's grave at Mortlake cemetary every Thursday without fail. After a loving marriage lasting 58 years she had been devastated to lose 'her Fred' to lung cancer. He had smoked when he served in the artillery during the war when cigarettes were given away free with rations. When he was demobbed in 1946, he stopped without any apparent difficulty and had never taken them up again.

His suffering had been short and he had died at home with his beloved Joan and their two children Rose and Alfie at his side.

She struck a lonely figure in her dark coat and hat as she walked slowly through the neat pale yellow gravel pathways of the large cemetery leading to Fred's grave. He had been buried over at the west side near the brick perimeter wall and Joan was pleased because he would be facing the sunsets. He had been a 'sunset' man all his life always marvelling at the changing fiery hues as the sun finally dipped beneath the horizon. An ancient oak nearby protected the grave from the extremes of weather. Joan would be next to him someday.

She clutched her usual posy of chrysanthemums in one hand and began to feel upset as she turned left along the last pathway before reaching Fred. She approached, stopped and read the headstone for the thousandth time.

PRECIOUS MEMORIES OF FREDERICK (FRED) KENNEDY

A DEVOTED HUSBAND, FATHER AND GRANDFATHER

BORN MAY 1920 DIED AUGUST 2007

REST IN PEACE TILL WE MEET AGAIN

She put down her small handbag on the ground beside her and knelt on the grass in front of the beautifully tended grave. She spoke to Fred for five minutes bringing him up to date with everything happening in the family and the recent price increase in petrol which had made everything more expensive for everyone. What could you do? When she'd finished she rose slowly, placing her hand on her right knee to stand upright again. She walked to the side of the plot and reached for last week's posy of flowers at the base of the modest granite headstone and gently eased them out of the grey and black ceramic jar, placing them behind her on the grass. She replaced them with the fresh ones and took from her pocket an old small medicine bottle filled with water. Unscrewing the glass top, she poured the contents into the jar of new flowers and re - capped the bottle.

'There, that should keep you till I see you next week,' she said to the flowers as much as to Fred. She turned round to pick up the partially withered flowers and that's when she saw it.

Something was sticking up from the ground four plots away. Without her glasses on she couldn't quite make out what it was and walked slowly towards the recently dug grave. As she approached it, a putrid smell filled the air, one she'd never sensed before. As she moved closer, the foul odour almost overpowered her and she had to catch herself as she stumbled. Then she let out a piercing scream and her hand flew to her mouth. What looked like torn fabric and the remains of an arm were sticking upright from the disturbed earth. She recoiled in shock and felt dizzy. The appalling smell assaulting her nostrils made her gag and in confusion she turned away and tried to work out the direction of the cemetery office. As she lurched along the path she almost collided with a middle aged couple walking towards her. They took one look at her and the woman reached out to support Joan.

'What's the matter dear? Are you alright?'

'Oh my God. There's a body up there. Please get some help.'

***

Within minutes of the police arriving, the blue and white crime scene tape went around the west side of the cemetery. When the SOCO team arrived, the digging began. As dusk fell arc lights were set up and a bright white light bathed the grave site. After an hour of careful digging a body bag was gently brought to the surface. The foxes had begun to do their work and a gash could be seen near the top left of the bag where the arm still stood exposed. It was plain to the trained eyes at the scene that the body had not lain for long and after further forensic tests had been carried out, the body in the bag was wheeled to an unmarked windowless grey transit van and transferred to the police mortuary.

As the van pulled away a policewoman turned to her colleague. 'There's no rest for the dead,' she sighed.

Chapter 28

London woke up to another hot day. At 7 o'clock the cafe pavements were being scrubbed and hosed down to clear the detritus left from the previous evening.

Xavier had slept badly, angry about the lack of progress. Khalid had snored loudly all night.

Xavier had to phone Sergei at ten o'clock with an update. Some update. He went to the kitchen and put water in the kettle for coffee then went back to his bedroom and collected his pistol from under his pillow.

He sat and sipped his black coffee thinking about what he'd say. All Xavier understood was getting results and being well paid for doing it. He didn't know right from wrong. Never interested him. This assignment was pissing him off. They had been in London for nearly a week and seemed no nearer finding their man. He made a mental note to ask Sergei if there was anything from Stanton's BMW.

He rang Sergei at ten o'clock precisely.

'What have you got?'

Xavier told him they had nothing more. Sergei grunted, 'There was nothing in the car.' Xavier knew what was coming next.

'So what are you doing today?'

As Khalid snored in the bedroom, Xavier outlined his plan speaking quickly to shorten the time he had to explain himself. 'The London investigator doesn't seem to have much so we're going to put the squeeze on Stanton's wife. Her husband must have been in touch. She has to know something.'

Xavier waited and Sergei said, 'OK, I'm going to call you tonight at 10 o'clock. Give me something, anything. The heat's getting turned up here so do the same there.' The call was ended.

Xavier went through to the bedroom and kicked Khalid hard in the backside. 'Get up. We've got work to do.'

Chapter 29

Jack's beating had slowed him but he was eventually ready to face the outside world. He put on sunglasses to hide his black eyes but as the whole world seemed to be after him, it might be safer to be Mr Incognito today. As he collected his car keys from the table his phone rang and the ID said, Jill.

'Hi, how's the wounded soldier this morning?'

'Getting better. Still technicolour under the eyes.'

'Jack, something's come up which you need to know about. A body's been found.'

Jack's heart missed a beat and suddenly he was lost for words.

'No, not Tom's. Sorry, I shouldn't have been so clumsy. There's still no word from him but a body has been found in a shallow grave at Mortlake Cemetery. The dead guy is a John Vanner and he used to be a client of Tom's. There could be a connection.'

Jack sat down as Jill told her story.

'They were quite friendly till they had a falling out. The police have just released his name. They say he was murdered. It's unbelievable and a bit spooky Jack. Do you think it means anything?'

'Maybe. How did you find out about it?'

'It's in the paper this morning. Front page.'

'Who thought it might be of interest to me?'

'Charles rang from the office. He said that Tom had asked his PA to get out John Vanner's file three weeks ago. Said he was thinking of trying to get him back on board but didn't return the file. Charles said it was too much of a coincidence and thought you should know.'

'Yeah, it could mean something. How old was Vanner?'

'I'm not certain, but around forty I think.'

'Can you ask Charles to do something for me? Would you ask him to search Tom's office again?'

'What's he looking for?'

'Anything he thinks might be relevant. Especially anything to do with Paris. And now, anything which might mention John Vanner.'

There was a short silence at the other end of the phone and Jill said, 'OK.'

Jack quickly changed the subject. 'Have you heard from Alex Mason yet?'

'Yes, he's on his way. I've rung my mum, and she and Dad are coming to stay for a couple of days. I need the company.'

'That's good. I'm pleased you've done that. Maybe you should go to them instead.'

'I thought of that but it's an important time for the kids at school and I'm already worried their dad's disappearance is affecting them badly. The summer holiday is coming up. Maybe we'll get away then. By the way, both Tom's credit card statements have come in the post. I haven't opened them but I know you want to see them.'

'I do. I've got things on today but maybe I could pick them up from you tomorrow?'

'Yes, OK. Would you give me a call later?'

'Yes, of course'.

***

Jill tried to keep herself busy till Alex Mason was due to arrive and switched on the radio as she went round to tidy the kids' rooms. When she got to the master bedroom she slipped off her dressing gown and pulled on her jeans and chose a white cotton blouse to go with them. She made the bed up and started on the en suite when she heard the doorbell chime above the sounds of the radio. She looked at her watch and saw it was twelve thirty. He's early. She went downstairs and saw a man in silhouette through the frosted glass and went to open the door. As soon as it was ajar, it slammed into her body, winding her as she staggered backwards. Khalid stormed in with Xavier just behind him. She screamed but as the door slammed shut, no one was around to hear. As she tried to scream again Khalid clamped her mouth with his huge paw like hand. She could smell his sour body odour as he dragged her through to the kitchen.

'Sit her on the barstool.' Xavier placed a small brown carton on the kitchen bar next to her before bringing a roll of duct tape from his pocket. Jill tried to kick Khalid as she saw Xavier lean across for a knife from the rack next to the sink and she began to panic whilst trying to draw air through her nose. Her eyes darted around with fear as Xavier crouched down out of her line of sight. She felt the ripping of the tape and her lower legs being bound around the chair legs. He wrenched her arms behind her making her sit up and taped them to the back of the chair. She suddenly wished she hadn't chosen the open necked blouse which was now stretched tight as her elbows were pinned behind her. She saw Khalid staring at her with a strange vacant look in his eyes. Xavier cut off a strip of tape and nodded to Khalid who removed his hand from her face. Before she had time to catch her breath and scream, Xavier had the tape stretched over her mouth. The combination of Xavier's breath and Khalid's body sweat was making her feel sick.

Xavier stood in front of her. 'Tell us what we want to know and we won't hurt you.' It was his best English. 'Do you understand me?' Jill nodded her head and without waiting, Xavier leant forward ripping the tape off her mouth. She winced as her lips took the brunt of the tearing action and she gasped for air as the gag came off.

'Where is your husband?'

Still desperately trying to draw breath she croaked, 'I don't know.'

'You're not hearing me. Where is your husband?'

'I don't know, I really don't. He's gone and I honestly don't know where he is.' Xavier took the knife and cut a new piece of tape. 'I don't think you are getting this, you must tell me where he is.'

Jill felt her heart thumping and her eyes moved to the knife that Xavier was still holding.

'Last chance, Madame Stanton.'

'Oh God, please, I don't know. I really don't.'

'I think you do.'

Sheer terror gripped Jill as Xavier put the strip of duct tape over her mouth.

Xavier moved away and went to the fridge whilst Khalid looked on as a spectator. Jill's arms ached from being pinned behind her back and she felt cramp in her legs. As Xavier turned round he had the cheese container in his left hand. Opening it he broke of a piece of cheddar and crumbled it in his right hand. He picked the cheese morsels and carefully started inserting them in the top of the gag next to Jill's lips. The smell made her want to retch.

Stretching behind her, Xavier picked up the small container he had brought with him and held it in front of her face. Jill heard a scraping noise. She tried to scream as he opened the top of the box and a rat's head popped up.

Oh, Jesus no.

She thought she was about to pass out as Xavier brought the box close to her face. The rat began to climb out of the box towards her mouth. As she began to lose her mind she vaguely felt the warm wetness between her legs as her bladder gave way. Xavier caught hold of the rat and stuffed it back in the box. As he wrenched the tape off, Jill hardly felt the ripping on her lips and she began weeping.

'Now where is he?'

Without warning the doorbell rang and this time Jill managed to scream out loud. Khalid jumped forward to close the kitchen door but not before Jill managed to scream again. Khalid saw the figure of a man at the front door as the bell started ringing incessantly. Xavier sprinted across and looked through along the hallway to the door. A voice started shouting Jill's name and she screamed as loud as she was able.

As the glass in the front door shattered, Xavier nodded towards the back door and Khalid ran to it and unlocked it. They dashed out into the back garden leaving Jill whimpering in the kitchen. The box still lay on the table.

***

Alex Mason broke in the front door as Khalid and Xavier ran round the side of the house and used a waste bin to climb over the side gate to the front of the house. As they started to run down the driveway, a man came charging towards them shouting incoherently. Patrick Flynn had been drinking since the bars opened early that morning and was out of his mind.

Khalid tried to dodge round him but the man kept coming at him, screaming. 'You bastards. I suppose you're in this too. I'm going to fucking kill you.'

Without hesitation, Khalid pulled his gun and shot him in the head. His massive frame buckled and he fell to the gravel driveway, a deep red stain forming a puddle around his upper body.

Khalid caught up with Xavier and they walked towards the road without looking back.

Chapter 30

Tom Stanton's first money delivery happened on a Tuesday. Everyone at the office knew he was off to see his clients in Paris and wouldn't be back till Friday for the partners' meeting. He'd seemed a little detached during breakfast at home that morning and Jill had asked him if he was alright.

'Fine, just a few work things on my mind.'

He told her he was going to miss gym that morning and see a client in St John's Wood before catching his flight from Heathrow. When he left home at nine o'clock he kissed Jill goodbye and drove directly to Victoria Coach Station in South London.

His instructions were to buy a copy of the Financial Times, go to the cafeteria and sit at a table near the window. He would be given a laptop bag by a man as he passed his table. The contents were to be taken to Danielle in Paris that day. He opened the newspaper and waited with a bad cup of coffee for company. He became increasingly nervous as the minutes ticked by and became convinced he had been set up.

At midday as his head was still in his newspaper, a laptop bag was placed on his table. He didn't look up and by the time he glanced round the side of the broadsheet newspaper, the courier had disappeared. He waited five minutes, picked up the bag and left the cafeteria. He headed straight back to the nearby multi storey car park and mounted the disinfected stairs to the fourth floor. When he got to his car he climbed in and opened the bag in the semi darkness of the corner parking bay he had chosen. It was the first time he had seen 'dirty money.' As he opened the bag an unusual smell hit his nostrils. He guessed what it meant but he was more intrigued by the actual sight of bundles of £50 notes. Although he talked and dealt in millions at SMG, he never actually saw it. He was used to rows of figures. Money without meaning. He felt strangely excited as he handled the bundles with white paper wrappers. He put the bag under his seat and drove out of the car park into blue skies. He headed west along the Thames Embankment and threaded his way through Earls Court. He joined the M4 and accelerated towards Heathrow and the long term car parks.

Chapter 31

Jack knew coincidences in life were rare but he also knew the death of John Vanner was connected to the disappearance of Tom Stanton. He scrolled the number for SMG and asked to speak with Charles McIntosh.

'Hello, it's Jack Barclay.'

'Mr Barclay, I was very sorry to hear of your injuries yesterday. How are you?'

'I'm getting better thanks but still a bit sore in places.'

'I'm sure. Bob feels the same.'

'How is he?'

'Like you, it'll take a few days. We should meet, Mr Barclay. There is much at stake here.'

'Yes I know. And please, call me Jack.'

'OK, thanks. How can I help you right now?'

'I'm sure the death of John Vanner is somehow connected with Tom's disappearance but it's difficult to see exactly how right now.'

'Yes, I'm sure too. You probably know John Vanner was an old client of Tom's and he was trying to get John back into the fold. He asked his PA for John Vanner's file a few weeks ago and never returned it. It's a strict rule here that files are always returned. No exceptions. Because of that I'm a little short on detail.'

Jack sensed Charles wanted to be helpful. 'What do you know about Mr. Vanner?'

'Well, without the file, only what I can remember. I have to say I am bound by client confidentiality and I'm sure you know all about that. The media are going to be all over this given the circumstances in the cemetery.'

'Can you just give me the basics?'

'I can say he was Caucasian. From the few times I saw him, I would put him just under six foot and he had a broken nose. We used to joke a little about their broken noses. They both played rugby in their day.'

Jack noted his second coincidence of the day. 'Address?'

'It's the one thing I can't do but you may find it is not a million miles from the centre court at Wimbledon. Would you just hold the line a minute Jack?'

Jack heard muffled voices and Charles talking to someone in the office. He came back on the line.

'I'll have to go. You may not know but there has been a serious disturbance at Jill's home. I've just been told.'

Jack froze and quickly said, 'Thanks, we'll speak again.'

After ending the call to SMG, Jack felt his heart racing and rang Jill. An unfamiliar female voice answered and without introduction said, 'Who is this please?'

'My name is Jack Barclay, a friend of Jill's. Can I speak with her?'

'This is DC Brighthouse of Thames Valley CID. I'm afraid you can't speak with her at the moment.'

'Is she alright?'

'I can't tell you anything, but you may like to call back later.'

Jack didn't want to get involved and decided to let it go and said he'd call back. 'Thank you.' The line went dead.

He immediately rang Alex Mason.

When he picked up, Jack asked if he was at Jill's.

'Yeah, I'm still here.'

'What's happened?'

'Chaos. Your two French friends were here.'

Jack felt the anger well up within him. 'Is Jill alright?'

'Yes, but she's in a terrible state. They tied her up and tried to get her to talk. 'Those two jokers were in the house when I arrived and I heard her screams. I broke in through the front door window. Jill had been tied to a chair in the kitchen but she hadn't been physically hurt. The two guys had run out the back door but after I got in they must have run round to the front. Some other bloke came running up the drive shouting and cursing and they just shot him.'

Jack was trying to take all this in. 'What, dead?'

'Yes, dead.'

'Jesus, who was he?'

'Don't know. The place is crawling with police and I'm one of their main witnesses. I'm going to have to go, Jack.'

'Hang on Alex. Do you think it was Jill's husband who got shot?'

'Not the impression I'm getting. Some Irish guy apparently. I'll call you as soon as I can.'

Jack was left listening to another dead line. He paced the floor of his small living room wondering what the hell was happening. He cursed himself for not advising Jill better. He should have known they would come back. She should have gone away with the kids. He should have made her do that. He couldn't believe he'd been so stupid. He cooled down and phoned Mike.

'It's Jack. Have you got anything?'

'Christ, you sound pissed off.'

'Sorry. I am. Bad day so far.'

'Well, I think I can improve it a bit. Tom Stanton's last call before he vanished was to Paris. He called a Danielle Bonnaire. His phone hasn't been used since.'

'You got her number?'

'Yeah, but don't get excited. That's gone too. Disconnected.'

'Pity. Good work Mike. Thank you. I'll square up with you when we meet. Could you check another one for me?'

'Go for it.'

'John Vanner. Wimbledon, SW19.'

'Leave it with me pal.'

'Thanks mate. See you.'`

His ribs ached and he took two ibuprofen.

He booted up his laptop and Googled John Vanner, getting over one million hits. Eventually he narrowed it down to John Vanner of London SW19.

He had been an author, publishing at least three books. They were all related to the effects of imprisonment on the human condition. He had been quite an authority on his subject travelling extensively giving lectures to governments and universities around the world. He had no doubt this was the John Vanner in question and walked painfully to his antique bureau in the corner of his living room. Pulling out a disc concealed in the bottom right drawer he slotted it into his

125

computer. In a minute he had John Vanner's address in Wimbledon. He rinsed his breakfast dishes and left his apartment for the drive to SW 19. As he turned into the Edgeware Road his mobile rang.

'It's Alex. I've got a bit more. Jill's OK but still shaken up. She's getting angry which is good.

'She's OK, isn't she?

'Yeah, she's not hurt. She's going to ring you when she can. The guy who was shot was called Patrick Flynn. Wrong place, wrong time, it seems. Had nothing to do with what was going on inside the house.'

'Poor man. These guys are insane. Thanks Alex, I really do owe you.'

'No problem. Speak later. Watch your back. These two are fucking lunatics

***

As Jack negotiated the traffic and headed towards South London, he realized he was thinking only of Jill. He started to see parallels in their lives. One day everything seems to be normal, almost hum drum. Then *wham* everything falls apart. How could he not have seen his own marriage disintegrating? How much had been down to him, to his absence from Kate as he worked impossible hours? In his subconscious, did he know the probable outcome would be so disastrous?

Perhaps Tom and Jill chased the dream of financial success thinking it would lead to personal happiness, or maybe only Tom was driven to win. He wished he was on his way to her to give some comfort. With his concentration lost, he moved out to pass a black cab and had to move back too quickly to avoid an oncoming bus. He heard the insistent blast of the horn behind him.

Jesus, why did I do that?

126

Chapter 32

Tom always flew business. The speedy airport processing was worth the extra money. It was his first money run and he was sweating. He was sure it would be noticed. The stomach cramps came on before he arrived at check-in and he went to the toilet. In the cubicle he sat down, opened a miniature of Smirnoff and downed it. He placed the empty bottle on the floor and tried to compose himself as he sat on the toilet.

He stood up and checked the distribution of money around his body. He picked up his carry on and opened the door. He walked to the huge mirrors by the wash basins and looked hard at himself. Normal. Fucking normal. He left the toilets and went towards security. He had been meticulous in making sure there were no coins in his pockets. No specs. No keys. No belt buckle. No watch. Nothing to set off the alarms. He watched his laptop and case go down the conveyer belt to the scanner and walked towards the security arch. As he went through he felt the wetness in his armpits. Sweet Jesus, let me pass.

Nothing happened.

Thank you. Thank you. He picked up his case and laptop and headed to the departure lounge for his second vodka of the day. Late the same afternoon he met Danielle and handed her a folded and sealed plastic carrier bag with £10,000 inside. 'Here's your duty free allowance.' She pulled him close and kissed him hard. 'You are so clever. I adore you.'

That night they had dinner and champagne at a small restaurant just off Boulevard Saint-Michel. Tom felt ecstatic at the ease by which he had travelled with the cash and he knew he had solved a problem for Danielle. 'Cheers darling,' and clinked his glass against hers. He smiled knowing there was bound to be more sweet reward on offer later that night.

Chapter 33

Jack had made good time through South London and found the Vanner address in a tree lined street in Wimbledon. He parked and bought three hours from the parking machine.

The house was an imposing detached Victorian residence with a gravel covered carriage drive. He walked up to the large black lacquered door and rang the bell. After a couple of minutes he heard the lock turn and the door opened. He was surprised there was no security chain.

Standing in front of him was one of the most elegant women he'd ever seen. She looked to be in her late sixties, tall and slender with strong grey hair tied at the back with a red tortoiseshell clip. She wore a burgundy blouse buttoned to the throat and a close fitting long black skirt which accentuated her height. Her face was kind and looked slightly suntanned. Spectacles hung from a silver chain around her neck.

'Can I help you?'

'My name is Jack Barclay. I'm a private investigator trying to find a missing person and I think you might be able to help me.' He held out a business card which acted as ID and she glanced down at it.

Her face crumpled and she stretched her right hand out to the door frame as if to steady herself. 'Is this to do with the loss of my son?'

'Yes, I'm sorry. It is. I can come back another time.'

She paused to collect herself and said, 'No, please come in. I'd like to help.'

She led him through a vaulted hall which to Jack looked quite splendid. It was beautiful in an old fashioned way.

They arrived at what Jack took to be the living room and he was invited to take a seat on one of the soft leather armchairs.

Fresh freesia filled a large vase on a mahogany coffee table giving a beautiful aroma in the room.

'Mrs Vanner, I can only guess what you have been through but I am here to try and help you get some answers.'

'He was murdered you know.'

'Yes, I know. Do the police have any idea who may have done it?'

'Well if they have, I haven't been told, but I don't think they know yet. Do you have some theories Mr Barclay?'

'Nothing concrete, but his death may well be connected to some of the ex prisoners he tried to help. They may have hired someone to kill him, empty his bank accounts at various ATM's in London and then bury his body. I'm sorry Mrs Vanner.'

She held her handkerchief to her face and he heard her sob.

'I believe John used to invest money with a company called SMG and his financial advisor there was Tom Stanton. They parted company some time ago but apparently Tom Stanton was trying to re-establish contact with your son.'

'Do you think he had anything to do with John's death?'

'No, but I think he may have taken your son's identity for his own good.'

'You know, Tom Stanton paid John a visit here. My son and I share this house. He lived at the top and I live on the ground floor. It would have been about six weeks ago. Do you think he has come to harm as well?'

'We don't know yet. Did your son see him when he visited?'

'I don't think he invited him in but they had a conversation on the doorstep and I seem to remember John saying he would get back to him.'

Jack made a few notes in his pad and asked about John's lifestyle.

'He was a workaholic. Never married. He didn't have much of a social life to speak of and the more successful he became, the less I saw of him. He travelled very widely and gave lectures at universities and institutes all over the world. He gave advice to governments and I don't know how he found the time to write. His books were very successful.'

'What did he do exactly?'

'He had some pretty radical ideas on how prisons should help rehabilitate the inmates. He believed they could leave as better people rather than the other way round.'

'Did he spend much time with prisoners?'

'Oh yes. He spent a great deal of time inside jails speaking with them. That's what gave his opinions credibility. He knew at first hand what they were going through. He always thought there was some good in everyone irrespective of past behaviour. They spoke freely with him and he usually managed to build trust even with the most hardened criminals.' Her voice faltered for the first time and her eyes misted as she went on. 'Maybe he placed too much trust in some of them. They knew he was quite well off and although he didn't specifically say it, I think he was giving money away to prisoners on their release. It probably wasn't the wisest thing to do and I think he sometimes worried things could get out of hand.'

As Jack listened, he realised John Vanner could have been a victim of his own well meant philosophies.

'Did he keep notes on who he had helped out financially?'

'The police asked me that. None that I know of. I think he just drew money from one of his bank accounts and used cash. The prisoners preferred it that way.'

Jack thought, 'I bet they did.'

'He did mention one name which stuck with me because it is the same as my dentist.' Jack looked up expectantly.

'It was Williams. I can't remember his first name. John was trying to help him in some way after he came out of prison.' Jack made a note of the name.

'When you were being interviewed by the police, did you mention Tom Stanton at all?'

'Well no. I didn't think it would be relevant.'

She looked at Jack and said, 'I asked the police if they thought John could be alive and they said they weren't hopeful.' She looked down at her lap before continuing. 'When I asked them why, they said his debit cards had been used at several cash machines in the immediate aftermath of his disappearance. The maximum amount was taken each time, always at night and always by a hooded person. The banks put a stop on the cards although one of his accounts was emptied.' She pulled a small white handkerchief from her sleeve and dabbed her eyes.

'They said it is possible that he was held against his will and he was made to divulge his PIN numbers. John was a kind man and genuinely interested in helping others whom he thought had been less fortunate than him. I miss him so much.'

Jack stood up and touched Helen Vanner on the shoulder. Just enough to try and convey his feelings.

'I'm so sorry Mrs Vanner. I'll do everything I can to try and find out who did this. I've no doubt the police will be working hard to do the same. They'll have contacts I haven't. The underworld is a small place really and people do talk.'

She walked him to the door and as he stepped out he turned and said, 'Thank you for seeing me.'

She held up a hand and said, 'Will you call me if you hear anything?'

'Of course. Goodbye Mrs Vanner.'

As he made his way back to the car an almost overwhelming sense of sadness came over him. She was a lovely woman and he had no doubt that her son had been an all round good guy who put his trust in the wrong people.

When he returned to his car he had ten minutes left on the ticket. He had to speak to Jill.

He pulled out his mobile and saw he had three text messages. Ignoring them he rang her number and she answered immediately.

'Jack, thank God, Where are you?'

'I'm in Wimbledon. I've spoken to Alex but only briefly.'

Her voice sounded hoarse as she blurted out her story. 'It was awful. Two men barged in to the house and tied me up. Threatened me with a rat. A bloody rat.'

'Jesus.'

'Your friend Alex Mason saved me when he arrived early and heard me screaming. He broke in and the two guys ran out the back door.' Her speech was almost getting ahead of her brain and it was as if she wanted to get rid of the words. They went round the side of the house to get away just as Patrick Flynn came running up the drive. He was drunk and screaming out my name. God, Jack, they shot him on the driveway. It was just horrific. Unbelievable.'

Jack listened with increasing unease. They will be the same guys who attacked me. They're animals. You must get away from there.'

'I know. I've spoken with Mum and Dad and cancelled them coming over.'

'Don't say anything more on the phone. I'll call you later. Are you sure you're OK?'

'Yes, sore mouth, but I'll be fine. Call me when you can.'

Chapter 34

Charles and Bob had worked long into the night trying to establish the extent of the damage. As they dug down, the realisation began to dawn on them.

Tom had hoodwinked them and the whole company. His cover up had been immense and for months he had milked money from clients' accounts. Everything he had done was going to end the reputation of SMG. As they ploughed through the files they became more horrified at what they found.

He had stolen money from long standing clients. People of stature in the local community and people with great influence. It was going to be a bloodbath and the press would have a field day.

As they itemised the sums he had siphoned off, they both realised they would not be able to repay the money from their own resources. Tom had been living a lie as far as they could see. He had removed money in a random way to avoid detection and even if they had the financial resources to replace it all, it could only be made good over a period of time. Their language became more coarse as the night wore on. By 2 o'clock in the morning they both realised the situation was beyond their control. Tom Stanton had milked the accounts of some of their oldest and most prestigious clients.

As they finally logged off, they realised he had been stealing money over a year. How could they not have seen it? Was this really happening? They had trusted him implicitly. He was the cornerstone of the company.

It was 3 am when they stopped and decided to meet again at ten o'clock to decide on how to manage the unmanageable.

Chapter 35

Xavier and Khalid retreated to the safe house in Paddington.

After leaving Jill Stanton's home they'd walked for over fifteen minutes before arriving at the local rail station. They knew they would have been filmed on CCTV at some stage especially on the platform but it was better than being seen at close range by a taxi driver. Outside of rush hour, the train was almost empty and they argued most of the way. Xavier couldn't believe Khalid had shot the guy.

'Why didn't you just drop him with a chop? You keep on about how good you are. Why kill him? You prick. That's going to put the heat on us.'

When they got back to the house, Xavier knew he was due a call from Paris and he knew Sergei would be furious. Not that an innocent man had been gunned down but because it didn't get them any nearer to finding Stanton and the missing money.

He told Sergei what had happened and the line went dead.

***

Tom had made his fifth courier trip to Paris from Heathrow in as many weeks and his confidence was now as high as it could get. He travelled business class and although he was subject to the same security as anyone else he felt it afforded a degree of protection.

He loved his trips to Paris and his nights with Danielle were sublime. He'd never known such pleasure. After his third run he'd stopped hyperventilating as he reached Heathrow. It was just routine now. He carried large sums of money on him as he travelled. No problem.

Dover woke to a grey day with low cloud blanketing the cliffs and another grinding round of arrivals and departures with the ferries at the docks. The weather had suddenly deteriorated after weeks of glorious sunshine. The Channel was relatively calm but for those who like sailing on a mill pond, it could prove difficult today.

Another large group of French students were on the mid morning sailing from Calais to Dover. Lots of laughing and squealing. Older passengers glared at them, some looking mildly irritated, others caught up in the unfolding docking procedures.

Frank Stevens was in his second year as a customs officer at Dover Docks and was beginning to be accepted by his older colleagues. They still played little tricks on him but he had been warned and expected it. Their attentions had been diverted to newer arrivals now and he was more or less left alone to do his duty during his shift.

The Channel had turned stormy and the air temperature had dropped as the ferry docked at Dover. Frank had taken up his usual position behind a one-way mirror to take an overview of foot passengers. He knew it was morally wrong to do this and he felt like a voyeur but it was necessary. If it reduced crime, it was in order to spy on people like this.

As passengers disembarked he spotted a large group of attractive young students. The girls looked gorgeous. Got to be French. He couldn't help looking at them. As he watched them moving through, it suddenly dawned on him. They were all wearing flip flops. Every one of them. As they all giggled their way through to their coach without hindrance he made some notes in his book. He didn't want to make a fool of himself but he was convinced there was something wrong. There was a decided chill in the air on both sides of the channel so why the flip flops? He submitted his report at the end of his shift specifically mentioning his concerns about the French students footwear and went back home to do nothing much until his next working day.

That night he dreamt of the young laughing French girls and woke with a hard-on.

Chapter 36

Jack's concern for Jill was gnawing away at him and he scrolled to her mobile number. 'How are you and where are you?'

'I'm at friends in Wiltshire. We're all here. We're fine and the kids have been great. We're going to lie low for a few days.'

'That's good. I'm pleased.'

'Jack, are you OK?'

'Yeah, I've seen a lovely lady in Wimbledon today and I think I know where I'm going now. I need to pull in a few favours tomorrow and I can move everything on.'

'How old was the lady?'

'Old enough to be my mother, but beautiful. John Vanner's mother.'

'Sorry.'

'That's OK. Have the police got any names yet?'

'They may have but I don't know. I saw them getting fingerprints off the fridge. The fat ugly one was in there helping himself to cold meat and chicken and then I saw him with a low fat strawberry yoghurt. And that's when I was tied up with a rat three inches from my nose. Bastards.'

That's the second time she's sworn thought Jack. Must be the stress of it all.

'You know they covered my mouth but not my eyes. How arrogant was that.'

They were going to kill you until they got interrupted, he thought.

'Their accents sounded French and quite a few prints were found from the kitchen and of course they left the rat. They reckon they can trace that.'

He paused and said, 'They can trace a rat?'

'No. The box it was in. Trace it back to where it was bought. You know, I have to tell you something. I peed my pants when he brought the rat out. I haven't done that since I was three. It was so embarrassing, I can't tell you.'

'Yeah, well who likes rats stuck in their face?'

'Yes, but I'm thirty eight.'

'Forget it. You're safe and the kids are safe. That's all that matters.'

'I suppose so. I'm never going to France again. Ever.'

'Ever?'

She managed a laugh.

There was a slight pause and she said, 'By the way, I tried to ring Lauren Flynn but it just kept going into message. I don't really know what I would have said to her. It's just all too awful for words. I mean, I set up the meeting between Tom and the Flynns.'

'Don't forget, Lauren Flynn initiated the meeting. You didn't ask for all this.'

'I can't see me ever going back to the club. If I hadn't stopped that cheque, he might not have come round. He might still be alive. I still can't believe what happened.'

'You could "*if only*" over just about everything you do in life but then you wouldn't do anything at all. You mustn't beat yourself up over this. The person who brought this on has vanished and you are a victim too. I'm afraid your husband has more to answer for each day.'

'I know. You're right, but when is all this going to end? I'm beginning to feel like a criminal myself.'

'It'll end when the people looking for him get back what he has taken from them. Whatever that is.'

She sighed and said, 'When will I see you?'

'I hope to get some information tomorrow. I'll call you then. And Jill, be careful when answering your mobile. If you don't recognise the caller, don't take it. You'll be fine but just be careful.'

'You too. Speak tomorrow.'

Chapter 37

It had been when Tom was sitting at a pavement café in St Germain waiting for Danielle, he realized how deep he was getting. He had just made his sixth money run and this time it felt different. On his way to business check in at Heathrow he had seen a sniffer dog trotting excitedly along the cases waiting to be checked in. Their owners looked on in an interested but bemused way. It was obvious none of them had anything to worry about. Instinctively he gave the dog a wide berth. No point in taking unnecessary risks but it worried him. He knew the money had been handled down the line at user level. His suit would have been a sniffer dog's paradise. He worried about it on the short hop to Paris and his mood worsened when he saw two passengers on his flight being pulled for a random search at CDG. He caught a taxi into the City.

By the time he got out to wait for Danni, he had made up his mind.

He was on his second espresso when she came up to the café. She had her usual jeans and a white T Shirt and a large black tote bag hanging from her shoulder. Her black hair was pulled back by a large bright red clasp and her eyes were shielded by sunglasses. She looked like a movie star and knew it. Even some of the old waiters gave her a look over.

Tom's mood softened when he saw her. He stood up, grinning broadly. 'Hi Danni.' He placed both arms round her and kissed her full on the mouth. No cheek kissing here. She was his.

She ordered an espresso, sat down and lit a Camel Light. Said it kept her weight down. Tom held her hand on the small round table top and waited for a passing police van to pass.

'I have missed you so much Danni.'

'Me too. Ca va?'

'I'm OK, but there was a lot of security at the airport today and I'm getting worried. The risks are growing for me and the money isn't just dirty, it smells of drugs.'

Danni inhaled deeply on her cigarette and flicked it twice in succession in the large clear glass ashtray. 'Do you have today's package?'

'Of course. It's here.'

He passed it under the table and she placed it in the tote bag sitting at her feet.

'So, what are you saying?'

'I'm saying the risks are outweighing the gains. Customs are putting more resource into money laundering. I have so much to lose. Everything. If you want me to carry on I need to have a bigger share. I want more of the action.'

He looked at her as she flipped open the pack and pulled out another cigarette.

'Tom, I don't have any authority here.' She flicked the wheel of her lighter, lit up and inhaled deeply.

'Ask for it Danni and if you don't, I will.'

'You don't know who to go to.'

'No, but you'll tell me.'

'I'm way down the line Tom. I only deal with the next level. That's how it works. Nobody knows anybody at the top.'

'Just send the message. I've proved my reliability. I deserve more.'

'Can we speak about it tomorrow? I need to get the package to my contact.'

'Sure.'

Danielle rose and kissed him on the cheek and they agreed to meet up at the Petit Maison at seven o'clock. In one way he regretted his aggressive stance. It had been brought on by events that day at Heathrow and Charles De Gaulle but nonetheless he had reached a point where he had to take stock. His financial position at SMG was weakening quickly. He needed to inject money to shore up his fictitious positions at SMG and he wasn't acquiring new clients.

As he had sat in his taxi on the way to his afternoon meeting at Canard Bleu, he made a decision. He needed a bigger piece of the drugs action and if necessary he would put his case to someone further up the chain than Danielle.

***

As soon as she was out of Tom's vision at the street café, Danielle stepped into a doorway and pulled her mobile from her bag. 'Sergei, it's me.'

'Ma cherie, ca va?'

'I need to see you.'

Sergei let out a low laugh. 'Yesterday not enough for you?'

Danielle laughed too and said, 'No, it was great. It always is. It's about Tom. I've just picked up the money but he says he wants more for the risk he is taking. Maybe a lot more.'

'What did you say?'

'Nothing, except I would speak to someone about it.'

'OK. Go to my apartment and let yourself in. I have a meeting in a few minutes but it will be short. I should be with you by 2 o'clock. And Danni, when I get there, let's work up a little appetite for lunch.'

'Make it a very short meeting then.'

They laughed again.

Chapter 38

The result of the post mortem on John Vanner was a shock to everyone. Not just because he had been murdered but because it appeared he had been assassinated. He had been shot with a small calibre gun pressed to his skull behind his left ear and death had been instantaneous. His wallet was missing and a ring which he wore on his right hand had been taken. No evidence was found around the grave site itself and whoever dumped him had been fastidious in leaving nothing on the ground. The only possible leads came from the crude body bag stitched from a builder's tarpaulin. Outside the perimeter wall, tyre marks had been found in soft grass 30 yards from the point where the body would have been pitched over the wall. By the treads it was determined they could have been made by a Toyota Land Cruiser and CCTV footage at a nearby junction leading to the M4 was being examined.

Thames Valley police started cross referencing using Toyota Land Cruisers as a base and they got over four hundred hits. One of them was the fatal road rage shooting of a young man just off the M4 at Junction 5 four weeks previously. No one had yet been charged with that killing but the two crime scenes were less than ten miles apart. Word was put out and Thames Valley Police waited for the snitches to get in touch with their contacts.

When Jack heard how John Vanner had been killed, he began to think of Tom Stanton in a different light. From what he had learned about him, he didn't seem the type to possess such callousness. Could Jill really have been attracted to someone capable of such an act?

***

'God, this changes everything.' Jack had bought the morning newspaper and Patrick Flynn's murder was front page.

'PLUMBER SLAUGHTERED ON DRIVEWAY IN ROYAL BERKSHIRE' He felt a chill as he recognized the descriptions of the two men. Surely it was only a matter of time before they were picked up. Tom Stanton really had brought the wrath of hell down on his family.

Jack, with his scant knowledge of the financial world, wondered how long it would be before the media publicity accelerated the withdrawal of client funds from SMG. The chain of events which was about to unfold seemed unstoppable.

Sitting in his living room with a coffee, he suddenly felt quite alone. He was in a city surrounded by millions of other people and since his divorce he realised his work had become his life. His only motivation in getting up in the morning. Everyone he dealt with had a problem for him to solve. He had no balance in his life anymore.

He still loved Kate. Probably always would. In the beginning it had been exciting for her to be married to a private investigator but in reality there was no glamour. Long hours led to cancelled restaurant reservations and missed birthday treats. Often those long hours would be spent sitting in the back seat of his car till the early hours waiting to photograph someone emerging from the wrong place at the wrong time.

When he was reporting back to a disbelieving client saying 'he had reason to believe' he really meant that he'd spent hours waiting for nightfall and the opportunity to rummage through black rubbish bags filled with all sorts of incriminating documents and receipts. Holidays were few and far between and even when they did get away, the mobile phone constantly intruded. One time when they drove to the Cotswolds for a romantic weekend, some crazy guy rang at midnight asking him if he knew why his wife would suddenly be buying more expensive lingerie.

'Maybe she's trying to get some action out of you,' he replied and threw the mobile across the room against the wall. The intrusion was too great and Kate turned her back and feigned sleep. In the morning they had breakfast over a stony silence, checked out, and went home.

As their marriage went into the third year maybe, just maybe, a baby would have helped ease the loneliness she felt when he was working the hours. But it never happened and the rows began. He'd analysed their failed marriage almost to exhaustion and he had concluded the only way for redemption would have been to take a safe job with regular hours and every weekend off. Even then, who knows?

He still missed her. They'd had great times together.

As far as he knew Kate had thrown herself into her job as an account director in a large marketing company up in the West End, working long hours. He often thought of the irony. The break up when it came had been unusually amicable. Without children it all came down to a split of their assets but the sadness had been almost unbearable and both parties wanted to ensure as much dignity as possible. Jack often thought about lifting the phone and ringing her. She lived in a one bedroom apartment only a few miles away in Camden. Some evenings he thought of her there, maybe with a new guy. Just chilling and enjoying each other's company. How could it have come to this?

He was pulled out of his melancholy when his mobile rang.

'It's Mike.'

'How are you buddy?'

'Good, and you?'

'Been better, but you know…'

'That name you gave me, John Vanner, there was quite a change in the pattern of use about a month ago. Could he have lost it or lent it to someone?'

'He was murdered.'

There was a pause as Mike took this in. 'That would explain it then.'

'Explain what?'

'Up until then his phone had been used perhaps five or six times a day. Below average use, mainly to landline numbers. Then suddenly it was being used dozens of times, day and night. It wasn't just the frequency, it was the nature of the calls being made. Lots of premium numbers in the evenings and five or six a day to a betting shop in East London. A huge number of calls to other mobile numbers. Very few landline calls. Everything stopped two weeks ago. Never been used since.'

Jack knew the user was probably the killer and that the listed calls were gold dust.

'Mike, just hang on to all this for me. I need to make a few calls myself. And thanks. You're the best.'

'No problem. Speak later.'

He was about to call Mrs Vanner to ask if she knew which prisons John was involved with when his phone rang. It was Mrs Vanner. 'I was just about to call you. How are you?'

'I'm alright I think. I'm not sure if I should be talking about this but I've just had a call from one of the banks John had an account with. Something strange has happened. One of his credit cards has been used.'

Jack quickly pulled a crumpled notepad from his pocket and searched for his pen. 'Go on Mrs Vanner. It's important.'

'They had asked to speak with him. It upset me that the person didn't know.'

'I'm sorry, I can imagine.'

'Before I could tell him, he asked if I knew if John was in Mexico on business.'

Jack tensed up. 'What did you say?'

'I said no, he's dead, then I burst into tears.'

Helen Vanner stopped talking and Jack heard her blow her nose.

'That is terrible and so insensitive. I'm so sorry Mrs. Vanner.'

'Thank you, but then the bank called me back and said they were terribly sorry, but their records said they'd never been told of his death.'

Alarm bells started to ring in Jack's head. If all his cards had been stopped by the banks after the funds had been exhausted at the ATM's, how come this card was still active? And who was using it?

'Mrs Vanner, if any more credit card statements come in for John in the next few days, would you please give me a call?'

'Of course. Do you think that John could still be alive?' Helen Vanner's voice trembled as she said, 'Could he be in Mexico?'

He knew his next few words had to be chosen with the utmost care. 'Well, I think there has been a mistake somewhere with the card. Some confusion over names maybe. I'm so sorry. Please don't get your hopes up.'

He heard her sob quietly.

'I know. I'm being foolish.'

'No you're not Mrs Vanner. You're his mother.'

***

When he had said goodbye to Helen Vanner, Jack dialled an old school friend. 'Simon. Hi it's Jack Barclay. Long time.'

'Sure is. How's things? I was sorry to hear you and Kate had split.'

'Yeah, 'fraid so. It happens, but it was grim. Trying to move on as they say. How about you?

'Ah, same old. Still looking, but having fun.'

'Simon, this is cheeky and you can tell me to piss off. I wouldn't be offended.'

'Go on.'

'Are you still involved with the GDS airline booking systems?'

'Yes, but not as closely as I was.'

'I need a lead on a person who recently flew to Mexico probably from Paris. Don't know the date; don't know the airline although it may have been Air France. I'm afraid I've only got the name.'

'Name the name.'

'It's Vanner. John Vanner.'

'OK. Going to take a bit of time but for you...'

'Thanks Simon. I owe you.'

'I'll get back to you.'

'I really appreciate this.'

'Speak to you soon.'

Jack sat down. He was puzzled but at the same time knew that he was making some progress at last.

John Vanner could have had a card that wasn't with him on the night he was abducted. It may never have had a stop put on it. In that case, who knew he had another card? One that was still valid. He looked down at his notes and leafed through them. It was on the second reading that he saw it. The bank had asked if he was in Mexico on business. It wasn't a personal credit card but one probably used for business to keep things separate. He picked out the number for SMG and asked for Charles. When he came on the line he sounded brusque.

'How can I help you Jack?'

Jack decided to skip the pleasantries too. 'I need to know something which you may get from Tom Stanton's files.'

Charles sounded weary. 'Go on.'

'I need to know if there is a record of a credit card in the name of John Vanner which was used in his business dealings with Tom.'

'How soon? Things are falling apart here.'

'I really need it as soon as you can get it Charles.'

'I'll get back to you when I know.'

'Thanks. It's important.'

Chapter 39

The customs teams at the Dover Port Authority had daily meetings to keep everyone aware of the complex surveillance operations which were constantly being mounted. Over one million passengers came through the customs halls every month. For the most part officers knew who they were looking for. Knew who to isolate for special attention. As they went through the previous day's reports they eventually came to one flagging up a party of young French students all of whom were wearing flip flops as they passed through. There was a chorus of laughter round the large table as it was read out.

'Mind you', said Fred, an officer with over thirty years service and a waistline which stretched his waistband to magical lengths, 'It was a bloody awful day. Why would a whole group decide to do that? I mean I wouldn't have worn flip flops in that weather.' This got them all laughing again. The team leader said, 'Let's check it out anyway,' and turned round to a small Formica topped table covered in used Styrofoam cups. He refreshed up his computer and went to passport frequencies. The supervisor entered the ferry code the students arrived on and scrolled to 'passports entry.'

It took a couple of minutes to make comparison checks and just as the group were losing all interest he shouted 'Whoa' and hit the print button.

It was enough to bring the meeting to order and as he turned back to face them he looked as if he had a winning lotto ticket in his hand. He studied the print out for a minute and said, 'We have something here. There were eighteen in the group and sixteen of them have come through every second week for the last three months. They are all from the Paris area and in random questioning, they were always headed for London. It seems to be on a Tuesday each time so we have some time to prepare for the next time they arrive. I'll have more for you at tomorrow's meeting. I'll put things in place just in case they arrive on an earlier date.'

They moved on to any other business and broke up at nine thirty. After they'd gone, Rob Terry, the supervisor, made a note to put in a commendation for Frank Stevens. Not bad work for a rookie. Then he set to work on his computer and studied the movements of eighteen French students who seemed to have an insatiable appetite for visiting the sights of London.

Chapter 40

Tom felt the thrill of excitement. All he could think about was Danni and the evening ahead. He dozed in the taxi on the way to Le Petit Maison. Even short haul travel was getting tiring. The hotel was deserted when he arrived and he rang the old fashioned brass bell on reception. Monique came out from the office and smiled when she saw him.

'Monsieur Stanton, how are you? You have your usual room.'

She turned to the wooden board behind her and pulled key number fifteen from the hook. 'Is there anything I can get you?'

'No thanks. I'll just do some work in my room. Danielle should be here in a couple of hours.'

'D'accord.'

'See you later.'

Tom climbed to the first floor and turned right. The corridor was tastefully decorated in pastel shades and his walk was punctuated by small pieces of furniture collected by Monique and her husband during their travels round the world. He loved it here. He always felt at peace and away from the realities of life. He put his key in the lock and went in to his room. It was exactly as he knew it would be. The large double bed was beautifully covered in a white satin bedspread with four white pillows. The walls were hand painted in the colour of sand and gave a hint of North Africa. The whole effect always filled him with joy. As he lay on the bed his thoughts drifted to the evening ahead. Danni would arrive and knock gently on the door. They would kiss deeply and she would immediately undress and take a shower. She would towel herself dry and with her long hair still wet, come to bed and they would lose themselves in each other and forget time. Tom smiled at the thought.

***

Four miles away in St Germain, Danielle was taking her shower. Sergei had been more demanding than ever she could remember and she had to lean against the shower wall for support. After they had made love for a second time and she was resting her head on a double pillow, she had asked him what to do about Tom's request for a bigger share.

'Tell him our overheads have gone up. Tell him we have payments to make other than his. Say we will look at it next month after we have assessed our position.'

'He will ask for a contact further up than me.'

'Just tell him you don't know. You only know the one above you. That's how it works.'

'I'll try Sergei, but he was serious about this and he'll be pissed off.'

'Let him. If he wants to take on the big boys, just point out that he could get hurt.'

Sergei was lying next to her and was smoking a large cigar. Danni lit a cigarette. As the room filled with smoke she got up from the bed and crossed to open a window. Sergei's apartment was on the sixth floor and the noise of early evening traffic filtered up to the room. As she leant over to pick up her cigarette from the ashtray at the bedside, he stretched his hand out and started to move it up her thigh.

'No Sergei, I have to go.'

'Once more.'

'No.'

She moved away from him and pulled on her jeans, then slipped on her T Shirt, tugging it down to her waist. He watched her do it and became aroused. She blew him a kiss from the middle of the room and smiled. 'I'll call you.'

'Damn right you will.'

She found a taxi and said, 'Hotel Petit Maison.' The taxi driver knew it and as he moved off she took out her mobile and scrolled down to her friend Sophie. She answered on the second ring and Danielle said, 'Please just listen. I will text you in about thirty minutes. When you receive it, ring me on this number. Talk about anything, it doesn't matter. I will listen to you, say nothing and thank you for the call, then you hang up.'

'OK, I will.'

She arrived at Petit Maison, walked in and smiled at Monique. She looked radiant and elegant as usual. She gave a large smile back.

'Monsieur Stanton is in room 15 Madame.'

'Thank you Monique. Ca va?'

'Ca va, bien.'

Danielle climbed up the stairs and knocked quietly on the door. Tom grinned liked a small boy when he saw her. She smiled back and Tom put his arms around her as she came in. He kicked the door shut and kissed her hungrily. Danielle responded as best she could but broke away and walked over to the small easy chair by the window and rummaged in her shoulder bag for her Camels. She fired a cigarette up and after exhaling looked across at Tom who was sitting on the bed.

She crossed her legs and leant back in the chair. 'How are you mon cherie? I've missed you.'

'I've missed you too darling. How's your day been?'

'OK, but boring. I took a long lunch with a couple of friends and went to one class this afternoon.'

'You look tired. Come to bed and we can rest.'

'Just give me a few minutes to freshen up.' She eased herself up, smiled and went to the bathroom. Inside she ran the shower, wriggling out of her jeans as she did so.

In the bedroom Tom lay back on the top cover and thought about what was to come. As Danni emerged naked and rubbing her hair with the towel, her mobile rang. Taking the call she listened and said, 'What now'? She looked round at Tom, rolling her eyes heavenwards.

She stayed on the line for a few seconds more and hit the stop button. 'I have to go. It's about the next shipment. It's the biggest yet and there are a few problems. I need to find a few extra students for the ferry run.'

Tom rose up on one elbow and said, 'But what about me?'

'I'll try to get back later darling.'

She went to the bathroom to get her clothes and Tom grimaced as she began to dress.

'I'll make it up to you darling, I promise. She came over to him and bending over the bed, caressed him through his trousers and kissed him slowly on the mouth. He responded and she straightened up, picking up her shoulder bag from the floor and turned for the door.

***

'Shit.' Tom looked at the closed door after she'd gone and lay back deflated on the bed. His mood changed as he lay there on his own. If they were upping the shipments and looking for more students to carry the drugs, there was more money coming in and more for him to bring back. He lay back on the bed, closed his eyes and started to plan his move.

Chapter 41

At Dover Docks the trap was set and there were over thirty officers involved in 'operation flip flop'.

As the 'Pride of Calais' approached Dover every custom officer was in place but passengers standing on the windswept upper deck would never have known it. Frank Stevens had been picked to be with the lead team and although he was nervous, he was excited. With the possibility of a haul of class 'A' drugs coming in, a whole dragnet of armed police had been deployed around Dover. The motorway slip roads were covered by a helicopter which hovered overhead. Frank shuddered as he thought how he had started this. It was probably the best day of his life.

The ferry docked on time and foot passengers began to disembark. After a few minutes the French students appeared. Had they known how many covert cameras were trained on them they might have laughed less as they made their way towards immigration. They were all wearing flip flops and they were all bunched together, still giggling nervously. As they came into the customs hall a young man in uniform called Frank stepped out in front of them. He held up a hand and asked them to move to the side. Suddenly the gaiety stopped and the students became silent. He motioned them over to desks at the side of the hall with their small rolling cases and they all obeyed his command. It was when older and more senior looking officers appeared from behind screens that panic set in. One girl started to scream and in seconds it was chaos. From an older girl the shout came up 'kick them off' and flip flops started sliding across the floor. Within seconds they were all barefoot.

The senior officer said, 'Won't change a thing. Let's get to work.'

Danielle had, as usual, hung back behind the students and in the general melee, casually strolled through and into arrivals. Picking up her pace, she made her way out of the building and once outside, stopped to rummage for cigarettes in her bag. She lit up and inhaled as if it was her last breath on earth. Desperately searching for her mobile, she found it and called Sergei. It went into message. 'The students have been busted at Dover. I've managed to get through and am outside arrivals. 'A police siren signalled it's approach and Danielle shouted, 'I'll call later.'

She walked away from the main entrance and keeping her phone in her hand, knew she had to try and warn Andrei who was waiting for the students at Victoria Coach Station. She sought cover behind an articulated lorry parked up on a slip road and phoned his number.

***

Andrei always made a point of arriving early at Victoria to make sure of being in position in the cafeteria for the students when they arrived. It was 1.30 pm and they were due in an hour. He was dressed in faded black jeans and a scruffy brown leather bomber jacket and carried a battered blue canvas bag over his right shoulder. A grey baseball cap completed the typical dress of a passenger waiting at the coach terminal.

'Shit.' He spotted the silver BMW 3 Series parked illegally on the yellow lines as he neared the entrance. Not unusual in itself but he saw how the parking attendant walked by without taking any action. Andrei stopped before crossing and looked down the road as a Transit van pulled up behind the BMW. He wheeled round and made his way up the pavement till he came to an empty shop doorway. He sat down and placed the holdall at his side, pulling the baseball cap down to cover the top part of his face. From his vantage point, he saw the BMW's rear passenger doors open and two men walking towards the coach station. As they did so, a dark blue Ford Focus approached slowly and parked a few yards behind the transit van. *The cavalry have arrived.*

As he slid further down into his doorway and peered from under his cap, his mobile rang. 'Danni, what's happening?

The police are all over the place. I saw them arriving in unmarked vehicles a few minutes ago.'

'Are you in the coach station?'

'I'm sitting in a doorway across the road. No one's giving a shit about me.'

'I do, honey. You've got to get out. The students have been busted at Dover. I managed to get away. Call me when you can.'

He levered himself up from the step and carrying his empty bag, turned left and walked slowly in the opposite direction.

Chapter 42

Jack received the call from Simon two days after he first called him about John Vanner.

'Jack, how's things?'

'Good, Simon. I appreciate you getting back to me so quickly.'

'No worries. Right, your man is in Mexico with his wife.' Jack let him go on.

'John Vanner and his wife Danielle flew to Cancun by Air France from Charles de Gaulle ten days ago and travelled first class. Used a credit card. All clean and above board according to the records. He bought a package for a hotel near Cancun airport and a rental through Hertz. Had it delivered to the hotel next day.'

'Do you know the hotel?'

'Yeah, it was the Mexicana. No expense spared'

'Simon, you've done me a big favour. Just tell me what you need.'

'Forget it buddy. You don't do it often. I might need you sometime so let's just say I'm in credit.'

'You're the best. Thank you Simon.'

When he finished the call, he knew what was going on. More or less. False passports didn't come cheap, especially those that passed all immigration checks. He walked across to his small drinks cabinet and found his bottle of Balvenie. He half filled a small tumbler, added some water and sat on the sofa propping his legs up on the coffee table. What he now knew was dynamite to SMG and crushing news for Jill. He sipped the whisky and thought through how he should handle the development. There was little point in suppressing it. Both parties would eventually find out and he should be the one to tell them. He thought of Helen Vanner. A lovely dignified lady who had lost her beloved son in a terrible way.

No mother should have to go through that. Now she was going to have to be told that her son's identity had been stolen and the thief was in Mexico. To add insult to her grief she knew the person who had assumed her son's identity and had received him on her doorstep. He drained his Scotch, stood up and re-filled the tumbler.. As the whisky caught hold he felt anger at Tom Stanton. How could he leave such a trail of misery for so many? What kind of guy was he?

Jack sat nursing his second drink and decided he would confirm with Jill that he should go to Mexico and find him. And Danielle, whoever she was.

Chapter 43

At lunchtime, Sergei arrived at Du Palais-Royal and was escorted to the best table on the summer terrace. It was his favourite time for eating since getting used to the Parisian way of life. He had been to the gym and had completed his full two hour workout on the treadmill and rowing machine, finishing with a punishing session on the weights. Francoise, his dining companion had turned the heads of diners in the restaurant as they arrived. The maitre'd led them to the best table.

'You always make me feel so special Sergei.'

'You are. You are so beautiful. I'm a lucky man.' It was after they had drunk their first glass of Bollinger and begun their grilled langoustine hors d'oeuvre that Sergei's mobile rang. He let it go into message. *Fuck it.* He looked across at Francoise and reached for her hand.

Just across the English Channel, his drug empire had begun to fall apart with a party of terrified young French students desperate to tell the UK Border Agency everything they knew. In Paris, top lawyers were being urgently called out of meetings by the apoplectic parents of a group of Sorbonne students arrested in Dover, England.

***

Jack wanted to tell Jill face to face about Tom but decided to break the news as soon as possible.

He awoke at seven o'clock, eased himself out of bed and stumbled through to the kitchen and made coffee. A shower helped his aches and pains. He shaved and had another mug of coffee before ringing Jill's mobile number.

'I have news for you and I'm sorry to use the phone but thought it best to let you know quickly. I think Tom is alive.' There was no sound.

'Are you still there?'

'Tell me.'

'I believe he is in Mexico.'

'Oh my God.'

She was becoming short of breath. 'Why?'

'I think he's gone on the run. He's taken a lot of money from the company. It's possible he has a woman with him.'

He waited and then heard the anger in her voice. 'Get him back here Jack.'

***

Tom figured he had another two weeks before his thefts at SMG came to light. He had ramped up the money he was siphoning off and the risks were escalating. He had stolen everything from one of his oldest clients who had recently died and he had been putting off meeting with the family's solicitor who needed a financial update to help wind up the estate.

Later on the evening after Danielle left Tom suddenly at Le Petit Maison, Tom walked to a local brasserie, 'Le Nocturne', ten minutes from the hotel.

He pushed open the door and picked a table near the window. It was a quiet night for customers. With only four tables taken the waiter was quick to bring him the menu. Tom didn't look at it but ordered moules mariniere with frites and a bottle of Sancerre. As he waited, he began to formulate his plan. He could feel the elation as he began drafting things in his head. The excitement of what was about to happen was overshadowing the sorrow his actions were going to bring to those around him. He assuaged his guilt with the knowledge that given his deceit at both SMG and towards Jill and the children, it would be better if he vanished. When they all realised the level of treachery, they would be devastated. It would be best if he wasn't there. Best all round and certainly best for him. He took a small notepad and pen from his breast pocket as the waiter returned with the wine. Tom watched as he expertly withdrew the cork - they always made it look so easy. He indicated with a hand gesture to pour without him tasting and with a slight grimace, the young waiter half filled his glass and moved to another table.

He sipped his wine and opened his napkin and doodled -
DISAPPEAR - CANCUN - SUN - LOVE. His mussels
arrived and when the waiter left he filled his glass to the top.
Looking at his notes, he realised they encapsulated the rest of
his life. The monumental change he had engineered for
himself. As he began eating and placing empty mussel shells
into the dish beside his bowl, he tried to understand the
reason for it all. For a moment he swept Jill and the kids from
his mind and blocked out the trust he had built up with his
partners and clients at SMG. He knew it was Danielle. She
was consuming his thoughts and he was besotted with her.

But there was something else happening between them and
he felt excited just thinking of her. If his plan was to work,
there were essentials to be arranged. New name, new
passports, new credit cards, new driving licences and
untraceable access to cash. He could arrange most of it but he
needed Danni's help with passports and driving licences. She
must have contacts who could supply the necessary
documents. He wanted the best.

He continued his checklist as he finished his meal by
dipping his bread into the remains of the white wine sauce.
He leant back and looked around the emptying room. Two
tables away he saw a copy of the London Times and stood up
to retrieve it before it was swept away by the waiter. He
glanced at the headlines and turned to the inside pages. He
felt his pulse race as he read of the discovery of John
Vanner's body in a London cemetery. Shock registered with
him and he put down his glass to read the story and read it
again just to make sure. He knew John had gone missing but
he never thought for a moment he was dead. The waiter
approached for a dessert order and Tom waved him away. He
felt a sense of loss although he probably had little entitlement
to it. For once, he could relate to a dramatic and tragic story
in a national newspaper. He knew the person involved. He
had gone drinking with him, had eaten with him and had
laughed with him. Although not close friends, they had met
often when discussing investment possibilities. He sat and
stared at the page. It was at that moment it came to him. He
would be John Vanner and he would go to Mexico. He asked
for a coffee and a brandy and sank into thought. John Vanner

even had similarities to him. Same age, same height and similar looks. He tore the page from the paper and stuffed it into his jacket pocket. As he indicated for the bill, he thought of calling Danni and then looked at the empty wine bottle. Get some fresh air and wait for her to call him later.

He made his way back to the hotel and felt good. He had a real plan. Now to share it with Danni. His immaculate love. He left his mobile by the bed and climbed under the duvet. She didn't ring and he fell into a deep sleep. His dreams were of Danni and Mexico.

Chapter 44

Jack flew Air France to Cancun from Paris. That was the chosen route taken by Tom and who knows, it could turn up something. At Jill's insistence he flew business class. The bruising on his face had all but gone and he settled in for the long flight. He was noticed by one female flight attendant and asked if he had everything he wanted.

'I'm fine thank you,' he replied.

Cancun was hot and humid when they exited into the terminal building. Jack collected his hold luggage and passed through customs and selected the car rental desk without a queue. The girl at the desk had a sweet smile and she swept her dark hair over her right ear as he approached.

'I'd like to hire a car for a few days.' He gave her his best smile too.

'We've had a bit of a rush and we only have a few smaller cars left. Maybe you wanted something a little bigger?'

'What would you suggest?'

'Let me see what I can do.' She peered into her computer screen.

'All I have is an Escalade available this moment but I can do it as an upgrade for you. Same price as a larger sedan.' When she looked up, he noticed her large brown eyes and he stared at her. Sounds good. Shall we just do that?'

'Sure, I'll fix everything for you Mr...'

'Jack Barclay.'

'OK, Mr Barclay, just give me a minute to load the details.'

Jack had no idea what an Escalade was, but looking at the illustrated list of rentals propped up on the desk, it was big, chunky and near the top of the price range. High-end stuff. She processed the documents and turning round to a key rack on the wall, selected a large keyless remote.

'Here we are Mr Barclay. I hope you will enjoy driving it. It's the black one on row eight. You can't miss it. It's got a full tank and to save time when you return it, just fill it up for us.'

'I certainly will. Would you have a map?'

'Of course.' She placed a folded map on the desk top and said, 'With my compliments Mr Barclay.' She looked at him and smiled. 'Would you return the keys to me, here please?'

'Nowhere else.'

When he reached row four, he spotted his rental further back. It looked positively presidential with the black paint and dark tinted windows. He noticed the badge on the tailgate and saw *Escalade*. Some upgrade. He placed his case in the back and climbed in behind the wheel. Studying the map, he jotted down the route to the Mexicana and moved off slowly trying to get a feel for the vehicle.

When he arrived it was late afternoon but the baking sun was still high. He was directed to a space near the front of the large car park close to the imposing entrance.

He walked straight up to reception and asked for a sea view suite.

'I am very sorry Sir, we have no suites available for tonight.'

'But I have to be here to meet with my good friend John Vanner. It is a very important business meeting. He is staying with you. Could you give me his room number so I can call him?'

'One minute please.' She bent down and tapped into her screen. 'I am sorry Sir, but we don't have a John Vanner staying with us.'

'There must be a mistake. He e-mailed me to say he would be here.'

'I'm sorry Sir. He and his wife were here but have left.'

Jack thanked her and moved out of her vision and out of the queue which had formed behind him. He walked across to the concierge desk where a kindly looking, portly man was dressed in a black uniform. Jack palmed him a ten dollar note. The man had slicked back silver hair and looked ready for retirement. He glanced quickly at the note and smiled. 'Yes Sir?'

'You may have looked after a guest called John Vanner. I'm a good friend of his and he asked me to meet up with him.

'Left this morning, Sir.'

'I can't seem to get a signal on his cell phone. He said he and his wife may move on and I wondered if you could just point me in the right direction.'

'I remember him. Good man. Looked after us well. I think he may have gone to stay by the sea at our sister hotel in Ciudad del Carmen. You can't miss him. He is driving a white Mustang convertible and his wife is unforgettable as you probably know.' He winked at Jack and went back to his desk phone which had started ringing.

Jack waved his hand to him in thanks and the concierge nodded as he spoke into the telephone. Jack left the glorious air conditioned lobby and went back out to the searing heat and made for his vehicle. It was only a three hundred yard walk but he could feel the sweat beginning to roll down the back of his collar as he used the remote and climbed in, thankful for the air conditioning. He checked his map again and left the parking area to make his way to Route 180 and the resort of Ciudad del Carmen.

Traffic was light. Maybe it was siesta and after driving for an hour he saw the sweeping azure blue of the Gulf in the distance. Within minutes he was driving across the causeway which connected Carmen Island to the mainland. The sea was a magnificent backdrop and shimmering on the horizon he made out the outline of an oil rig. After months of working in London, Jack gazed at the view which was no doubt taken for granted by the locals.

He began his sweep at the east end of the palm lined promenade and began working his way along the front line hotels until he spotted the Mexicana. It held a commanding position on a small headland overlooking the Gulf of Mexico. Tom Stanton had chosen well especially if he had a suite overlooking the sea. Jack indicated and moved into the left lane in preparation for his turn into the hotel. On the green light he moved slowly, aware of heavy traffic around the intersection. The white Mustang came from behind him with a prolonged blast on the horn. As it careered round the

Escalade into the hotel entrance, Jack saw a girl with dark hair in the passenger seat and the male driver who looked to be laughing as he put the car through its paces.

Jack carried on into the parking area and moved off to the left where it was relatively quiet. He stopped inside a marked bay and looked across towards the hotel. The Mustang had been parked at the main entrance and he saw Tom Stanton for the first time. Then he saw Danielle. As the top began to glide up over the car, they put their arms around each other and the driver lobbed the keys to a young man in black trousers and a cream waistcoat. The car valet hid his deformed right hand at his side as he deftly caught the keys with his left. 'Thanks my friend. Don't park it too far away.' Tom held out a folded note and the valet glanced at it and smiled as he began unloading the cases.

Jack's camera was in its case on the floor behind the driver's seat and he twisted round and brought it over to rest on his knees.

He changed to his telephoto lens and opened his side window to be hit with a blast of scorching air. He squeezed off a shot of the Mustang and checked the result. Replacing the camera in its case he climbed out and walked to the back of his vehicle and opened the door. He rummaged in his soft bag and found his shorts and green baseball cap before getting in behind the wheel again. When he climbed out he looked just like any other tourist and slinging his camera bag over his shoulder, sauntered towards the hotel lobby.

Once inside, he looked up at the giant fountain in the central area of the lobby and the vast array of palms and tropical ferns. Five star without a doubt. There was no sign of Tom and Danielle and as he ambled across the lobby he picked up a couple of free magazines from a narrow wicker table. He saw the sign saying 'pool area' and walked outside into the stinging heat. Although it was after 6 o'clock there were a few people on sun loungers by the pool and a small group were laughing and drinking cocktails at the swim up bar. An elderly lady in a bright yellow one piece was swimming lengths.

He picked a lounger where he could see the door leading from the hotel lobby and lay on it with his camera bag open at his side. Pulling the visor down over his nose and placing a magazine on his chest, he looked like any other resident having a late snooze.

He wanted to see them at close range. The sounds of laughter from the swim up bar increased as the next round of cocktails were served. As one man tried to sip his drink with a snorkel and mask on, Jack caught sight of the lobby door opening from the corner of his eye. Tom and Danielle strolled onto the pool area. Danielle looked up to check the position of the sun and pointed. They moved away from Jack and chose a spot near the shallow end, away from the happy hour guests.

He watched as they draped towels over the loungers and adjusted the backs to the sitting position. After they had given the pool waiter an order they leant towards each other for a lingering kiss before leaning back and closing their eyes.

Jack waited until the waiter had returned with two drinks before easing his camera out of its case and placing it under the magazine. They looked as if they were dozing and, lifting the camera and the magazine in one movement, he squeezed off three close ups of the couple and placed the camera back in its bag. He waited fifteen minutes till they lowered the back rests to turn over and quietly rose and walked slowly back into the lobby. Walking round the hotel's car park he spotted the white Mustang and made a mental note of the registration number and returned to his rental. He jotted the Mustang number down in his notebook and then checked the images on his camera. In one, Tom was looking straight into Danielle's eyes. They could have been honeymooners. In all three, she looked stunning and his thoughts went to Jill back in England, still waiting for news. He gunned the engine and moved off.

The car valet used his good left hand to write down the registration number of Jack's Escalade as it passed by. He tucked it into his cream waistcoat pocket as he walked back to his desk by the hotel entrance.

Jack found a Holiday Inn a block away and checked in to a high floor room overlooking the sea. He sat on the bed and looked again at the images he had captured by the pool. He knew the pain it would cause Jill if she saw these but he couldn't change facts. He picked up his mobile. Jill answered quickly, 'Jack, how are you? Have you found him?'

There was a slight pause and he said, 'Yes, I've seen him. I'm in seaside town called Ciudad del Carmen on the Gulf of Mexico.'

'So he is alive?'

'Yes.'

It was Jack's turn to hear a pause at the other end.

'Does he look happy?'

'He seems to be, but who knows.'

Her voice began to break. 'What do we do now?'

'I'm going to watch him for a day or two although I don't expect he'll to be going anywhere in a hurry. I think you should phone Bob and Charles in confidence and let them know I have found him and he's alive. I need a little more time to dig around. I'll call you again tomorrow.'

Jill's voice was shaky. 'Is he on his own?'

Jack hesitated. 'No, he seems to be with a woman.'

'Pretty?'

'Yes, she would be classed as pretty. I'm sorry to give you this news. I really am.'

'It's alright. I probably knew from the start he wouldn't be alone. I must tell the children their dad is alive though.'

'Put a call through to the police to let them know he is no longer missing. I'll call you tomorrow Jill.'

Jack ended the call and he felt bad for her. But he felt nothing but anger for Tom Stanton.

He stood under the shower and switched it to cold and towelled himself down before stretching out on the bed. It was dark when he woke. 'Damn.' It was ten o'clock and he had slept for nearly three hours. He dressed quickly and going out of the front door, turned right and walked along the promenade towards the Mexicana. The night was hot and the humidity seemed even higher than in the afternoon. Within seconds he could feel the sweat trickling down his back. The almost deafening sounds of the cicadas in the nearby reed grass drowned out the sound of the surf on the other side of the road. He approached the Mexicana and walked by the main entrance looking into the car park. Moving along till he came to where the Mustang had been parked, he saw an empty bay. He cursed himself as he went along and checked the rows in case it had parked elsewhere. It had gone.

'OK, they've gone out for the evening. Big deal.'

As he turned to retrace his steps, he saw the car valet look across in his direction with a smirk on his face.

Jack woke early next morning and walked by the shore to the Mexicana. He checked the parking bays to find there was no sign of Tom Stanton's rental.

A new valet was attending to a family checking out from the hotel and Jack waited till he was free. He was fresh faced and looked straight from school. He smiled broadly as Jack sauntered up to him and shook his hand, palming him a fifty peso note.

'How can I help you Sir?'

'My cell phone has died on me and I've missed my pal John and his wife. I was supposed to hook up with him here. He would have been in his white Mustang rental. Loves that car more than his wife, but don't tell her eh.'

They both laughed. The young man looked conspiratorially at Jack. 'His wife didn't look too happy. I had some trouble getting their cases into the trunk. Went about an hour ago.'

Jack smiled, patted him lightly on the shoulder and thanked him. He went through the automatic revolving door into the lobby and circled round. Looking through the large plate glass window he waited till the valet had gone to collect another vehicle and headed outside towards the exit. He returned to his hotel, packed his case and checked out. He turned right and drove towards Route 180 and Cancun. He was cursing his stupidity.

He checked each gas station as he headed out but saw no sign of the white convertible. By the time he made it on to the causeway he knew he had lost them. He drove at the speed limit towards Cancun and pulled in at Carmelo's truck stop near the city boundary. He hadn't eaten properly since the day before and hunger had hit him.

Jack had ordered sausage, ham with scrambled eggs and coffee from a cheerful waitress with long frizzy blonde hair tied back with a red ribbon. Around him, weary truckers were telling driving tales as they enjoyed their time away from the wheel. He put copious amounts of ketchup on his meal and finished in record time. The waitress offered him another coffee but he declined and stood up to head for the bathrooms. He pushed the door open and walked across to the urinal aware the door had opened behind him. The blow when it came was hard and straight to the side of his head. He felt himself falling and then a vicious pain as he was kicked in his right side. He reached out for support and the last thing he remembered before the darkness was the glimpse of small wooden truncheon being held awkwardly in a deformed hand. When he came round, he was lying along the seat in a booth near the back of the diner. He was vaguely aware of people hovering over him and as his eyes came back into focus, he recognised his waitress who was now holding a blood soaked towel to his head.

As he opened his eyes, she adjusted the cushion placed behind his head, 'You're going to need a couple of stitches in that honey.'

His mind began to re-engage and he remembered he had stopped for breakfast. He recalled going to the washroom but nothing else.

'It looks like you got yourself mugged,' she said. You should check your wallet and stuff. How are you feeling?'

Jack looked up at her, 'Like I need to go to the bathroom,' and managed a weak smile. He managed to gingerly feel his pockets and realized he still had his wallet and keys.

'Hang on a bit longer, we need to get you to the hospital. It's not far.'

No one had noticed the young man, trying to hide his cruelly deformed right hand, leave the diner and walk away, nodding to the driver of the Mustang parked in the far corner of the parking lot.

Jack heard the approaching two tone siren and closed his eyes as he began to feel the shooting pain behind his eyes.

The journey in the ambulance was a blur and he woke up in a hospital ward. As he tried to prop himself up on one elbow he felt a stabbing pain in his side. He fell back on the bed and slowly raised his arm to feel the turban like bandage around his head. He guessed he had been given painkillers and he lay there waiting for someone, anyone, to come to his bedside and let him know when he could leave.

The doctor's lapel badge said 'Dr P Hernandez' and he was adamant. 'You will be staying overnight for observation. You have received a severe blow to your head Mr. Barclay and have concussion. You are very fortunate there is no fracture to your skull. We must wait a little time to make sure there is no deep damage. You also have bruising to your ribs.'

As he lay there, he couldn't believe how he could have been so unaware. Jesus, he was supposed to be a private detective. He had to get released from the hospital. As of now, his trip to Mexico had gained him nothing apart from the knowledge that Tom was here with Danielle. And a very sore head.

Next morning he saw the doctor and asked to be allowed to leave.

'I can't stop you leaving, but if you insist, I will ask for the administrator to visit you and arrange things.'

'Thank you doctor.'

An hour later a serious looking young man dressed in an open necked white shirt and dark trousers arrived at his bedside and asked him to confirm he wished to be discharged. 'Yes, I do' said Jack.

'We will ask you to sign papers to say that you are leaving of your own accord and absolve the hospital of any liability in the future. The nurse will help you get ready Mr. Barclay and I'll meet you at main reception a little later.' His face broke into a warm smile. 'Would you like me to arrange a taxi for you?'

'Yes please, that would be most helpful.'

He nodded to the nurse and moved down the hospital ward.

He hadn't seen her before and she helped him get dressed. She looked to be in her forties and as she put his arm into his shirt, he winced as the movement stretched his rib cage.

Her badge said she was Maria Martinez. 'You really will have to take things easy for a few days. We'll give you some painkillers.' Jack grimaced as he manoeuvred his other arm into his shirt sleeve and said, 'Thank you, I will.'

When she had finished helping him to dress she scanned the bedside to make sure he had taken all his possessions.

She walked him to the front entrance and the young administrator he had seen on the ward was waiting at main reception.

'Here are the papers to sign, Mr. Barclay and an invoice for your treatment.' The amount was less than the cost of a return flight from London to Paris. Jack pulled out his wallet and gave him his VISA card. He briefly looked at the discharge papers and signed them. His Mexican wasn't too good but he knew from the treatment he had received and the kindness of everyone at the hospital, it was safe to sign.

Jack saw a taxi pull up outside as he signed the credit card slip. The young man and the nurse were standing at his side and he turned to them and smiled. 'Thank you. I am very grateful.' As he shook their hands they smiled back and said almost as one, 'Look after yourself Mr. Barclay.' He picked up his wallet from the desk and headed outside and the furnace like heat hit him full in the face. He climbed into the taxi and waved weakly in the general direction of the hospital entrance.

'Where to Sir?'

'Carmelo's diner on the 180.'

The Escalade was where he had parked it and he opened the rear door of his rental. The bag was lying there with his passport and mobile phone. He glanced over to the diner entrance and cast his eyes around the parking lot but saw nothing. No white Mustangs. He climbed into the stifling vehicle, started the engine and after waiting a minute, switched the air conditioning to full. As he drove off and turned left into the main road, he kept checking his rear view mirror. Spotting a small strip mall ahead, he pulled in and spotted a BANAMEX cash machine next to a run down grocery store. He eased himself out of the Escalade and felt the pain coursing through his body as he shuffled over to the ATM. He withdrew 3,000 pesos and retreated to the comfort of his vehicle before driving back onto the main road to pick up signs for the airport.

Traffic was heavy and it took him fifty minutes to make the journey.

He had no idea when the next flight to London was but he headed into the rental returns and parked up near the exit. He checked the interior and collected his bag before heading for the coolness of the airport building.

When he got to the rental desk, he was greeted by a young man.

'Hello, Sir.'

'I'm returning my vehicle as I received it. No problems, except the tank is empty. I've had some problems and couldn't fill up. I'll pay cash.'

The young man looked at Jack and saw the heavy bandaging on his head. 'I'm sorry to hear of that Sir.'

'It was my own fault.'

He signed off the rental and left the bemused young man watching him as he walked away. The first flight to London Heathrow was in five hours and he booked with British Airways.

After passing through security he bought a novel featuring a hotshot private investigator, sat down in a far corner of the lounge and tried to become anonymous.

***

When the valet had come out of Carmelo's, he walked across to the Mustang and took the envelope that was offered from the driver's window and without a word, turned and headed quickly for the exit.

Danielle turned to Tom and said 'Would you mind telling me what's going on?'

'We need to go.' He gunned the engine and slammed it into first. Trying to dodge the biggest potholes he almost hit a truck as he barrelled over the cinder track before reaching the exit. He fishtailed onto the main road and accelerated hard towards Cancun.

'Why the hurry?'

'We've got problems.'

'What sort of problems?'

'We need to get out of Mexico.'

Danielle looked sharply at Tom as he drove over the speed limit towards the City. 'But I haven't been to Cancun yet.'

'Our cover has been blown. Don't ask me how, but people know we are here. I need to think about what we should do.'

As he approached the outskirts of the City, he pulled into the car park of a shabby looking building with a faded pink cinder block frontage. The flickering neon sign said, 'Welcome to Ocean View Motel'. Danielle pulled a face. 'I'm not staying in this shit hole.'

Tom nosed the car towards the far side of the car park and chose a bay hidden from the road.

'We have to lay low tonight. A man has been following us and I had him stopped back at the diner.'

Danielle stared at him but said nothing. Tom went in and waited by the reception desk. A young acne faced man with black greasy hair clutching a comic appeared from behind a door and looked sullenly at him.

'I need a room for tonight.'

'It's 800 pesos in advance.' Tom produced his wallet, counted out the notes and put them on the counter. The boy took the money, turned to a cupboard behind him and lifted a key from one of the hooks. 'Room 22. You need to be out by noon.'

Tom looked hard at him. 'You think I want to stay that long?' The man shrugged and turned away as they began wheeling their cases towards their room. Danielle hung back. Tom grunted, 'Come on, it's only for tonight.'

The door would only open half way and they wrestled their cases into a dark green room which smelt of stale tobacco and sweat. Danielle grimaced as she threw her handbag onto the stained blue bedspread and walked over to the window. The neon welcome sign was still promising an ocean view.

'I don't see any water.'

'Take a shower'

She pushed past him and into the bathroom, slamming the door behind her.

Chapter 45

Jack's flight touched down on schedule at Heathrow at six am. Although he'd slept for most of the flight, he felt weary and his bandaged head made him self-conscious. After collecting his case, he went through immigration and exited from Terminal 5 joining the short queue for a taxi. The cabbie was friendly and wanted to start talking about Mexico but Jack said he hadn't slept for three days and the driver shut up. Traffic was light and he pulled up in Maida Vale in 40 minutes.

He met the usual avalanche of 'pizza' mail behind his door and ignored it all. He switched on the heating and took a shower to get rid of the odour of the long haul. His head was hurting and he swallowed two of his Mexican painkillers with water and fell exhaustedly into a cool bed. He woke to the sound of his phone, not knowing the time of day or even the day.

'Jack, it's Simon.'

He collected his thoughts, 'Simon, how goes it?'

'Good, thank you. I thought you might be interested in a little piece of information. I left a tag on your Mexican man. He and his wife have just boarded a flight from Cancun to Paris. Business and economy were full so he paid for First. I thought it might save you a wasted trip out there.'

Little did he know. Jack smiled. 'Thanks Simon. I really do owe you.'

'No problem buddy. Keep in touch.'

'I will, I promise.'

Jack put the phone down and lay back on the pillow. Maybe his trip hadn't been in vain after all. Whoever attacked him in the diner had set off a chain of events which had sent Tom and Danielle scurrying back to Paris. He checked the time on his bedside clock which said 11.00 am.

He closed his eyes and drifted off. He was groggy when he awoke but the headache had subsided. He pulled the duvet back and sat up feeling dizzy as he lowered his feet to the floor. After a couple of minutes he stood up stretching his arm out to the wardrobe door for support. He reached for his dressing gown and tied it loosely before moving slowly to the kitchen to brew some coffee. After his second mug he felt almost human. Almost.

He called Jill and she picked up quickly. 'Jack, are you home?'

'Yes, I'm back. Just got up. Jetlag.'

'How are you feeling?'

'I've felt better but I'm OK. How are things with you and the kids?'

'We're all fine. Back home now. I sat them down and told them you have seen their dad in Mexico'

'How did they take it?'

'A mixture really but mainly joy of course. They just want him back home.'

'Do you want that too?'

She paused before answering. 'I don't know what to think anymore. I just feel overwhelmed by what's happened. I am so angry over what he has done to us. How did he look?'

'Tanned and fit.'

'And the girl?'

'The same.'

Jill just said, 'Bitch.'

He changed the subject and asked if Alex Mason had completed the security work at her home.

'Yeah, he's done a terrific job. Even a squirrel would trip all the outside flood lights.'

'Or a rat.'

'Don't even mention one of those things Jack. Your humour is warped.'

'Sorry, I couldn't resist it.'

'Well try.'

'I will. Look, I'll call you tonight.'

Chapter 46

Sergei was in bed at his luxury penthouse apartment. Francoise was in the shower and he could smell his own sweat after their lovemaking. He had missed six calls and stretched across for his phone to check his messages. He took Danni's first.

'The students have been busted at Dover.' Danielle was shouting above background noise. Sergei swung his legs round and came off the bed.

'They're all in custody and we've lost the consignment. I got through. Have to go. I'll call you later.'

Sergei froze and hardly noticed rain beginning to spatter against the huge picture window. He rang Danni and it went straight to message. 'Jesus Christ.'

Francoise came from the en suite and saw him throw the phone onto a side table. She walked across to the bed and sat on the black silk sheets. When he turned back to face her, he had paled and looked anxious, almost unsure of himself.

'I have business to attend to. Get out.'

Francoise sulked but didn't argue as she took off the large white towel and began searching for her clothes.

When she'd gone, he quickly showered and dressed. He had to make the call and dialed his immediate boss in St Petersburg. 'Gregor, it's Sergei.'

'I know. You're on my ID. What's up?'

Sergei came straight out. 'We've been busted at Dover. Looks like we've lost the whole consignment. All the couriers have been arrested.'

There was a silence, then, 'So what are you doing?'

'I'm on the case now.'

'Get back to me in two hours. Whatever happens to the couriers, remember, no fall out for us. Where's Danielle?'

'She got away. I'm just waiting to hear from her again.'

'Two hours Sergei. We need to know why this happened?'

'I'll get back to you when I know more.'

'That would be a good idea.' The line went dead.

Reaching into a drawer in the cabinet next to his flat screen TV, Sergei brought out his Sig and pushed it into the inside pocket of his jacket. He grabbed his wallet and phone from the table and strode towards the door picking up his car keys from the kitchen on the way. He took the lift to the basement car park and remotely opened the doors of the 911 as he exited the lift doors. His mind was working furiously but not coming to any conclusions. She was in charge of the courier runs. Why hasn't she called again? Where has she been? What had gone wrong?'

***

He gunned the car through the narrow exit lane and out into the street. He threw his phone on the passenger seat and concentrated on getting to Danielle's apartment.

He parked in a bay marked 'residents only' at the back of her building and walked quickly to the front entrance. He took the stairs two at a time, his breathing unchanged when he reached her door on the sixth floor. Taking out his key fob, he quietly opened the door.

The apartment was quiet and in semi darkness. It smelled slightly musty. He inched his way along the narrow corridor and kept close to the wall tapping the living room door open with his foot as he drew his gun. All the blinds were drawn and a vase on the low walnut table in the centre contained a posy of withered roses. By the dim light he looked round and saw nothing but a deserted looking room. He lowered his gun and walked through to the bedroom he knew well. The double bed was made up and the room was neat and empty. He looked inside the wardrobe and saw gaps where clothes would have hung. He quickly checked the bathroom and found all her stuff cleared from the glass shelves. He returned to the sitting room and sat down on the sofa. He rang her mobile again to make sure. Disconnected.

Thoughts were tumbling into his mind but his anger was mounting. He rang Xavier. 'Have you got anything?'

'Nothing yet.'

'We've got some new problems. Wait for my call.'

He started to look round the apartment and began in the bedroom. He searched in the wardrobe again and saw all her winter clothes. He moved across to the dressing table and started checking the contents. He felt between her folded clothes and under the protective layer of paper at the bottom of each drawer. He found nothing unusual and walked across to the bedside cabinet.

Each drawer was a jumble of odds and ends and paperbacks. He lifted the round pink rug near the bed and found nothing and walked through to the small living room. Danielle had shopped at Printemps on Boulevard Haussman and there was a certain grandeur about the furnishings. Magazines and newspapers which were usually scattered around had been stacked in a neat pile on a white shelf next to her small flat screen television. He flicked through them and found most were fashion and beauty with a couple of lifestyle titles. One of them carried a cover flash featuring Mexico as the hot new holiday destination. He placed them back as he found them. He carried on to a small drawer unit behind the door and found an old cigar box. Inside was a bank book tucked inside a folded bank statement.

It was recent and when he looked at them, he could hardly believe what he was seeing. The balance was over 16,000 Euros. The money had been deposited in tranches of around 2,000 Euros over a period of two months. The exact timescale which Danielle had involved Tom in bringing money back from the UK. 'Bitch.' Two thousand Euros had been taken from the account fourteen days previously. He sat down and taking a scrap of paper from his pocket, wrote down the account number, the balance and the date of the first and last deposit. He returned the bank statement and book and opened the three drawers above it. There were various CDs and an assortment of paraphernalia found in any home. There was no sign of her passport. He went to the bathroom and opened the wall cabinet above the wash basin and found only various medications and cosmetic products. Turning round he lifted the cistern lid, placing it on the toilet seat. He pushed up his right hand sleeve and dropped his arm into the cistern, feeling to the corners around the bottom.

Cold water. He dried his hand on the small towel and replaced the cistern lid. Moving out to the hallway he looked up for any overhead hatch cover to a loft area but with apartments above, there wasn't one. He took a last sweep around the apartment, checking to make sure he hadn't missed anything. Satisfied, he opened the front door and checked both ways along the corridor. There was no one around and he quietly clicked the door shut and made his way to the stairway and out to the street. He sat in his car for a minute to collect his thoughts. She's gone with him. He began to shake and had to wait a few minutes before starting the engine.

He drove to the Meurice and parked in the space reserved for him at the back of the restaurant. As he let himself in at his private door he knew the next few hours would be the most important since he became the boss of the Paris operation. He had given everything to be where he was and no one would be spared if they had been found to have betrayed him.

He sat down heavily in his chair and rang through to the restaurant for a pot of coffee. He waited until he heard the soft knock at the door and Henri came in carrying the coffee and a bone china cup and saucer on a silver tray. The old waiter looked at Sergei and said nothing. He put down the tray and left quietly.

Sergei put a call into his police contact in London. 'I need to find out about a drugs bust at Dover today. Can you get anything on it for me?'

The voice at the other end said he would get what he could but Dover was a little out of his range of contacts. 'Give me a couple of hours. I'll get back to you.'

Sergei sat back in his chair and put off making the call to Gregor. He had sleepwalked into a trap. He had become complacent. The courier system using the students had been working like clockwork and the money came back regularly from the offshore accounts. But he had taken his eye off the ball. Danielle was a first class operator managing the student runs across the English Channel and he had trusted her. He had also found her enthusiasm in the bedroom a wonderful bonus but now he knew he had been distracted. His masters in St Petersburg wanted the drug deliveries made, money paid, cleaned up, and returned upline, on time, every time. Now Danielle had disappeared. And as he enjoyed the trappings of his wealth, he hadn't noticed.

When Gregor called him his voice was quiet but deliberate. 'Sergei, I gave you two hours for a report and you've failed me. Dover is bad, but there are also reports of missed payments from your division. Big numbers. Solve it as you wish. You have 48 hours and a lot to do. Your family still live here and you know what happens. I will not be able to help you.'

The line went dead and Sergei stared into his mobile as if he would get a message saying it was all going to be alright. That nothing bad would happen. That his sister in law in St Petersburg wouldn't go home and find her husband hanging naked in the hallway from a cord attached to a post at the top of the stairs. There was no hiding place, no mercy when the mob wanted their money. Sergei rang through to the restaurant and said he didn't want to be disturbed. They knew anyway.

Khalid and Xavier had let him down. They should have eliminated the private investigator after they got information on Tom Stanton. He would find the missing money with or without their help. Stanton was behind this. He was a financier and understood money and it was all too much of a coincidence. He called a mobile in London and the voice answered saying only the last three digits of the number.

'773'

'It's Sergei. I need some work done.'

The Land Cruiser turned left into a side street in East London and pulled into the curb.

'What do you need?'

'I want the Stanton daughter taken into our safekeeping. You need to take her to an address I'll give you in Paddington. There will be someone at the house to receive her.'

'When?'

'Tomorrow, as school comes out. It's near Windsor. Can you do it?'

'Yeah, I scoped the place a couple of weeks ago for Xavier. I can do that.'

'I'll call you tonight.'

Then he rang Xavier again.

'You'll have company at Paddington from late tomorrow afternoon. Prepare a room for a female guest who will be delivered to you. Treat her well till I tell you otherwise. Make sure Khalid understands this. I'll give you more details tomorrow.'

Chapter 47

Jack checked the arrival times of Air France from Cancun to Paris CDG and realised they would have already landed and passed through immigration.

He dressed and walked to the local newsagent. Just for normality if nothing else. He got back and let himself back into his apartment, sat down and opened the morning paper. Page four carried the story on the drugs find at Dover and he tried to picture the scene as dozens of flip flops were impounded. Crazy.

He rang Jill and asked if she was going to be home.

'Yes, home all day apart from the school run this afternoon.'

'I need to update you on my trip. How about I come over about 2 o'clock?'

'Good, I'll see you then.'

When he arrived, Jill answered the door quickly as if she had been waiting for him. She was dressed in tight blue jeans with a black T shirt and sandals. She took one look at the bruising on the side of his face and uttered, 'Oh God Jack, not again.'

He saw the tiredness in her face as he extended his hand but she ignored it and moved forward to embrace him. He was taken by surprise but felt the need in her. He could only guess what she had been going through since he had told her Tom was alive and well in Mexico. The knowledge he was with a girl must have made the pill very bitter to swallow.

'It's good to see you Jack. The coffee's on.'

They walked through to the kitchen and he sat down on a bar stool as she poured the coffees. He noticed the security monitor next to the toaster showing sequential pictures of the front, back and side of the house.

They looked at each other and, as one, said, 'Good to see you.'

She put his drink down in front of him, 'OK, what's been going on?'

He recounted his trip to Mexico and his sighting of Tom and Danielle, holding nothing back. He told her of Tom's change of identity to John Vanner and her new name of Danielle Vanner. Her husband had taken on the name of a previous client who had been murdered. Jill blanched when he told her how John Vanner had been found.

'It all finished up badly. I'd gone into a diner near Cancun for breakfast and got attacked from behind. It was probably Tom who set it up.'

Jill touched his arm. 'What happened?'

It's all a bit hazy but I'm pretty sure it was the valet from their hotel who jumped me. Probably Tom giving me a warning. Anyway I finished up in the local hospital and they patched me up.'

'So, where do you think they are now?'

'They're on their way back to Paris as far as I know.'

'But why go all the way to Mexico to fly back so soon?'

'He'll have his reasons. If he knows his cover is blown and he could get arrested, he probably doesn't fancy seeing the inside of a Mexican jail. His original plan may have involved staying in the country for some time. A lot depends on how much money he has access to. There is £900K missing from SMG but we don't know if he has it. There could be another explanation.'

She looked up from her coffee, trying to make sense of what he was saying.

Jack started to spoon the froth from his cup, 'With the heavyweights who are looking for him, I'd say there is a lot more to this than the fraud at SMG. He's in big danger and Paris could be the worst place for him to be in.'

Jill thought for a moment, 'That's why I can't understand them heading back if they were going to start a new life in Mexico.'

'We don't know they were. It's a huge thing to do. Just leave and go and live in a far off country, not even speaking the language.' He was trying to figure things out as he spoke. 'Cancun could just have been a holiday. With the change of identity, maybe they plan to live in France. It's a big place.'

Jill chipped in. 'Maybe the girl had something to do with the decision to come back. They could have fallen out.'

Jack looked up from his empty cup, 'We could speculate all night on the reasons why, but one thing is for sure, he's in big trouble on both sides of the Channel.'

'What happens now?'

'We've got to find Tom. He has to be in this much deeper than he thinks. No matter what we think of him and his actions, he has upset some nasty people. Danielle has to be part of the bigger picture. I don't think he'll see it till it's too late and I'm going to try and find him again.'

Jill looked up at the large round wall clock and said she'd have to go and collect Sarah.

Jack slid off the bar stool and touched her arm as he headed towards the hallway. 'Stay strong. I know how bad it all must feel for you and the kids but at least you're together. We'll get you through all this, I promise.'

She looked at him and smiled. 'I hope so. Thank you Jack.'

She let him out and he watched as she closed the door behind him. Looking up he noted Alex's work with the lights and closed circuit cameras perched high on the house. A professional job.

***

Sarah waved to her friends as they went in different directions at the school gate and as she spotted her mum's car near the end of the long line of parked vehicles, started towards it. She had to stop as the door of a parked 4X4 swung open in front of her with a man leaning over the empty front passenger seat with a map in his hand.

'Excuse me, can you help me?' and gestured to her to come over to the open door. Instinctively she moved towards him and as she ducked down, felt her body being wrenched into the front passenger seat. She felt little as his fist smashed into her face knocking her out cold. In seconds he had hauled her into the vehicle and pulled the door shut. The 4x4 swung out into the slow moving traffic and careered down the road forcing drivers to mount the pavement to avoid a collision. Horns blared as the large vehicle roared away from the school with no one really knowing what was happening.

Jill was changing stations on the radio and when she looked up Sarah had gone. A dark 4x4 raced past her with horns blasting all around. Mothers and schoolchildren scattered as the vehicle mounted the pavement to gain speed round all the slow moving cars. She was startled and wondering what was going on. She opened her door and started running towards the spot where she had seen Sarah. A mother was shouting, 'Someone took her.'

Jill started to scream as an outstretched arm stopped her falling. 'Oh, my God. She's gone. Please help me.'

Within minutes, police vehicles began arriving and the area was sealed to retain witnesses. Statements were taken but it had all happened so quickly and details were scant.

'It was a large 4x4 and dark. Maybe Japanese.' This was about the best they could get from a shocked and confused crowd of mothers and daughters. Jill eventually climbed back into her car and phoned Jack. She managed to utter the words 'Sarah's been kidnapped. They've taken Sarah,' and began crying hysterically.

***

The Land Cruiser came off the motorway before entering London to avoid the dense number of CCTV cameras. As he approached Paddington he called Xavier to let him know he was ten minutes away. Sarah was bundled in front of the floor area and began to come round as he threaded his way through heavy traffic towards the safe house. She looked groggily towards the driver. Her whole body ached and her mouth seemed as if it was on fire. He looked down and said, 'Make a move and I'll kill you.' She began to remember what had happened. Her legs were jammed underneath her and the pain from cramp was becoming unbearable.

'Can you move the seat back? My legs hurt.'

He just looked down at her and grunted.

She felt the vehicle slowing down and he told her to keep still.

As it drew to a halt the door was opened and before she realised what was happening, a heavy woollen hat was placed on her head and pulled down over her face. She was dragged roughly out of the vehicle and the pain from the sudden movement shot through her legs making her scream out. A strong smell of stale garlic hit her and the tightness of the hat almost made her retch. A voice next to her face said, 'Just shut up.'

She was half dragged through what she took to be a doorway and another set of hands pulled her inside. Only seconds had passed and she heard a door close behind her. She felt herself being guided along a carpeted floor and through another door. As she sat on a bed the smell of garlic receded and the other set of arms pushed her down into a sitting position. She leaned back, knocking her head against a wall behind her. There was a low gruff laugh and a feeling of terror gripped her for the very first time. Then the door opened and a voice said, 'You will stay with us till we find your father. If you try to escape we will kill you. Do you understand me?'

Sarah managed to nod and her voice croaked as she asked if she could use the bathroom. She was taken a few yards along a damp smelling corridor. She was pushed in and quickly turned as the door was closed behind her. Her hand flew to the lock and she slid the bolt as far as she could before whipping the hat off. She was in a small toilet with a tiny hand basin. A dirty looking blue towel hung from a ring fixed to the wall. She looked up and saw there was no window and no escape.

***

Jack had been in traffic in Kensington High Street when Jill's hysterical call came through.

'Oh, God Jack, Sarah's been kidnapped. They've taken Sarah. It was outside the school.' She was sobbing and Jack could barely make out what she was saying. 'If I hadn't been late, I would have been able to park closer. It's all my fault. What will they do to her Jack?'

An ambulance screamed past Jack's car and he shouted, 'Where are you?'

'I'm back home with the police.'

'I'm on my way to you.'

As he turned and began driving west again, he knew what this had turned into. The kidnapping of a schoolgirl in broad daylight was front page stuff. Everything was about to become public. There would be no hiding place and someone, somewhere had escalated the disappearance of Tom Stanton to the highest level.

The police were with Jill when Jack arrived and he had to explain his involvement and show ID to get past the two police constables standing on the road outside the driveway. A gaggle of photographers stood by the gates and one squeezed off a shot as Jack turned in.

He drove up to the house and parked behind two police cars. The door was opened by a WPC who asked again for ID. Jill saw him from the kitchen and broke off talking on her mobile to come down the hall to him. Her mascara was smudged and her eyes were red. Exhaustion and fear were etched into her face.

'Oh God, Jack. It happened outside the school. It was so quick. I couldn't do anything.'

She broke down and he took her in his arms and held her. As her sobbing began to subside, he said quietly.' Is Oliver safe?'

'Yes, he's here with me.'

'We'll find Sarah, I promise you.'

They walked slowly into the kitchen where different conversations were taking place with backs turned to hear and be heard on mobile phones. Jill motioned him through to the living room.

'I need a minute on my own, it's been non stop questions.' She walked towards the sofa near the side wall away from the window and they sat down, still hearing the sounds of voices in the background. Tears began to well in her eyes and she used a balled up tissue to stem the flow. As Jack took her right hand in both of his, he realised how much she had gone through since Tom vanished. Her life had been turned upside down and now her daughter had been taken by force. Life had become unbearable.

They sat in silence for a minute and he said, 'Do they have anything at all on the vehicle?'

'I heard one of them in the kitchen say they had a part of the registration number from one of the mothers outside the school. It was a big dark 4x4, probably Japanese. I think they're checking CCTV in the area and on the M4. They seem pretty hopeful they'll get something. Oh God, Jack, I'm so scared. My poor Sarah. If anything happens to her, I'll never forgive myself.' She started to sob again and he put his arm around her shoulders.

'You couldn't have stopped this. She'll be OK I promise you. This is just to get Tom to make contact. She'll come back to you.'

Jill just sobbed, 'Please God, you are right.'

He said he would keep in touch and he kissed her lightly on the cheek as he let himself out of the front door. As he turned his car in Jill's drive and drove slowly out, he knew the only person who could get Sarah freed was her father. He might be the only person who knew where she was right now. He drove straight into London and to his apartment. Online, he booked himself on the first flight out of Heathrow to Paris. He threw some clothes into a bag, showered and poured himself a whisky, taking it through to his bedroom. He thought of ringing Jill but decided there were probably still too many people there. He finished his drink, switched off the bedside lamp and tried to sleep.

Chapter 48

He bought four newspapers from WH Smith's at Terminal 5. The kidnapping was front page on all of them. He stuffed them in the outside pocket of his case and carried on to the gate. When he had settled in to his seat he began reading all four. They had made the connection with Tom Stanton, the missing father and the mounting financial calamity at SMG. Two had gone further and speculated on bigger and darker things with international connotations and Jack wondered how they got their information. Probably the same way as me, he thought. All featured speculation as to the vehicle used in the kidnapping and it was now generally agreed it could have been a Toyota Land Cruiser. The police were said to be following up promising lines of enquiry. There was a photograph of the Stanton's taken at a recent party. The irony was there for all to see. A family with everything to live for and now in desperate danger.

He exited the airport in Paris and headed for the taxi rank. In an hour he was in central Paris. The taxi stopped short of The Petit Maison and Jack got out and paid off the driver.

Without breaking his stride he entered the small foyer. It was only 10 am and tourists were still checking out. He joined people of all nationalities milling around the reception and moved towards the desk. Jack didn't recognize the girl on duty who was looking harassed as the desk phone began to ring. She broke off to take the call. Jack leant across and extended his arm between two middle aged ladies as he picked up the guest book. They looked round at him and he smiled as if he was checking in. They turned away and continued their conversations. His eyes darted down the names and he flicked back one then two pages. And there it was. Mr. and Mrs. Vanner checked in two days ago and were allocated room fifteen. A London address which was probably a building site. He smiled sweetly at the ladies and placed the book back on the desk.

He walked slowly towards the stairs, carrying his case and climbed to the first floor and came to room fifteen. The maids had not yet arrived to start cleaning and it was quiet in the narrow corridor. He listened at the door but heard nothing. He looked up and down and seeing no one, tapped softly on the door. He heard some rustling and knocked again.

'Who is it?' It was a male voice with an English accent.

Jack covered his mouth and called in his best French, 'We have a problem with the gas, Monsieur. I need to check your heater quickly.'

There was a pause and Jack heard the lock turning. The door opened a fraction and Jack came face to face with Tom Stanton. Before Tom had time to query him or ask for ID, Jack looked him straight in the eye and said, 'I am from London. Your daughter Sarah has been kidnapped and is in grave danger. Please speak with me.'

A look of disbelief came over Tom Stanton's face and he tried to slam the door but Jack already had his foot against it.

'I have this morning's papers Mr. Stanton. Read the front pages. Only you can save Sarah.' He held up one of the papers and Tom saw himself and his family smiling from the front page.

Jack watched as Tom slumped against the door frame and a female voice called from inside the room. 'Who is it? 'Tom half turned and said, 'It's OK, Danni.' When he turned back to face Jack he took hold of the newspaper and let the door swing open. He looked incredulously as he tried to take in the front page and it began to drop from his hands. The door had now fully opened and Jack saw Danielle lying in bed covered by a white sheet.

Jack took a step forward and said, 'We haven't got much time.' As he peered over Tom's shoulder into the room, he saw Danielle sit up, doing nothing to cover her nakedness.

She shouted, 'Who the hell are you?'

Tom turned to her and said, 'Shut up Danni. Something terrible has happened.'

Jack knew the next thing he said had to work. 'What the papers don't say is that Sarah is going to be tortured before being killed. Only I can help you stop that happening. We must get away from here now.'

Tom looked hard at him. 'Give me a minute to get packed and dressed.'

'I'll wait here. Don't forget your passport and be quick.'

The door closed and Jack heard Danni's voice. 'You can't go. You don't even know who that guy is.'

'I'm going. Stay here and I'll call you later.'

The door opened and Tom Stanton re-appeared looking pleadingly at Jack. What do I need to do? Oh my God.'

They went downstairs to reception and Tom crossed to the desk where the girl was now free of guests. He told her, 'I have to leave on business. Just use my VISA for the room. Danielle will be down shortly.' They walked outside and Jack took hold of his arm. 'Let's go. We need to talk.' They hailed a passing taxi and Tom told the driver, 'Charles De Gaulle.' Traffic was light and as they moved off Tom asked, 'Were you in Mexico?'

'Yes, I'm working for your wife.'

'How did you know I would be at The Petit Maison?'

'I know quite a lot about you.'

Tom flushed. 'Yes I know. I caused you a lot of trouble and pain in Mexico. I'm very sorry. I didn't know who you were.'

'Yes, you caused me a lot of problems, not to mention a very sore head. How much did you pay the valet?'

'A month's wages.'

Jack stared hard at him as Tom's head dropped to avoid his gaze. 'There are some very dangerous people trying to find you and that is why they have taken your daughter. You have put your whole family huge danger. You must be involved with more than defrauding SMG.'

'I'm not sure I know what you mean.'

Jack became angry. 'We are way beyond playing games. I need every bit of help I can get to have any chance of saving your daughter. It's not about saving your skin now. Do you understand that?'

Tom murmured, 'Yes I do.'

'Before you start, I should tell you we are going to London on the first flight we can get. That is, unless you think we can do more good by staying in Paris.'

'I don't know anyone here apart from Danielle and her friends at the University.'

'Is that true?'

'Yes, I did business with a small restaurant chain here but the rest of the time was spent with Danni.'

'Where is the money you took from SMG?'

'It's in a bank account. Look, please, what has happened to my daughter?'

As the taxi drove towards the airport the suburbs gave way to light industrial units and soon they heard the overhead roar of jets on their final approach to Charles De Gaulle.

Tom brought him up to date. 'Sarah was kidnapped as she left school yesterday afternoon. It was over in an instant and although there were witnesses everywhere, no one actually got any details. It was all too quick. She's disappeared into thin air. Just like you Mr Stanton or is it Mr Vanner?'

Tom stared at Jack. 'All I know about John Vanner is that he disappeared. I took his identity and nothing else.'

Jack held eye contact. 'And you opened a credit card in his name.'

Tom Stanton's composure left him and he held his head in his hands and sobbed. 'I've been a bloody fool.'

The drop off area was hectic when the taxi arrived at the terminal. Tom climbed out and Jack reached for his wallet and asked the driver for a receipt. The taxi pulled out of the parking bay and when Jack turned round, Tom was gone.

Jack ran towards the terminal building looking right and left as he went. Going inside he checked the immediate area and saw nothing but a mass of people. He pushed his way to the escalator and looked up but couldn't see him amongst the throng. Dashing back outside, he was met with the same sea of vehicles parking and disgorging more people and more luggage. He stopped when he reached the edge of the paved area and knew he'd lost him. He walked back inside the airport building heading for the café where he ordered a coffee and watched the departure area. There was no one looking like Tom Stanton to be seen.

Chapter 49

Sergei picked up on the first ring from Xavier, 'Have you got her?'

'Yeah, she's at the house in Paddington. In the spare room.'

'Has she told you where her father is?'

'We haven't asked her anything yet.'

Sergei felt his whole body stiffen and shouted, 'I want her to tell you where her father is. Keep her alive, but get the information. Call me back when she talks. I don't care what time it is.'

Xavier just said OK and finished the call. He wasn't used to disrespect and his lack of results was beginning to anger him. He went through to the kitchen to find Khalid eating spaghetti bolognaise. Juice was running down his chin and onto his shirt. Xavier looked away and said, 'I'm going to speak with the girl. Stay outside the door.'

'Don't you need me?'

'No.'

Xavier walked down to Sarah's room and let himself in. It was almost dark when he entered and she was lying on the bed. She was startled when she heard the door open and sat up. Xavier walked over to her. 'I'm taking the hood off now. Don't look round at me or I will have to kill you.'

She nodded and as he took off the hat she exhaled before taking in breath.

'I need to know where your father is.'

'I don't know where he is. I really don't.'

'That's not good enough, Sarah. Try harder.'

'If I knew I would tell you. He hasn't been in touch with us since he disappeared.'

'We need to know and if you won't tell us, we will hurt you.'

She was crying and started to shake uncontrollably. 'I haven't a clue where he is. That's the truth.' Her words came out in gasps as she caught her breath between sobs.

He slid the hood back on her and left the room. When he returned he had his mobile phone with him and his cigarette lighter. He picked up a chair and sat it in front of Sarah, making her lie back on the bed.

'Last chance.'

She could only manage to shake her head and repeat, 'I don't know where he is.'

Xavier took a cigarette from the packet and lit it. He held up his mobile phone, switched it to video and pressed the lit cigarette into the calf of Sarah's right leg. As she screamed he kept the cigarette stubbed into her flesh for longer than he needed. He filmed her screaming and writhing and a smile crossed his thin lips. This would get the result he needed and help restore his reputation with Sergei. Whatever it takes.

Khalid heard the noise and stuck his head round the door taking in the scene. 'Need any help?'

'No. If I need you I'll call you.'

Xavier knew that would annoy Khalid. There was violence being meted out and he wasn't involved. Khalid scowled and slammed the door shut.

Xavier watched Sarah's face contort with pain and he asked her again to say where her father was. She could only croak that she hadn't a clue where he was. Then she passed out. He hadn't got the information he had wanted but he knew the video would give Sergei the means to get it and he felt better about himself. When he returned to the living room Khalid was watching some daytime reality shit on TV and looked up sullenly at Xavier.

'Don't know why you brought me along if you're doing everything yourself.'

'Your time will come. Go and have some lunch.'

'I've just had some.'

'Have some more. You're wasting away.'

Khalid threw the remote at Xavier and missed. 'Fuck you,' he said and went back to watching television.

Chapter 50

Tom Stanton knew he had to get out of the taxi and back to Danni. He shouldn't have left her. As he listened in horror to Jack relaying the news that his daughter had been kidnapped, the slow realisation came to him that this was nothing to do with SMG. This was to do with the drugs. He had to get back to Danielle and find out what she knew and how she could help. She had the connections. She could feed things up the line. When he stepped out at CDG he saw Jack turn his back and speak with the taxi driver and he took his chance. He darted left into a crowd of American tourists bunched up in front of the revolving door waiting to enter the terminal. He ducked down and ran through the crowd at waist level and in seconds found himself clear at the other side. He spotted a covered area set apart from the entrance doors and ran towards it. He turned in to it and found himself alongside uniformed airline personnel smoking and talking. He smiled weakly and moved towards the end of the shelter and searched for his cigarettes. A young airport employee offered him a light and he accepted gratefully. He smoked the cigarette slowly and then peered out towards the main entrance. Jack was nowhere in sight. He moved out towards the taxi rank and kept his head down. Within minutes he was on his way back to the City to find Danni. He rang her from the taxi but the call went into message. His feeling of panic rose and he came close to ringing Jill. He asked the driver if he could go any faster and received a nonchalant shrug in return. He phoned the Petit Maison and the girl recognised his voice.

'Could you put me through to my wife please?'

'I'm sorry but she left about fifteen minutes ago.'

'Of course, thank you.'

He leant forward and told the driver to take him to Arrondisment 6 and gave him Danni's home address. He had never felt such blind panic. Slumping into the seat he started praying. 'Christ, help me, what have I done?'

***

When Danni left Le Petit Maison she took a taxi and went to Sergei's apartment. He greeted her at the door and kissed her on the mouth. She knew the layout intimately, going straight to the living room and sat down on the sofa.

Sergei followed and moved across to the oak drinks cabinet. As he opened it, the interior was filled with a soft light. 'What would you like?'

Danni asked for vodka straight and ice. He poured himself a Scotch and picked up her drink. He sat down and handed her the drink. As she lifted the glass to her mouth, he hit her with his free hand and caught her on the side of the face. As the glass flew out of her hand she felt a sharp pain in the inside of her mouth and fell sideways onto the sofa. He gripped her throat and said, 'So, where have you been? You've been stealing from me, haven't you.'

She tasted her own blood as she tried to push herself back upright and he struck her again. 'Tell me Danni, what's been going on?'

'I don't know what you mean. I've been visiting friends. I told you that. Anyway, what money?'

'In your bank account. The sixteen thousand euros'

She desperately tried to think through the pain in her jaw. 'It was from Tom. He just gave it to me.'

She knew he'd bound to have worked out she'd skimmed from Tom's regular money trips. She tried to hide her fear and watched him saunter over to his drink and hoped he wouldn't ask about her absence and the friends she'd been visiting. Her face was hurting and she felt the swelling beginning to rise on her cheek. Lifting the tumbler from the top of the cabinet, he downed the whisky and walked back to Danni.

Look Sergei, 'I'll make sure the money gets back to you. I don't know where Tom is right now.'

'What do you mean; you don't know where he is?'

'Apparently a man visited him this morning. Said he should go with him as his daughter was in great danger.'

'Who was this guy?'

'I think it may have been the private detective from London.'

The mobile sitting on the drinks cabinet rang and Sergei went over to check the caller ID. It was Xavier.

As Danni looked on, he took the call and walked through to the kitchen, shutting the door behind him..

'I've got something for you.'

'About fucking time. What is it?'

'I'm going to send a video to your phone. It's Stanton's daughter and she's in a lot of pain. You'll like it.'

'Keep her alive.'

He finished the call and waited for the video to download to his phone.

He smiled as he heard Sarah scream and after he'd watched it twice, went back to Danielle.

'Give me Tom Stanton's mobile phone number.'

As she scrolled down her contacts she kept her phone away from his line of vision and called out Tom's number to him. He added it to his list of contacts.

The violence in the video had sent his mind spinning. He turned to Danielle and yanked her up from the couch. 'Come on,' and he pushed her roughly towards the bedroom.

***

Tom paid the taxi off and walked up the stairs to Danni's door and rang the bell. There was no reply so he fished in his pocket for his key and let himself in. The curtains were drawn and the rooms were in semi darkness. There was no sound as he made his way to the living room and sat down on the sofa. A feeling of complete helplessness had come over him and he agonised over whether to try and find out about Sarah. He rested his head in his hands and tried to work out why someone would go to these lengths. His mobile phone rang and he saw it was a withheld number. He clicked on the receive button and the video began playing. He watched in horror as his daughter screamed in agony and without being able to move, vomited over the carpet.

'Dear Jesus.' He was sobbing and punching the side of the sofa when he heard the key in the front door.

As he squinted through his watery eyes, he saw Danielle come in and recoil as the smell of sickness reached her nostrils. She called out his name and Tom stumbled into the darkened hallway, tripped and fell down at her feet. She jumped back and screamed. As he lay on the floor his mobile rang again and he hit the button without checking the ID.

'Mr. Stanton, you will have seen my little video presentation. That is just the start. A mild dose of persuasion. We will move on to stage two with your daughter in two hours time and it will be filmed for your private viewing. You have two choices. Return the £4 million or watch your daughter undergo some unusual manicure treatment. The choice is yours. Get your answer to me quickly. The clock is ticking. I will ring you again.'

There was a click and then silence. Tom let out a loud wailing sound and looked up at Danielle.

Her nose wrinkled as she saw the mess on the carpet. She turned and went into the kitchen, pulled on rubber gloves, filled a bucket with cold water and threw in a large yellow sponge. After the worst of the vomit was cleaned up she sprayed the carpet with some deodorant.

Tom had gone into the kitchen and she carried the bucket of dirty water in and emptied into the sink.

'Who was that on the phone?'

He was barely coherent but managed to say, 'Someone has kidnapped my daughter. They're torturing her somewhere. I was sent a video on my mobile and I can't believe what they're doing to her. My little girl. Oh my God.'

Danielle stared at him as he sat on the bar stool still looking at his mobile phone in disbelief.

'What's happened Danni? The voice asked for his money back. He sounded Eastern European. I don't know what he means.'

After she rinsed the bucket out and put it back in the cupboard under the sink, she turned to him, 'There's been missed payments from the banks you set up. I don't know the amount involved but I think it's big.'

'And he thinks I've got it?' Tom studied Danni's face. 'That's impossible. I had nothing to do with that.'

'Tell that to Sergei.'

'You've got to help me.'

'Only finding that money will save your daughter Tom. You need to get it back to Sergei.'

'I don't have it to give back. You know that.'

'Do I?'

He stared at her as she stood unblinking next to the cooker and realised he didn't know her at all. She believed he had stolen the money. The taste of his own vomit lingered in his mouth and the reality of his situation hit him like a thunderbolt. His head fell forward and he began to tremble uncontrollably.

Danni looked down at him and ripped off her rubber gloves, 'You don't really have any options. Just get the money back.'

He walked to the bathroom and gargled with mint flavoured mouthwash. When he returned she was on her mobile phone. 'OK,' she said and quickly switched it off.

'Who was that?'

'A girlfriend from college. I am meeting her tonight.'

'You didn't tell me.'

'God, I don't have to tell you everything. It's nothing, just girls meeting up.'

He couldn't have cared less and sat down on the opposite end of the sofa to where he'd thrown up. 'Danni, tell me something. Why would I steal the money knowing I would never get away with it? I mean, you know, drug money.'

'I don't know why.'

'Do you know who has my daughter?'

She looked away, 'No, I don't.'

Tom knew he must leave and do some thinking. 'I'm going back to the hotel.'

She nodded, pushing herself away from the kitchen unit before walking across to him, kissing him quickly on the cheek. 'Keep in touch with me. If I hear anything, I'll call you.'

He picked up his mobile phone and let himself out. As he walked down the staircase to the first floor, he felt light headed and realised what little he'd eaten he'd thrown up. He wasn't hungry but he needed a drink. He stepped out into a late afternoon gloom and turned left, not really knowing where he was going. As he stumbled along the pavement he became aware people were looking at him. He straightened his body and as he came to an intersection, saw lights coming on in a small brasserie across the street. He picked up his pace and walked over to the dimly lit bar. He asked the barman for a large Scotch with ice and was served a Johnnie Walker Black. He carried on ordering another every ten minutes and the young man behind the bar just left him to it. Tom was in turmoil and as the whisky took hold, he began to feel the anger rise within him. He thought of his precious daughter, how much he loved her and what he'd seen on the phone video. He wanted to leave Paris now and go to her. Save her from further pain. But where? He had no idea. He kept on drinking until the barman said, 'I think you could use a taxi Sir.'

Tom managed to focus on the face which had just spoken to him and said, 'OK.' The taxi arrived at the door and the barman went out to him as Tom found his way back from the toilet. On his return the young man asked, 'Where are you going?' Tom managed to slur Hotel Petit Maison and the barman helped him outside. It was the last he remembered until he was awakened by his mobile phone. His room was dark and he heard a sound like chimes. He tried to sit up and his head exploded. He fell back on the bed and went into unconsciousness. Had he taken the call, he would have heard Sergei telling him his daughter's time was up.

Chapter 51

Jack was furious with himself. He'd lost Tom at Charles de Gaulle and had no idea where Sarah was being held. Sitting in his Maida Vale apartment he was sifting through notes he had made since his return from Paris. They were written in a random fashion. Why had they gone to Mexico? New life? Launder money? Where was SMG's money? Had TS taken it? Danielle's role? Why return to Paris?

He looked at all his questions and wished he could put an answer to at least one of them.

He walked across to his CDs and chose Julie London and pressed play. His mobile chirped as he sat down and he saw a withheld number.

He clicked it on and held the phone to his ear.

'Mr. Barclay, this is Tom Stanton. I am sorry about running today but I do need your help.'

Jack said, 'Go on.'

'I ran because I was scared and I thought I could save Sarah by staying in Paris and appealing to Danni.'

Jack eased back in the sofa chair and said, 'And did you?'

There was a silence and then he heard Tom Stanton voice breaking as he spoke.

'She can't or won't help me. I'm in your hands now.'

'Where are you?'

'In Paris.'

'Have you had any further contact from Sarah's captors?'

'I had a video sent to my mobile phone.'

'Send it to me now.'

'Must I?'

'You have screwed up in every possible way. Don't start asking questions. Just send it after we finish this call. There may be helpful background in the video. Your daughter is probably somewhere in London but the decision maker is likely to be near you. I need names and contact numbers of everyone who you think may be connected.'

'I will take the first flight from Heathrow to Paris tomorrow morning. I'll tell your wife I have spoken with you but for tonight I will say no more. Tell me where to meet you?'

'Just come to my hotel. I am still at Le Petit Maison.'

'You need to leave there now. Check out and ring me when you have found a new room.'

'Are you being serious?'

'You and your family are in great danger. Just do it.'

He heard an intake of breath at the other end of the phone and then, 'Of course. I'll ring you later.'

Jack finished the call and went over to the table, booted up his laptop and booked a flight to Paris. Then his phone rang. He received the video and was appalled. 'Bastards.' The stakes had been raised beyond anything he'd imagined. He went to pack his carry on and took a shower.

Two hours later he received a text from Tom Stanton with a new hotel address near the Metro in Madeleine.

Jack climbed in to bed and lay awake thinking of Sarah.

The video was so horrific; Jack decided to wait before calling Jill. What he had seen was beyond any level of reason and he thought he knew who was holding the video phone. There was only one person who was capable of doing that and he thought he had already encountered him. He left home at 4 am and drove to Heathrow.

When he met Tom Stanton, he couldn't believe the difference in 24 hours. His hands were shaking and he looked ten years older. He could smell stale alcohol on his breath. The hotel he had chosen was modest and in a side street near the Metro. Jack had phoned ahead and arranged to meet him in the small restaurant inside the hotel. Most of the residents had checked out and they were left alone near the back of the poorly lit subterranean room.

Tom ordered another pot of coffee and asked Jack if that was OK for him.

The girl arrived at the table saying, 'We are closing soon. Would you like to order breakfast?' Jack said no and Tom poured coffee into two mugs although his trembling hand could barely manage it. 'Did you see the video?'

'Yes.'

'I need to get her back before anything else happens.'

'Then you'd better tell me everything. And I mean everything.'

Tom told his story as if in confession. 'I took money from my company to help fund my new lifestyle. I was travelling to Paris often and I met and fell in love with a young French girl. She liked the good things in life and my expenditure got way out of hand. I found out she was involved in the running of cocaine to London and she asked me if I could help launder the UK drug money back to her bosses in Paris.' His head dropped then he glanced at Jack and carried on. 'I was besotted with her and agreed to help. I knew I would eventually get caught for what I had done at SMG and decided to disappear.' He shifted on his chair and began to look embarrassed. 'I took on the identity of an old business client who had disappeared. I became John Vanner and Danielle became Mrs. Vanner. We went to Mexico on what was going to be an extended holiday before deciding where to settle, but you found us. I thought you were someone from the mob. I'm sorry.'

Jack listened as Tom reduced a chain of calamitous events into a few sentences.

'We returned to Paris and all hell broke loose. I can't believe where all this has led.'

Jack watched a broken man in front of him and almost felt pity. 'You took the money from SMG to finance your new life.' Jack said it as a statement.

'Yes, that was the reason.'

'And you still have that money?'

'Most of it.'

'Have you stolen any other money?' Tom's head jerked up and he said, 'No, what do you mean?'

'Your daughter has been kidnapped and is being tortured, your wife has been attacked and tortured. One of your colleagues at SMG has been beaten up and so have I. Twice.

Someone wants to find you very badly and if you want to see your daughter again, I suggest you start opening up.'

Tom hung his head. 'I only really know Danielle but I have spoken with her boss Sergei by phone. No one gets to see him. Something must have gone badly wrong. I think they believe I have stolen a lot of money.' He looked up. 'Becoming involved with the drug business was the worst decision I've ever made and I regret the day I agreed to help, but I haven't stolen any money from them. Ever.'

'If you want to see your daughter again, you may have to let them believe otherwise.'

'What?'

'You need some bargaining power or at least you need to let them think you have something to trade. They're not going to let your daughter just walk away. If she has seen the faces of her abductors she can identify them. They know there is only one way to protect themselves.'

Tom listened in growing horror. 'But I can't offer them what they want.'

'Maybe you can but just don't realise it. As long as they think you have their money, you can negotiate. You need to send a message through Danielle. Tell them you want your daughter back and you will get their money for them.'

'But what if it all goes wrong.'

'Well, you could go to the police. But if they find out you have done that, I wouldn't like to guess what would happen. If you negotiate yourself, you keep control. It's your call, but we should move quickly.'

Tom Stanton's face went white and his hands began to shake at the realisation of what lay ahead. 'You'll help me then?'

'Yes, but I need to clear a few things up. Did you kill John Vanner?'

Tom's face contorted in a look of shock. 'Jesus, no. Who has said that?'

'No one yet. I just need to know.'

'I knew he had disappeared and I took a chance. He was involved in prison reform and trying to help some pretty desperate people. I admired him actually. When I learned he vanished, I was pretty sure he'd paid the ultimate price for trying to help rehabilitate these criminals. He wasn't street wise enough to be dealing with these types. When they left prison and contacted him, it probably wasn't for social purposes. They were broke.'

'John Vanner actually looked a bit like me you know. I had all his personal details from dealings with him, so I took his identity. A friend of Danielle in Paris provided the passports. It was surprisingly easy. Then we flew to Mexico.'

'So what was your exact financial involvement with the gang?'

'Danni was my link. She is placed higher in the organisation than I thought and is tight with Sergei. She gave me the bank accounts which should be credited as the money washed through. I set up ways for the money to return from the UK through different offshore accounts. At each stage it was getting cleaned up and becoming more distanced from its origins. It wasn't too difficult to arrange.

Jack listened and made some notes.

'I took a percentage every time money moved. Then Danielle asked me if I would carry cash with me when I came across to meet her in Paris. She said it was for Sergei to help with his outgoings. It was crazy but I did it for her really. It was usually a few thousand pounds. Always well below the legal limit for cash going across the UK border but it was drug money and I must have reeked of it. Heathrow is known to be well policed. I was lucky.'

Jack sat and listened as Tom told his story. He wondered how an intelligent man had been drawn in to such a dangerous web of drugs and danger.

Tom looked across at him. 'It was all for Danielle. I couldn't resist her. I can't believe what I have done to Sarah and my family. Whatever it takes, I'm going to get my daughter back safely.'

Jack stared at him half in contempt and half in hope. 'OK, here's what you need to do.'

Chapter 52

Sitting in her living room, Jill was beyond consolation. Her mother and father had arrived and had taken over the running of the home. Oliver had taken his sister's kidnapping badly and was alone in his room. Armed police were in a vehicle parked at the bottom of the driveway and any visitors were being vetted.

The atmosphere throughout the house moved from one of despair to one of hope. Her parents had not seen Jill for two months. Her father, Robert, was a retired insurance manager and although lost in all the drama was spending time with Oliver to give him support. Her mother Ruth was also staying strong and sat close to her daughter on the sofa. Both had a glass of white wine in front of them and Jill's hand shook as she brought the glass to her mouth.

She had hardly eaten for twenty four hours and was frustrated at the lack of progress. It was late when she phoned Jack. 'It's me.'

Tom was still next to him as he took the call. He got up and walked away from the table but kept an eye on him. 'How are you?'

Her voice trembled. 'Not too good. Have you heard anything?'

'Nothing yet, but I'm working on something. It won't happen tonight or tomorrow for that matter but I'll tell you more when I can.'

He glanced over at Tom and saw him stare wearily into his coffee. He wasn't going anywhere this time.

'Have you heard from Tom?'

'No, not yet.' He hated lying but it was too dangerous to say anything else. 'Are your mum and dad with you?'

'They're here and are being absolute treasures. God knows what this is doing to them.'

'We'll get Sarah back. Try to stay calm. I'll call you tomorrow.'

'OK, thank you. Look after yourself.'

'And you.'

He walked back and sat down.

'OK, here's the plan. I want you to call Danielle. You need to buy some time. Tell her you have found out one of the banking intermediaries has let you down. There has been a mistake and you think the money may have been lodged in a wrong account.'

'Why would they believe that?'

'They're not bankers, Tom. Make them believe it. You're the money man. Divert blame away from yourself. Put some detail on your story and make it sound good. They're drug distributors. They know nothing about the workings of offshore banking.'

Tom took his spoon and stirred the dregs of his coffee absentmindedly. 'And what comes after that?'

'Let's worry about that later. We'll feed them enough explanation to let them think the cash is retrievable. Someone has screwed up. But you must say to Danielle you want your daughter kept safe. No more harm to be done to her. She has to pass that up the line. No more torture. Whoever has her, must back off. That is a condition of your co operation.'

A flicker of hope crossed Tom's face. Maybe he could do something to bring this nightmare to a close. Jack heard him mutter 'God help me.'

Chapter 53

Danielle cursed herself for leaving her bank statement details so casually placed in a drawer at her apartment. She sat hunched on a bench on the left bank of the Seine watching the river traffic coming and going. Barges vied for space with large pleasure boats as they negotiated the heavy swell at one of the broadest expanses of the river.

She had emptied the cash from her account and returned it to Sergei. It was just a matter of time before she paid the price for her dishonesty. The tumbleweed had started to blow through her dreams. She had been a few weeks away from becoming financially independent. The plan had been virtually foolproof. Sergei had only asked for eight thousand Euros per trip and Tom had no idea she was skimming two thousand each time he couriered the money. The amounts were tiny in comparison to the mass of money flowing within the organisation. No one was getting hurt and it allowed her to indulge in the designer clothes she loved. When her mobile rang and she saw it was Tom, she didn't want to answer it, but did.

He sounded a broken man and his voice was hoarse as if he'd been crying. 'I need your help Danni.'

'I'll do what I can for you darling.'

'We need to meet up. Can I come round to your place?'

'Yes, but I'm not there yet. Can we say an hour? Where are you?'

'I'm nearby. In an hour.'

He ended the call and she rang Sergei. 'He's just called me and wants me to meet him.'

'Where is he?'

'Didn't say. Wants me to meet him tonight alone. He said he'd call later on where to rendezvous.'

'Call me when you know.'

Danielle took a last look at the river, rose from the bench and started walking back to her apartment. She let herself in and hurriedly took a shower before choosing a low cut white top to go with her jeans. As she checked herself in the mirror she heard a faint knock at the door.

'Who is it?'

'It's me, Tom.'

The chain kept the door secure and she checked it was him. 'Are you on your own?'

'Yeah, just me. Let me in, Danni.'

Unfastening the chain, she opened the heavy dark painted wooden door and Tom stumbled in. He looked a spent man and there was a day's growth on his face. He walked through to the living room and turned to face her. 'You must help me save my daughter.'

She followed him into the room and sat down on the end of the sofa.

'You need to tell Sergei I will help him get the missing cash back but I need to know my daughter is not being harmed anymore.' His voice shook as he talked and he slumped into the chair across from Danielle. 'I haven't taken any of his money. Not one penny. I want Sarah freed. There has been an error in the transfer of money from one account to another. It hasn't gone. It's just in the wrong place.'

Danni watched him go through his agony.

'I'll meet with him and explain what has probably happened. It's not uncommon when cash is being transferred around the world. There are always risks but in the end it is your money and the banks will have to make good any loss attributable to them. You need to get that across to Sergei and if you can't, then I will. I must have my daughter back before I get the money flowing again.'

Danni went across to him. 'I know what you're saying darling and I'll make it all clear to him. Trust me.'

He put his hands to his head and his elbow slipped off his knee as if he was about to fall forwards out of the seat. She reached out to help him and he grabbed her by the wrist. 'Danni, nothing in the world is more important to me than this. Nothing. I'll get the money back but you let him know that without my daughter being released now, there is no deal.'

A fire had come into his eyes and for the first time she saw the other side of the man who had built up a successful business. His hold on her wrist intensified and she squirmed in pain as the anger registered in his face. 'Just do it Danni. He needs his money. I need my daughter. Simple.'

He let go of her. 'I need an answer by first thing in the morning. Either he calls me or you do.'

She stood up and went to him but he turned and made for the door. He opened it and walked out, closing it without a backward glance.

She watched him from the window as he made it down to the street and lean against a lamp post. He looked desolate and she wondered if he would be able to carry it all through.

***

Danielle sat down and thought through the options. She had to wait a little time before getting in touch with Sergei but she felt sure of what she would say. She put on her leather jacket, collected her purse and stuffed it into her pocket. Her mobile phone and cigarettes were on the kitchen table. She walked through and picked them up knowing she had three hours to kill before calling Sergei. She left the apartment and headed back to the river to think.

Chapter 54

Xavier was furious with himself at his lack of results. He needed to get back to Marseilles and do some fishing. He entered Sarah's room checking he had his mobile phone in his pocket. Khalid wanted to come in with him to watch. 'Stay in the kitchen.' Khalid gave him the finger as the door slammed shut in his face.

Sarah was lying curled up on the bed and heard the door open.

'Last chance bitch. If you love your family, tell me where your father is. Talk now or we take your mother. When we make her tell us, you'll watch too.'

Sarah felt her body begin to knot up. She felt paralysed and before she could stop herself, she screamed. Xavier brought his fist down on the back of her head and as soon as the pain hit her, she descended into darkness.

'Shit.' He shook her to try and make her regain consciousness but she remained still and lifeless. Khalid opened the door and took in the scene. As he approached the bed staring at Sarah, Xavier saw the lecherous look on his face and drove his fist into his stomach. Khalid went down trying to hold his huge stomach with his right hand, clawing the air with his left. He fell in a heap on the floor shouting and cursing.

'I told you to stay out of here.'

As Khalid made to reach inside his jacket, Xavier kicked him hard in the ribs. Khalid groaned as the boot penetrated the heavy flesh in his gut and he rolled over before staggering to his knees. Xavier saw the fury on his face as he rose and turned for the door. He missed the handle and landed heavily against the thin door splintering the wood as his weight crashed into it. He wrenched the door shut behind him and limped to the living room.

Chapter 55

Tom picked up his mobile and rang Jack. 'I've told Danni to speak with Sergei. Said I can get all his money back. This better work because I'm in no man's land here. I don't know where their money has gone. I just set up the offshore clean up routes for the cash. I don't even know how much is missing.'

Jack listened. 'How did Danielle take it?

'She was cool. I said it was a missed payment between three banks. Happens a lot. The money was still there, just in the wrong place. I said I could get it back to them but I wanted Sarah freed first. That was a must before I intervened.'

'How did you leave it?'

'I told her I wanted to hear by tomorrow morning that Sarah was to be let go with no more harm done to her. I would get the money back to them when I knew she was OK. She said she would get that message to Sergei. That was it.'

Jack listened and he could only hope Sergei's lack of knowledge of the financial sector would influence him. With the muscle he had sent to London, there had to be serious money missing.

'Where are you Tom?'

'In a café. What do I do if Sergei goes along with this?'

Jack told him he was thinking. 'Keep your phone switched on. I'll get back to you.

***

Danielle found the same bench as before, sat down and lit up a cigarette. There was no doubt in her mind. She was the one in the middle with the knowledge. Tom was desperate to get his daughter back and Sergei was in big danger if the money wasn't found. She could help them both. She inhaled deeply and prepared what she would relay to Sergei.

She waited until the lamps on the embankment began to flicker on. As the pale yellow light played on the water, she took out her phone. It felt better talking after dark. 'Sergei, it's me.'

'What've you got?'

'He changed his mind about meeting me. He's just phoned.'

'Why didn't he meet you?'

' He was suspicious. But said he'll get the money back to you.'

'So he's got it?'

'Seems so.'

'When?'

'He wants his daughter freed with no more harm done to her.'

'Right, tell him he can have his daughter back. The money comes back to a bank account here and he can collect his daughter in London. I'll tell him where and when after I know he has the money ready to transfer.'

'OK, I've got that. He said he might have to make some of it in cashable bonds if it had to be done in a hurry.'

'Fuck him. The offshore loss has been confirmed at £4 million and that's what I want transferred in cash or his daughter's dead. Just tell him that.' The connection went dead.

Danni lit another cigarette and leaned back on the bench staring out at a barge as it made its way up river. It was a warm evening and she was aware of nearby laughter as couples and families walked by the river. She picked up her phone and called Andrei in London.

'It's me. How are you my darling?'

'I'm fine. Missing you. Where are you?'

'On our bench by the river. On my own. Where are you?'

'Having a pizza. On my own. Just delivered. I miss you Danni.'

'I miss you too, but soon it will be OK. Things are moving quickly now. I've just spoken with Sergei. Not long now sweetheart. Good luck tomorrow. I love you.'

'I love you too.'

Chapter 56

Jack checked into the Petit Maison under his own name and was given a small room at the front of the hotel on the first floor. Anyone looking for Tom would start here and he could see the street in front of the entrance to the hotel.

He lay on the bedspread and heard the sound of distant laughter from somewhere downstairs. How he wished he could just go out and enjoy some of the many pleasures the City had to offer. In a few moments he dozed off. When he awoke, a weak shaft of light from the street lamps filtered through his window. He looked at his watch and saw it was midnight.

'Damn.' He checked himself in the mirror before grabbing his jacket and descending quietly to the small lobby. The night porter had come on duty and Jack went straight to the desk. A man in his late sixties with thinning white hair and a tired look on his jowly face glanced up as Jack approached.

'Monsieur?'

'I am in room fifteen. I wondered if anyone had called looking for me or my friend Mr Stanton?'

He pushed a ten euro note across the desk and the clerk palmed it.

'It has been quiet tonight. There was a gentleman came in about two hours ago and asked if he could check the guest book. He was very generous. I had to check something out in the office and when I got back to the front desk he was gone.'

Jack slipped another ten Euros across and asked if he could describe him.

'Ah oui, he was quite young and very expensively dressed. Sounded as if he could be Russian.'

Jack thanked him and walked outside looking both ways as he exited the main doorway to the street. It had been a lucrative shift for the night porter and Jack now knew Sergei had a little more information on him. It worked both ways.

He turned left out of the hotel and after walking for a couple of minutes found a small bar still open. Its round neon sign hanging outside was in pale pink letters and said 'Le Globe'. The darkness of the interior suited his mood and he walked up to the bar. A range of spirit bottles were displayed in front of an ancient mirror carrying the branded imprint of Dubonnet along the top. Three lamps fixed to the bar top were spaced a few feet apart and cast a shadowy glow across the room. There was a soft rendering of an old Richard Anthony classic 'The Autumn Leaves' coming from a speaker at the side of the bar.

A young, dark haired man with a white open necked shirt moved to where Jack had taken a barstool and asked what he wanted. He ordered a double whisky and a small jug of water. The barman set down his drink and the water jug and went back to the end of the bar where he stared vacantly out of the window, maybe wishing he wasn't here.

Jack poured a little water into his whisky and took a gulp before setting the tumbler back on the bar. He had an urge to call Jill but he had nothing new to tell her and put the thought out of his mind. He signalled to the barman and had one for the road before paying and leaving.

He made his way back to the hotel. He had wanted to stay longer in the bar but knew tomorrow was a big day. The biggest for everyone.

The night porter was still behind his desk and reading a magazine as Jack went towards the stairs to his room. They nodded knowingly at each other. As Jack climbed the stairs, the porter picked up the phone and called the number he had been given.

Chapter 57

Jill Stanton was being besieged by the media who were camped outside her home every morning. The story had caught the public's attention and had every element possible to sell newspapers and attract viewers to TV news channels. The tabloids were frantically digging around and Jill hardly knew what to expect when she checked the headlines each morning. Trips to the local shops had become all but impossible with photographers around every corner, desperate for a candid shot of her looking distressed.

Most newspapers led with the kidnapping of Sarah and the disappearance of Tom and the possible reasons behind it all. There was little mention of the financial scandal beginning to envelope Stanton, McIntosh and Goldman although the broadsheets were beginning to include more detail on this. It was front page news and likely to be until such time as Sarah was found.

Jill had decided to stay indoors for the day in the hope that the mass of photographers at the front gate would be moved on to a bigger story. She rang the headmistress at Oliver's school and asked that he be allowed a few days off. She received a sympathetic response and the offer of 'any help at all'.

As her mother called through from the kitchen that 'coffee was ready', her mobile rang. As far as she knew, the press hadn't got hold of the number and she walked across to the sofa where she had left it when checking her messages earlier. There was no caller recognition and she wondered whether to accept it.

It could be Sarah.

As she pressed the green button and said, 'Hello,' she heard the caller say 'Jill' and her legs gave way. As she began to lose her balance, she sat down heavily on the sofa and was unable to speak.

'Jill, it's me. I'm so very sorry. I can't begin to tell you how very sorry I am for everything that's happened.'

A tear formed in Jill's right eye and as it began to roll down her face, she let out a loud sobbing sound and threw the phone down on the seat beside her. She held her head in her hands and began crying. Her mother came through quickly from the kitchen and, sitting down, took her daughter in her arms and held her tightly.

***

When the line went dead, he immediately regretted making the call. What a fool. He had nothing to offer. No news of their daughter. All he really wanted was to hear Jill ask after him. Any signal that at some time, some place, they could be together again. As he sat in his sparsely furnished hotel room, he resolved to do anything to get Sarah back. Whatever it took, he would do it.

***

Sergei put a call in to Xavier who was sitting in the kitchen of the safe house keeping one eye on Sarah's door and the other on Khalid who was sitting on the sofa with a sullen look on his face. Xavier turned his back to take Sergei's call.

His Russian accent seemed even harsher than usual. 'Don't harm her any more for the moment. I need to have her alive. Just keep her fed and watered and make sure she doesn't get away. We may have to move her in the next twenty four hours, so be ready.'

'No problem. I'll be glad when this one's over.'

Xavier stuck his phone in his pocket and went down the hall, unlocking Sarah's door. She was lying prone on the bedspread and unhooded.

'Don't turn round or I promise I'll kill you.'

She lay completely motionless and Xavier went across to her and felt for her pulse.

'I'm still alive if that is what you are worried about.'

Xavier leant back to keep his face from her line of vision.

'You've given me a headache and my leg is in agony. I need some ibuprofen and I have to go to the bathroom.'

He put the hood over her head and helped her up from the bed. 'Leave me alone.' She shook herself free from his hold and walked in front of him as he leaned forward to open the bedroom door. The right hand sleeve of her school shirt was pulled down over her hand and she hoped he didn't notice the blood which had begun to seep through around the cuff of the light blue material. She had spent most of the previous night working one of the large springs free from the bedstead and her fingers were raw from the hours of twisting and straightening the metal. She felt better knowing that she at least had some means of defending herself or even escaping. As she felt the door in front of her, she said, 'You can leave me now.'

Locking herself into the windowless bathroom, she removed the hood. Running her hands under the cold tap, her cuts hurt and she winced as the water hit her skin. There was a small bar of soap on the sink by the taps and she rubbed it into her cuff to take away the worst of the bloodstains. She stood on tiptoes to check her appearance in the small mirror and was taken aback by her dishevelled look. 'Oh my God.' Her hair had not been combed for nearly two days and she did her best with her good hand to bring some order to all the loose strands. Pulling her sleeve back down over her right hand, she pulled the hood over her head. She knocked on the door and pulled back the locking bolt. Xavier was standing back when she opened the door inwards and she waited till he checked nothing had been removed. He walked behind her and led her back to the bedroom. As he turned to leave he muttered, 'Are you hungry?'

'Yeah, I'd like a burger and fries and a Coke.' As soon as he'd left and locked the door, she felt under the mattress to check for the dislodged spring. It was still there. Someone, she presumed Xavier, had left a packet of ibuprofen next to a glass of water on the bedside table and she took two. The pain she felt was in her fingers and her leg rather than the blow she'd taken on the head. She lay down and waited for the tablets to take hold and was dozing when someone came in with her food. She sensed it was the other guy because of his laboured breathing and as she heard him place the bag and drink carton on the bedside table, she moved as near to the back wall as she could.

Chapter 58

The Dover Port Authority had never had so many drug smugglers to cope with at any one time and after statements were taken, many of the students were held together. Most were terrified and because of the ages involved, strenuous attempts were being made to contact their parents in the Paris area. Most of them spoke good English but interpreters had been used during the interviews to ensure there were no misunderstandings. The young couriers said they had no idea who was behind the organisation that employed them. They met up at a specific time at Eurostar Paris and sometimes at the Porte de Bagnolet for the onward coach journey to Calais if it was to be a ferry crossing. They were given the flip flops either on the coach or as they travelled in the train across Northern France towards the channel tunnel and fellow passengers really didn't take much notice. They were just teenagers messing about and laughing. The change of footwear was carried in a holdall by a female who, to anyone taking notice, looked just liked their schoolteacher. By the time the group was ready to make the crossing to England either on the channel or under it, their own footwear was packed in their rucksacks and the group leader had slipped away.

As they were interviewed one by one it became clear they didn't know exactly what was hidden inside the built up soles and heels of their flip flops. They'd never asked. Most thought it could be ecstasy but none said cocaine. If they'd been drilled on what to say, they were fine actors but all denied knowing about class 'A' drugs.

After all the sandals were examined, the haul came to ten kilos of high grade, uncut cocaine with a street value of half a million pounds.

It had been a good day for UK Border Agency but they needed to find out who was further up the chain. After the initial questioning sessions all the students were being as helpful as they could and the method of their recruitment was a constant. They all described a girl they knew as Veronique who had approached them in the cafés and bars around the Sorbonne. She made it sound so simple. Just make trips to London every couple of weeks and earn yourself 100 Euros per trip, all expenses paid. She implied they would be taking a small amount of contraband with them but it was just a harmless thing. Everybody had a little smoke from time to time didn't they? There would be no risk.

From all the descriptions, a photofit of 'Veronique' was made up and sent to Paris.

Chapter 59

Last night's whisky had given Jack a light headache and he took a few seconds to remember where he was. As he raised himself up from the narrow hotel bed he swung his legs out and sat motionless before attempting to get up. The curtains hardly met and morning light was streaming in through the window. He leant over, looking through the small gap and saw it immediately. The black Mercedes 320 with tinted windows was parked on the other side of the street about 100yards from the hotel entrance. It stood out amongst the more modest vehicles around it but the thin trail of cigarette smoke coming from the open window on the driver's side was the giveaway.

Jack turned and looked left up the street and saw nothing unusual. He quickly ran his hand through his tousled hair and splashed some cold water on his face. Packing his things into his flight case, he cast his eyes round the room to make sure he'd left nothing. When he reached the bottom of the stairs, the lobby was busy and there was a group of British tourists checking out. He hung back and waited for the last couple to pay their bill and as they did so, a touring coach pulled up outside. The noise levels rose as they all began to pick up their wheeled cases and make their way outside. Jack casually moved across the lobby and mixed in with the crowd keeping a fixed smile on his face. No one took much notice of him as he exited the hotel using the coach as cover before walking up the street for thirty yards before turning left down a side street. He took two more lefts before arriving back on Rue Jacques and guessed he would be at least 500 yards away from the hotel. He put his mobile to his ear as if stopping to take a call and covered most of his face as he did so. He saw the Mercedes still in its bay on the other side of the street and he moved slowly up the opposite side towards the back of the car. He kept the phone to his ear and walked till he could read the registration number. Moving into a doorway, he brought out his pocket book and wrote the number down. There were two men in the car and although the front windows were open a few inches to let the smoke out, the tints obscured their faces.

He was about to leave his vantage point when the passenger door opened and a man stepped out. He looked to be in his late twenties and could have been Eastern European. He bent back into the car and said something to the driver before flicking his cigarette butt into the gutter. He looked round and walked towards the Petit Maison.

Jack waited a few minutes before the man reappeared and walked back towards the Mercedes with a grim look on his face. He wrenched open the door and quickly slid back inside the car. Jack saw the two men talking and could just make out the outline of the driver holding a phone to his ear. A minute later it pulled out and drove away slowly past the hotel.

He watched it go out of sight and then phoned Tom Stanton.

'It's Jack.'

'Where are you?'

'I'm in Rue Jacques, near the Petit Maison. It's been an interesting morning. We need to move things now. Do you know the Deux Magots?'

'Yeah.'

'Be there in fifteen minutes.'

Jack waved a taxi down and gave the driver the address.

***

The 'Deux Magots' was a noisy place at any hour. The waiters were young, handsome and surly and the women loved them.

Jack was there first and was shown to a table near the back. There was a lot of noise but that was good considering what he was there for.

Tom arrived five minutes later and spotted Jack. He came across and sat down quickly. 'I rang Jill last night. Big mistake.'

Jack couldn't believe what he had just heard. 'You did what?'

'I know. You can't believe what I've been through. I had to do it.'

Jack looked at him. 'You prick. I don't even know why I'm here. You don't deserve to have a loving family at home.' The silence was palpable between them. The waiter arrived and the deadlock was broken. They both ordered coffee.

Jack stared at him. 'Ok, you haven't many options. Right now, your problems at SMG are almost incidental but you'll have to resolve them eventually. You have stolen a great deal of money from a lot of reputable people and they are furious.'

Tom glanced away with a look of embarrassment.

'What we have to do is save Sarah and believe me, you are running out of time.'

'They think I have stolen their drug money.'

'How can I be sure you haven't?'

'You'll just have to believe me.' Tom slumped back in his seat. 'Look, I told you. I only sorted out the banking routes for their cash to get cleaned up. I never saw any of the money. That's all I did.'

'That's not going to get Sarah back if they think you've stolen it. Have you spoken to Danielle?'

'I left a message on her mobile to call me but she hasn't got back yet.'

'Try her again.'

Jack sipped his coffee as Tom dug in his pocket for his mobile. He called the number and held the phone closely to his ear.

'Danielle, it's Tom. What's the news?'

'You have to find four million sterling and transfer it in the next 72 hours.'

'What?' Tom shouted, 'Four million. They're crazy. How can I find that sort of money in three days?'

'You're a banker. Borrow it. Find a way.'

Tom was about to start protesting but knew it would be pointless. She was the messenger. There was a pause before she said, 'Don't go to the police Tom. They're well connected and they'll know.'

'Assuming I can get this sort of money together, how do I know Sarah will be returned safely?'

'The exchange will take place in London. In a public place. I don't know where but you'll be able to see she's OK. After the money lands in Sergei's account she will be back with you. That's all I know.'

She sensed his growing apprehension.

'You have to ring me by this time Thursday morning to confirm you have arranged it and you will get your instructions for the exchange. You've got to do it Tom. I'm sorry.'

He ended the call.

'What did she say?'

Tom picked up his spoon from the saucer and stirred the froth on his coffee.

'They need four million pounds into a named account by Friday and no police. The exchange for Sarah will be somewhere in London.' He said it all matter of factly as if it was an everyday piece of news. 'I have no idea where to get that sort of money. Especially in 72 hours.'

Jack looked up at him, 'How about trying to find out where it went in the banking system? If that's where it went. Somebody must have it.'

'Trouble is, nobody will speak. I've made enquiries and no one is even admitting to handling any of the cash being routed through to the mob. The cash is funnelled through a lot of shell companies around the world. It's a fucking nightmare.'

'So where should the money have ended up?'

'Your guess is as good as mine. The money trail may only be known to one person at the top. For all I know someone inside the organisation has it or part of it. It hasn't all gone missing at once. It'll have been going on for months but with payments being staged during the laundering, it's taken time for the fraud to surface.'

As Jack listened, he noticed Tom's hand begin to tremble as he lowered his coffee cup to the saucer.

'Jesus, I'm used to dealing with money but I don't know how to handle this. I really don't.'

Jack pushed his cup and saucer away from him to the middle of the small table and said, 'I do. You're going to get them their money and you'll get Sarah back.'

Tom was astonished. 'You a magician or something?'

'Maybe. Oh, and you're going to repay SMG as well.'

***

Jack found a small hotel near Boulevard Saint-Michel and booked into a room at the back paying cash. Looking out of the window, the view of a high, grimy brick wall suited his mood. He needed to be alone. He unpacked his small case and checking his phone still had battery charge, he made his way down the narrow stairs and walked out onto the street to find a brasserie. Le Tambourin was just around the first corner he came to and he entered, choosing a small table at the side of the restaurant where he could see the door. He ordered a steak tournedos with salad and then rang Jill. She picked up immediately.

'Jack, any news?'

'I've just left Tom.'

'Yeah, he rang me.'

'To say what exactly?'

'To say sorry. That's as far as I got. I put the phone down on him. I was just too angry and upset.'

'How are you doing?'

'I'm trying to stay calm for Oliver as much as anything but it's the lack of any news which is getting to me. I'm feeling frantic and I haven't really slept for three nights. Do you think she's OK?'

'I think so. They want money. It seems incredible but the amount missing is £4 million but Tom is adamant he hasn't got any of it. It's in everyone's interest to keep Sarah well. I think there will be an exchange in a couple of days.' Jack dropped his voice as a waiter glided by the table holding a tray of drinks at shoulder height. 'We have to keep the police out. I don't like doing it but they have made that very clear. We have to keep this to ourselves for the moment if only for Sarah's sake.'

'I'll do whatever you say. Will you call me later?'

'Of course. Are the press still around?'

'It's thinned a bit but there's still a pack of photographers at the gate.'

'Try and stay positive. I'll call you early evening.'

Jack laid his phone on the table as his meal arrived. As he ate, he thought of the problems with trying to get Sarah back alive. He believed the only reason they were asking for such a ludicrously large sum at such short notice was because they thought Tom really had siphoned it all off to his own bank account. Why else would they think anyone could gather such a huge sum together in a matter of days? He began to believe Tom when he said he hadn't stolen the cash. He would give it all back to get Sarah freed.

So if Tom didn't have it, who did?

He signalled the waiter over and asked for a glass of water.

He hadn't outlined his plan to Tom because he couldn't be sure who he was talking to or in contact with inside the organisation. He knew that Danielle was the key. She wasn't high in the hierarchy but she probably knew who was and that would have to do.

He finished his meal and asked for 'l'addition' as the waiter went by. He left the money on a small silver plate adding a tip. Leaving the restaurant he turned right and looked for an internet café to check his e-mails.

***

Danielle luxuriated in her bath with a large glass of Sancerre. Her mobile phone sat on the side next to a large flickering white candle. She loved being naked. As far as she was concerned, things were going to plan.

Tom was terrified of losing his daughter and Sergei was terrified of losing his life. The drugs bust at Dover was a huge blow but it was going to keep everyone in the mob busy. New methods would have to be found to get the packages to London. Not her problem.

She smiled to herself when she thought of the description the students must have given to the police at Dover. She had always worn an expensive chestnut wig when recruiting new couriers and contact lenses had changed the colour of her eyes from a deep mahogany brown to a much lighter shade.

Some clever make up made her look at least five years older. She hardly recognised the reflection in the mirror.

She reached out as her phone cheeped.

Sergei was agitated. 'Where are you?'

'In the hallway. Just got back.'

He grunted and asked if she had contacted Tom.

'Yeah, he's on board. I said he had 72 hours to get the money together.'

'What did he say?'

'He's shitting himself. He promised he would get it. Said not to touch a hair on Sarah's head or there's no money.'

'Fuck him. OK. I'm sorting out a place to do the exchange. Ask him how he is going to transfer the cash. No police or she's dead. We'll know if he's not alone when he meets me.'

'I told him that.'

'Well tell him again. He'll get instructions later. What are you doing tonight?'

She couldn't face another onslaught from Sergei. 'I'm feeling bad. Think I've got a cold coming on. I'm going to bed.'

Sergei grunted with annoyance and said he'd speak to her in the morning. She picked up her drink, lay back and prodded the hot tap with her right toe. She closed her eyes and dreamt of a life away from Sergei.

***

Jack had just finished checking his e-mails and was leaving the internet café when his phone rang. There was no caller ID but as he stepped out into the late afternoon sunlight, he pressed the phone against his ear to drown out the passing traffic noise.

'Jack?' He didn't recognise the voice. It's Rob King. I need a favour, so thought I'd do you one first. I may have some news on the Landcruiser used in the Stanton kidnapping.'

Jack realised he was talking to an old acquaintance who'd finished up on the fringes of the London underworld. He hadn't heard from him in months.

'How did you know I would be interested in him?'

'Someone would have had to be on the moon not to know about the Stanton kidnapping. I heard you were involved and

I may be able to speed things up a bit for you. Are you OK to talk?'

'Yeah, I'm fine. Just turning into a side road which is quieter. I appreciate your call.' Jack moved further down the tree lined street to get away from the din of the early rush hour traffic.

'There's a lot of chit chat about the road rage murder just off the M4 near Windsor a couple of weeks ago. My contact thinks it's the same guy.'

'Are the police onto this yet?'

'Bound to be. This has come from a snitch in Wandsworth. Hadn't heard a peep from him for months but he needs some quick money.'

'How about a name?'

'He's working on it but he's asking a lot for any more information. Said he'd call me back.'

'It won't be a problem Rob. There's no limit here. Just give him what he asks. It's life or death. Call me when you have anything. Doesn't matter how late it is. What can I do for you?'

'I never thought it would happen but I think my wife is seeing somebody and I need some help.'

'I'm happy to do what I can, Rob.'

'Thanks. I'll get back to you.'

'Speak later.'

As Jack thought about the call he'd just taken, he phoned the airline and checked flight times to London.

Next morning Jack arrived at CDG in good time for his flight to Heathrow and was on his way to security when the call came.

'It cost me a grand, Jack.'

'I'm on my way back to London now. I'll sort the money out with you today. What have you got?'

'You're looking for a Frank Williams and he's thought to be living with a woman in Streatham. Pendennis Road. I can't get the house number but he's still using the same vehicle so shouldn't be hard to find.'

Jack asked him to spell it and he wrote the name and address down on the top of his newspaper.

'No doubt about his credentials, Jack. He's a pro and works for anyone if the money's right. Everyone's using him because he always delivers. He's doing jobs all over London apparently. Provides the full service.'

'What do you mean?'

'Hit, clean up and disposal. Take care. He's got to be an evil bastard.'

'Thanks, Rob, I'll be in touch later today to sort out the cash with you.'

'OK. Thanks.'

Jack knew he had just had the break he thought would never come. The name he had just been given was probably the hit man who had killed and buried John Vanner. The name remembered by his mother.

He went through to the first café he could find and ordered a coffee with a croissant. His flight was scheduled for departure in 60 minutes.

Jill was in the kitchen when he rang. 'You said you'd call last night. I was worried that something had happened.'

'I'm sorry. I got caught up and ran out of time. I'm on my way back to London. I have things to set up. All I can say is, I think I'm making progress but I won't know till later today. I'm going to have to switch my phone off at some time so don't worry if you can't get through. Have the police made any progress with finding Sarah?'

'I think so. They're working on the 4x4 which was used to snatch her. That's all I know.'

'How are you doing, Jill?'

'Not too good but Mum and Dad have been great. Thank God they're here. Oliver is morose and he's not sleeping well. It's just awful.

Jack listened and said, 'I'll get back to you today, definitely. If I can get over to see you, I will. Try to stay strong and give my best to Oliver and your parents. Tell them we are doing all we can.'

'Thanks. Speak to you later.'

Chapter 60

Jack collected his car from the long term at Heathrow and drove into London. Crossing the Thames he turned south towards Streatham. It was an area of London unfamiliar to him and as he approached Streatham High Road he watched for Pendennis Road. When he saw it he quickly turned left, driving slowly between parked cars. He spotted it tucked into a front garden which had been converted into a parking area with concrete slabs. It was a black Toyota Land Cruiser which almost dwarfed the front of the London-brick semi-detached house behind it. A handwritten 'For Sale' sign with a phone number had been taped inside the back window.

Weeds sprouted from the ground where there was no concrete and some unruly perennials clinging to the brickwork around the door made the house look almost derelict. Dirty white net curtains covered the front windows. Jack carried on past and parked a hundred yards beyond the house. He felt his heart rate begin to accelerate but he knew it was a chance he may never get again. A piece of luck had got him here and he knew he had to do it for Sarah.

He brought out his wallet and notebook from his jacket and placed them in the glove compartment. Before he closed it, he rummaged around and found the small knuckle duster lying at the back and pushed it into his left hand pocket. As he locked the glove compartment and leaned back in his seat, he tried to push any thoughts of fear from his mind. It was no time for doubt. He was about to confront a stone cold killer and Jack could be next on his list. He thought of Sarah as he climbed out of the car, locking it before walking slowly back to the house with his left hand in his pocket. He felt the sweat gather at the back of his neck and go cold as it travelled down his spine.

Squeezing past the 4x4 he went up to the flaking dark green front door and rang the bell. The woman who opened the door did so hesitantly and Jack could only see her head and shoulders. She could have been in her late twenties and had auburn hair cut in a bob. Her small features and soft mouth made her attractive and when she spoke, showed the whitest teeth Jack had ever seen. He smiled at her and apologised for troubling her but asked if it was possible to look at the vehicle for sale. As she half turned in the doorway, a tall, lean figured man came up behind her. A black leather bomber jacket covered a white open necked shirt and he looked as if he had been ready to leave. As he looked over the top of the woman holding the door, Jack saw a scar which had marked him from his left ear to his upper jaw line. It had come to an end at his top lip giving him a sneering look. Underneath his black cropped hair, a crooked nose sat on a tanned thirty something craggy face which could have been on an older man. He certainly looked like a hit man.

'I was just goin' out.' His accent sounded vaguely south London.

'I was just passing by and saw the 4x4 for sale. It looks just what I'm after. It would be cash.'

The woman smiled at Jack before turning and ducking away into the dark hallway leaving them to talk about the vehicle. Jack watched him raise his right arm and check the time on an oversized black faced watch. 'OK, but we gotta be quick.'

Jack stepped back as the door was pulled shut and half turned, easing the fingers of his left hand into the knuckle duster inside his trouser pocket. He let the man pass by him and watched as he drew a set of keys from his jacket pocket and remotely open the driver's door of the vehicle.

'Could you just start her up for me please?'

As he leant in and aimed the key towards the ignition, Jack swung his right leg back and drove his foot straight in between his legs. He heard the scream as his toe found its target. The adrenalin rush hit Jack as he took hold of the man's waist and threw him forward, forcing his face onto the gear stick. He thought he heard a bone crack. As blood spurted over the interior, Jack began moving forwards but didn't see the next move coming. His victim shouted, 'Bastard' and lashed out with his right foot, catching him with full force in the kneecap. Jack gasped as the pain shot through his right leg and fell backwards grabbing desperately for the side of the vehicle to stop himself falling over. Before he knew it, the man had managed to twist round and Jack saw the contorted rage on his bloodied face. He lunged at him, kicking wildly, and aimed a second kick, this time sweeping his foot up to crunch under Jack's chin. A tidal wave of pain shot through his jaw and he fell towards the pavement. Through misted eyes he saw his prey levering himself out of the vehicle and he knew he was out of time. He summoned his remaining strength, sweeping his left arm round and drove the knuckleduster as hard as he could towards the man's face. He heard the crunch as it connected and it gave him time to regain his balance. As the hitman fell forward, Jack brought his knee up and caught him straight in the stomach. He heard a loud 'oomph' and his body went limp. He collected his strength and pushed him back inside the vehicle and across to the passenger seat punching him in the kidneys for good measure. As the man groaned and slumped sideways against the passenger door, Jack saw the bulge under his jacket. The element of surprise had prevented him from reaching for the gun but Jack knew he'd been lucky. He wrenched the pistol from its holster and jabbed it into the man's already aching groin and took hold of the back of his shirt collar jerking his head back. As blood poured from his nose, covering the front of his white shirt, it mixed with the saliva coming from his smashed teeth and torn mouth. Jack tightened the grip on his shirt, constricting his intake of air.

'Where did you take the girl?'

There was a grunt as he began to try and heave himself off the seat. Jack pulled on his shirt and heard a loud choking sound as blood came in a torrent from his mouth.

'Last chance. Where's the girl?'

He started pulling the shirt again and he could see the man's eyes beginning to bulge.

Jack could barely make out what he said as he tried to speak through his damaged mouth. Jack loosened the hold on his shirt collar.

'Paddington.'

'Where in Paddington?'

'I dawed noaw.'

Jack tightened the hold on his shirt till his eyes began to roll and his head fell sideways. The blood and saliva was still spewing from his mouth and when he tightened his shirt collar again and he told Jack the address. He made him repeat it just to make sure he had understood it correctly.

Jack sat back in the driver's seat, exhausted. His face was on fire and he checked in the mirror to see if he still had teeth. The pain grew more intense but he had to move away from the house. He turned on the ignition and hoped his lady would think they were off for a test drive. As the bloodied form lay slumped on the passenger seat, Jack checked him for any other weapons but only found his mobile phone which he pocketed. Before moving off he fastened the safety belt over the crumpled body and tightened it till it was biting into his clothes. He reversed the Land Cruiser out to the road and headed towards Streatham High Road to cross the river towards Paddington.

Chapter 61

In West London, Sarah's fear was turning to despair but she kept her spirits up thinking what she could do with her weapon. She thought of her mum and her brother. She wondered if her dad had been forced to run because of something beyond his control. The thought of him doing anything dishonest was beyond her. He was her dad after all. The one who had taught her to swim and ski on all those wonderful family holidays. Something weird must have happened. There would be a logical explanation. She was just thinking of her best friend at school when she heard a voice outside the door.

'Is your mask on?' It sounded like the wheezy one.

She slipped the hood over her head and moved back on the bed as far as she could towards the wall and curled into the foetal position. She heard the door close quietly and his laboured breathing as he got nearer the bed. She felt the bed creak under his weight as he reached her. As his hand touched her knee and began to move up her thigh, she let her left hand fall below the bed feeling for the weapon loosely attached to the bedspring. She was sure she would be spotted. She heard his rasping breath and tried to keep her thighs tightly together. She felt her trembling hand land on the makeshift knife and as she managed to dislodge it, brought it up from below the bed, curved her arm and plunged it in his general direction. She heard a scream which seemed to last forever. As she pulled the hat from her face she saw blood over her hand and wrist and down the back wall of the room. She turned and saw him on the floor, the makeshift knife sticking from the side of his neck. As he rolled on the floor he pulled the knife out and a torrent of blood spurted in a high arc onto the wall. His face was contorted with pain and his arms flailed as he writhed in agony. As he began coughing, a projectile spray of blood landed as mist over her legs. Sarah stared in horror and her heart was racing as she looked away, unable to take in what she was seeing. She swung her legs to the floor and stumbled across the room towards the door. When she heard a key being inserted in the outside door and the soft click as it shut, the sense of fear was almost overwhelming. She frantically looked round the room but knew there was no hiding place.

When Xavier came in to the house he knew something had happened. Dropping the takeaway pizza boxes on the chair, he drew a Walther.22 from his jacket and moved slowly towards the bedroom. As he edged towards Sarah's room he heard a low moaning sound. He kept close to the wall and moved towards her room and kicked the door in.

His outstretched gun arm swept the small room and his first vision was Khalid lying on the floor. He saw the gash in the side of his neck and the massive dark red pool widening on the carpet by his head. Blood had spattered across the dirty beige carpet and reached the bed giving the white eiderdown a bright red pattern and sprayed further to reach the back wall. He lowered the gun as he took in Sarah in a kneeling position at the side of the chest of drawers her face to the wall, sobbing and shivering uncontrollably.

'What did he do?'

She managed to gasp, 'He attacked me.'

'Are you hurt?'

'No.'

'You sure?'

'Why should you care?'

'I don't.'

He wrenched her up by the arm and pulled her through to the kitchen and threw her onto a wooden chair. Searching in drawers he found some twine and began tying her arms to the back of the chair before securing her ankles to the legs. The thinness of the hemp cut into her skin and she cried out in pain as he finished knotting her ankles in place. He just looked at her without expression. He turned round and headed back to her room. She heard a scream and a muffled bang. She shuddered, closing her eyes, knowing what he had just done. He returned almost immediately with the same vacant look on his face.

He walked towards the sink and said, 'You're almost through now.'

**

Jack drove the Land Cruiser through south London and headed for Battersea. He chose a side street near a semi derelict industrial estate where there was no one around and no CCTV cameras. He pulled in and parked. Unfastening the seat belt he propped the still unconscious passenger upright and stepped out. He leant in to the vehicle and dragged the man into the driver's seat. Wiping down all the surfaces inside and outside the vehicle he emptied the gun and locked it in the glove compartment. He finished by taking the keys from the ignition. As he stepped away from the vehicle he locked the doors and wiping the key fob, lobbed the keys fifty yards into the dense rubbish filled scrub.

He walked casually back towards the vehicle picking up a discarded brick on the way. As he passed the vehicle, he smashed it against the side window setting off the alarm. He made his way towards the sound of traffic and saw no one. Someone would hear the alarm and find him but even if they could understand him, he wasn't going to be making phone calls anytime soon.

Chapter 62

Tom had been trying to get in touch with Jack for over an hour and left messages to get back to him. He found an internet café and paid for two hours of time. Looking round he saw an unused screen at the back of the small room and squeezed past some excited students. He sat down and booted up the computer taking a small hardback notebook from his inside pocket.

Within an hour he had made contact with all eight banks he had used to launder the mob's money. With the huge cash flow he'd given them over the past months, he was seen as a platinum investor. No face to face contact had ever been made with any of them and his password and his status got him the required attention. His message to each was the same. He had a mega deal going through very soon. It was going to treble the funds they had been receiving but he needed a little more seed capital to ensure the venture was properly funded from the start. It was a short term arrangement and the loans would be repaid with interest in four weeks. Thereafter the increased cash flows would be sustained for some time to come. It was a win win for everyone. One by one the responses came back and Tom smiled as each popped up on his screen. They were falling over themselves to give him their money. Four of them promised more flexibility if it was needed. 'No problem. You only have to ask.' In ninety five minutes he had raised the £4million pounds and the cash was already on its way to his personal account at his bank just over a mile away in the Sorbonne. He had called the manager there to confirm he would be able to withdraw the whole amount in one transaction.

He logged off before his time was up and tucked his small notebook back into his pocket. He nodded at the café owner as he walked by and strolled out into the late afternoon sunshine with a feeling of satisfaction and unbridled relief.

***

Sergei sat in the back room of the Meurice. He went across to the bar and filled a large brandy goblet before moving across to the sofa. He took a gulp of his Remy and tried to think of a way out of the mess. His Paris operation had lost a drugs consignment and all their couriers in one bust and £4million had been stolen. One of those would have been enough to finish off his career but all three put his life in danger.

His home country was awash with drugs and with the prices being driven down, he was part of the grand plan to move deeper into the UK market. When Vladimir Ivankov had appointed him almost a year ago he said, 'Set up the route, make it watertight and grow it. Paris and London will be your exclusive territory and if you get it up and running we will have you back in St Petersburg in two years. You will be made for life.'

As he turned his goblet on the table top, he felt his anger rise. He took another gulp of brandy as his phone rang.

Tom Stanton said, 'I've got your money. I want my daughter.'

Sergei felt his pulse quicken and he put his brandy glass down slowly on the table. 'Your daughter is alive. It's down to you now.'

Tom stalled. 'I have arranged for the money to come through in the next twenty four hours. I need to keep on top of it to make sure it is ready for transfer to you. Is it the usual account number?'

Sergei confirmed the account number and sort code.

Tom went on. 'There are global time differences to take into account. You will have to be patient.'

Sergei jumped up spilling his brandy. 'Don't fucking tell me to be patient. You have my money. I have your daughter. Which one of those two is replaceable?' Sergei knew the answer was neither but his outburst had silenced the voice on the other end. He started pacing the room, breathing deeply, waiting for a reply.

Tom asked, 'How do you want to play this?'

240

Sergei sat down again. 'We'll do the exchange in London. I need to know the money has been deposited and you can have your daughter. You'll only get the one chance. Any police, you'll have to live for the rest of your life with the next phone video of your daughter. You can watch her die. We'll even get it on the internet for you. Understand?' Sergei managed a low growling laugh and began to relax. He wasn't sure whether it was the pleasure he got from handing out death threats or the Remy kicking in. 'I'll call you tomorrow at 10 am. Make sure the money is in place and ready for transfer to my account.'

***

The line went dead and Tom looked blankly at his phone, hardly able to believe the conversation he had just had. He ran his hand through his hair, sat down and bowed his head. He now knew what people meant when they said 'it was the worst moment of my life.' It was his first ever experience of that and he was paralysed with fear.

When he had recovered, he called Jack. 'I've just been speaking to Sergei. I've raised the money and he wants to do the exchange somewhere in London. Said he would film Sarah being killed if I involved the police and I believe him.' His voice began to break and Jack said, 'You sure about the money?'

'Yeah, it'll be there. I've raised it through the banks.'

'How's the exchange going to be done?'

'He said it would be somewhere in the open but with nobody about. He would call his bank and make sure the money had been transferred, then I'd get Sarah back.'

'You believe him?'

'I have to. There's nothing else to believe in.'

Jack was quiet for a moment. 'You still there?'

'Yes, I'm here.'

'Has Sergei ever met you?'

'Nope. I've only spoken with him since the problem arose.'

'He's not going to let you live.'

'What do you mean? I've got the money together.'

'Maybe so, but you've humiliated him. He's dead meat with his masters. He knows he's at risk now. He'll kill you as soon as he knows the money has hit his bank account. It'll restore a little of his credibility.'

Tom listened with growing alarm. 'You really think that?'

'I'd put money on it.'

'Jesus, I just assumed that with the money going back, this would be all over.'

'Only in fairy tales. But there is another way. Catch the first Eurostar you can get tonight and head back to London. You'd better travel as John Vanner. I'm on my way back to collect my car from Streatham. Call me when you get to St Pancras.'

Chapter 63

Sergei had phoned St Petersburg and reported developments. There was a slight tremble in is voice as he spoke. 'The £4m has been recovered. It will be transferred to you in the morning. Absolutely one hundred per cent. It has been a misunderstanding inside two of the banks.'

Vladimir asked quietly, 'How are things at Dover?'

'It was a random search which happens all the time. The students have no idea of the existence of the organisation. There will be no fall out for us.'

Sergei tried to hide his nervousness and heard Vladimir say, 'The money must be back in the main account by noon tomorrow. Just make it happen.'

'Of course. I am travelling to London tonight to arrange it.' Sergei sat back feeling relieved as the line went dead.

***

London woke up to a normal day for most of its inhabitants. It was going to be hot and probably cloudless. Jack was desperate to get to Sarah but knew the money had to be in place or the mob would just go after someone else in the family. He and Tom waited with growing apprehension for the call.

Sergei rang Tom at nine o'clock. 'Where are you?'

'Waiting for you. Just give me the place and the time.'

Sergei named a street in Paddington behind the mainline station. 'There's a yard next to a boarded up newsagents which you can drive into. Just come up to a red and white hut you will see on your right. Wait there. Have your phone ready to call your bank. Remember just you. What are you driving?'

'It'll be a BMW 5 Series, white.'

'We'll be waiting.'

Jack was next to him as he took the call and could hear the conversation.

As they drove across London to the location, Jack looked at him. 'You're not going to do the exchange.'

'What do you mean?'

'Just what I said. I'm going to meet Sergei and do the deal.'

'So where do I fit in?'

'You don't. Stay hidden in the car. I'll bring Sarah back to you, I promise.'

'Jesus, you don't know how to do the bank stuff.'

'Maybe, but it can't be that difficult. Put the phone number in the memory and I'll call it. I'll just tell Sergei I'm you. Tell me what to say when the call is answered. If the money's there I can get it transferred same as you.'

Tom turned on him and shouted, 'No way. I'm going to get my daughter back. No one else.'

'He'll kill you both. Let me handle it. You want Sarah to get out alive.'

Tom drove on but almost hit a car as he took a late left turn.

'You ever fired a gun, Tom?'

'Never.'

'Sergei is bound to have one. Maybe two.'

'Come on, all he wants is the money.'

Jack rounded on him and shouted back. 'You should have stayed in your little world. You are so far out of your depth, you'll kill your daughter. Just listen to me.'

Tom went quiet.

'Just let me handle it, OK.'

Tom's phone rang. The caller was withheld. 'It's Sergei, where are you?'

'About two miles away. I'm in traffic.'

'You on your own?'

'Yes. Have you got my daughter?'

'Yeah, she's with us. She's well.'

'She better be. I should be there in fifteen minutes.'

'Just drive into the yard like I said and pull up by the hut. Step out of your car and walk away from it.'

'Then what?'

'You'll see me and your daughter. Hold your phone up and be ready to phone the bank. I'll take the call and I need to know the transfer has happened.'

'You will. I guarantee it.'

'If you fuck up on the money, your daughter is dead. Believe it.'

'I believe it.'

Jack heard the line go dead and turned to Tom. 'Pull up when you can.'

He pulled into a side street and looked across at Jack. 'This better work.'

Jack got behind the wheel and told Tom to get into the back and lie on the floor. As he turned back to the main road and drove on he felt his stomach begin to churn.

When Jack drove in to where he thought he should be, he saw nothing. It was a dismal looking piece of land adjacent to a rail siding. All around were rows of grit boxes and pieces of rusty equipment which saw action in London's mid winter. He looked right, saw the hut and drove towards it. Before getting too close, he stopped the car and switched off the engine. He sat without moving and looked left and right.

***

Sergei and Xavier were crouched down behind a stack of old rail sleepers with Sarah kneeling in front of them. They saw the BMW arrive with one person inside.

Sergei nodded to Xavier and both got up dragging Sarah to her feet. They moved out and kept her in front of them. As they walked towards the car, its door opened and Jack got out slowly. He moved out to meet them with his phone in his hand. Xavier had the pistol. They edged towards each other and when they were close enough, Sergei called out, 'Stop.'

As they stood, Sarah said nothing. This was her dad.

Sergei was ten yards from Jack. 'Make the call.'

He pressed call and asked the recipient to, 'Wait just a moment. I'm in a meeting and need you to confirm to my colleague that our agreement is complete and that the money is in place. The four million pounds. Would you mind?'

'Not at all Sir.'

'I'll pass you over now. Please wait.'

Jack walked towards Sergei with the phone held high and handed it to him.

Sergei just said, 'Hello.'

'Good morning Sir. This is to confirm that £4 million pounds sterling has been paid into your named account this morning. It is deposited now.'

'Good. Please give me your name and main switchboard number so I can call you back. I will do this immediately. I'm sure you understand.' He was given the name M. Sangret. He rang the number and the bank's main switchboard answered. He asked to be put through to M. Sangret who confirmed what he had himself said moments before. Sergei grunted his thanks and ended the call.

He placed the phone in his pocket and a small smile creased his face.

Jack looked straight at him and started walking towards Sarah who was standing three yards away. Sergei looked round at Xavier and nodded. As Jack kept walking, Xavier's gun arm stiffened and he seemed to take aim at Sarah. She shouted out and Jack dived towards her and brought her down to the ground, shielding her beneath him as they fell. Xavier turned and stared at Jack, pointing the gun straight at him. He had run out of options and as he waited for the inevitable, Xavier's arm kept moving round before shooting Sergei twice in the body. He watched without expression as Sergei's eyes widened in disbelief. He clutched his stomach and screamed in agony as his legs buckled and he fell to the ground. Xavier glanced at Jack, shrugged and walked away, pulling out his phone as he retreated from the now silent assassination scene. He called St. Petersburg and Vladimir answered. Xavier just said, 'C'est fait,' and flipped his phone shut.

***

To Jack, he'd just witnessed a re-run of Lee Harvey Oswald and Jack Ruby.

Tom heard the shot and looked up from the back of the car. All he saw was bodies on the ground, a pool of blood forming round the middle of one of them.

Sarah disentangled herself from Jack and she looked in disbelief as she pushed herself up to a sitting position and saw from the scene of horror in front of her.

She turned to Jack and he embraced her, rubbing her back with his hands. It was then she saw Tom opening the back door of the car and her eyes locked onto him. Sarah gasped as her father walked slowly towards them leaving the car door open.

She saw the wretched look in his face as he pleaded with his eyes. Unsure what to do, she clung to Jack and buried her face in his shoulder. The silence was broken when Sarah turned and whispered, 'Hello, Dad.' As the awkwardness continued, Jack said to no one in particular, 'Let's have a seat in the car.'

Sarah opened the front passenger door and climbed inside. She heard Jack call for the police and an ambulance. When he'd finished talking, she said to him. 'Can I borrow your phone to call Mum?'

Within minutes the yard was a sea of police and blue and white tape. Tom sat on the ground with his head held in his hands.

'I'm OK, really Mum.' Sarah could hear her mother laughing and crying. As Sarah began to sob, she handed the phone back to Jack.

'It's Jack. Yes, she seems OK and very brave. She's being looked after by a paramedic and he's covering a wound on her leg. She will have to have proper treatment for it but just wants to see you. I'll keep in touch and hopefully we can get her back to you later.' He listened at the mix of laughter and hysteria in her voice and Jack felt his own emotion as he gave out the good news.

'Thank you so much Jack. Thank you for everything you've done. You've been wonderful.' As her voice faltered, he just said, 'I told you I was persistent.' They both laughed.

'Will you bring Sarah home yourself?'

'Of course. I'll call you when we set off.'

'Is Tom still there?'

'Yes, he's here but I suspect he will be going to the police station.'

'I don't want to speak to him now. I just wanted to know he was there.'

Chapter 64

The police allowed Jack and Sarah to leave after some intense questioning. They would be interviewed again in the morning. A policewoman was with Sarah. 'You have been through so much. The paramedic says you need to go to hospital and have your leg properly dressed.

Sarah thanked her. 'I just want to get home to see my mum and brother and have a bath. I'll go to my local hospital in the morning.' She was already imagining sleeping in her own bed.

When they pulled into the driveway there were balloons hanging around the front door. Sarah looked a little embarrassed when she saw the decorations. They had managed to beat the press to the house but Jack pulled up as near to the front step as he could. Jill had seen them arrive and flung open the front door. Jack waited by the car as Sarah and Jill cried and hugged each other. Oliver burst out of the door followed by Jill's mum and dad.

***

When they were all inside, Jill turned to Jack and flung her arms round him. He felt a kiss on the side of his cheek and then he felt his own emotions welling up. They all trooped into the kitchen making lots of noise. As the champagne flowed, Jill stole a glance at Jack, who looked pale and exhausted. She came over to him and linked her arm through his. 'I can't tell you how happy I am. You've done everything you said you would and more.' She pecked him on the cheek again and he kissed her back. He held on to her and said, 'It was a close call at times but there was too much at stake to lose.'

'What will happen to Tom?'

'He'll be charged with fraud at least. Custodial sentence almost a certainty.'

He turned to her. 'How do you feel about him?'

'I'm just going to take one day at a time as they say. We'll see. What are you going to do Mr. Super Detective?'

'Have a bath and a shave and a good night's sleep.'

She smiled. 'Same as Sarah really except for the shave.'

They laughed and Jill asked, 'Will you keep in touch?'

'Yes'

***

Tom was released on bail pending charges of fraud and participation in money laundering. He left West End Central police station in a daze not knowing who to contact or where to go. He had not washed or shaved in over a day and his travel stained clothes only added to his crumpled appearance. He had been held at a central London police station and as he stumbled away following hours of questioning, he hailed a taxi and for no good reason asked for SOHO. He walked into a small café in Greek Street and ordered a full English breakfast with coffee. He sat in silence avoiding all eye contact until his breakfast arrived. When he had finished eating he pulled his mobile phone from his pocket and checked the battery. He had two units of power left. Taking another swallow of his coffee, he rang home. 'Hello Jill, it's me.' There was silence and he said, 'Please don't hang up. I'll never forgive myself for what I've done. I'm so very sorry.' He broke down and started to sob.

'Where are you?'

'I'm in a café in central London.'

'Why did you do this to us?'

'I'll never know. It was madness.'

There was another silence and she said, 'There's nothing I want to say to you right now.'

He sensed the deadening in her voice. 'Can I ask how Sarah and Oliver are?'

'They're doing OK. Pleased their dad's alive.'

'Tell them I love them. I love you too.'

'Goodbye, Tom.'

Chapter 65

Next morning, Air France flight AF444 took off on time from Paris for Rio De Janeiro.

As it climbed out towards Atlantic air space, two passengers sat in first class enjoying one of the many cocktails they would have over the next eleven hours. They clinked glasses and the cabin staff were delighted to see a young couple so obviously in love.

It had been Andrei's idea to point the finger of suspicion at Tom for the theft of the £4million and Danni had found it easy to fan the flames with Sergei.

The cost of their new identities so professionally crafted, was a drop in the ocean compared to their new riches. Danielle's nights with Andrei in London had been known to no one and they had longed for the time when they could be free to be together. Danielle's systematic theft of financial data from Sergei had allowed Andrei access to the offshore bank account details and withdraw the mob's funds. It would mean both would be forever be on their hit list but South America was a very big place and they had the money to buy all the surgical anonymity they needed.

As the steaks arrived he looked at her and laughed.

She started grinning and said, 'What's so funny?'

'You know they say bankers have no sense of humour. When I was siphoning the money and spreading it around our bank accounts, one of them said it was unusual to get such large amounts in cash. I told him I was an international drug smuggler and he burst out laughing.'

Danielle wrapped her arms around Andrei and smiled. She had fooled them all.

Lightning Source UK Ltd.
Milton Keynes UK
UKOW04f0824041215

264021UK00002B/31/P